I0687626

# Happy Endings

**Grete DeAngelo**

Lighted Path Press

Cover design by Audrie Thompson

# 1

I gingerly pulled a thorny branch out of my hair and away from my face after it struck a stinging line across my cheekbone. Part of the rose bush had attached itself to my coat, the thorns leaving little prickly holes in its wake. I rose up on tiptoes, careful as I peered into the dining room window not to fog up the glass and give myself away. This had to be the stupidest thing I'd ever done.

I watched John, the man I love, cutting his daughter's chicken while his wife tilted back her head and laughed at something he was saying. She refilled his wine glass and topped hers off.

As she reached over to straighten the back of his collar in the way that wives did, a wave of jealousy hit me. John's visits with me were stolen moments a few times a week, with sometimes a whole day or a weekend when he padded some time onto a business trip or his wife happened to be busy with their kids.

So here I was, scratched up and feeling punished, both emotionally and now literally too. The lash across my cheek should have been the final warning that this had to end, but I ignored common sense because it had always been my habit to do so.

I thought about all the times John had spent in my bed with me, telling me his marriage was a sham. There was a sense of power I felt in the fact that I knew so much about his wife while she knew nothing about me. I knew her history, her fears, her habits, her mothering style. John's stories about Georgia were my guilty pleasure. I loved it when he told me her shortcomings and all of the things that made him fall out of love with her.

We did things together she wouldn't do with him. Not just in bed either. Once, we both took off from work and skipped town to go to an amusement park on a school day. We jumped out of one roller coaster and skipped through the empty lines to the next ride until we were both dizzy and exhilarated and a little nauseated. "Georgia likes to keep her feet on the ground," John said. "You make me fly."

I felt now like *she* was the other woman. I dared to press my nose a little closer to the glass, angry to think I'd never be inside this house with John, no matter what he promised. So what if she saw me? They looked too happy to notice I was here. I balled my fist, ready to bang on the window, but stopped myself from taking it that far. Not yet.

The realization was slowly dawning on me that John was using me for free therapy. He got the chance to vent and gripe and blow off enough steam so that he could go back to his family and not end his marriage.

I began to realize, too, that I could never be taken care of the way John took care of Georgia. Whenever she called, he dropped everything and spoke to her immediately. I envied the way he would tenderly reassure her that he would be home soon and that he loved her. Sometimes she called when we were lying in my bed facing each other, each with a cheek on a pillow, and he rolled his eyes in a silent apology for her cutting into our time as he answered his phone to talk to her.

He told me he loved me too. Was he as insincere about that? Or did he really love her? Either way, he was lying to me. Part of me got it: She was the mother of his children, and for that, she'd always hold a place in his heart. But mostly I wondered why he was staying with her if he really wanted to be with me.

As I watched the family eat, my calves burned and my fingers froze and I resolved that I would delete John from my contacts list and never talk to him again, but even as I said it to myself, I knew it wasn't true. I couldn't give up John because I loved him desperately.

The whole family was completely oblivious of the woman who stared into their window longingly from the cold night, imagining herself as the wife whose cheeks were warmed by the wine, whose eyes were sparkling as she looked around her table at her beautiful family, the two perfect children with good table manners, the remains of a roast chicken on a platter, the bowls of mashed potatoes and green beans being passed from one to the other.

My dinner had been a soggy fast food burger scarfed down on the drive across town, the wrapper balled up and tossed on the passenger side floor of my car to roll around with the others.

As the kids started pushing their chairs back to leave the table, I dropped back onto my heels, carefully parted the rose bushes so I wouldn't get caught by the thorns again, and walked back to my car parked up the street, my hands in my pockets and my head down.

Maybe I'd come back another day and knock on the front door. First I'd give John a chance to reassure me that he loves me and needs me and I'm the only one he thinks about when he's sleeping with her.

# 2

I was attracted to John as soon as I met him, but I didn't plan to act on it. He came to see a massage therapist at the spa where I work, and I happened to have an open block the day he walked in. Actually, it was my lunch, but I was willing to forgo my free hour when he asked nicely if I could help him right away and flashed a disarming, dimpled grin as he leaned over the reception counter. Everything about our relationship was on his schedule, right from the beginning.

Some of the married clients have the nerve to try to pass themselves off as single, but I'd see the dent in their finger where they took their wedding band off right before they walked in the door. In contrast, John was wearing a wedding band and told me his wife suggested he get a massage to see if it would help his sciatica pain.

The first thing I did was ask him to get out his wallet. He pulled out a fat trifold from his back pants pocket. I told him half of the problem was right there, that a man sitting on his wallet all day threw his back out of alignment. The rest we should be able to fix with a massage and some stretching when he got home.

I must confess that when a person is attractive, I am going to have certain thoughts about him. After all the time I spent in school memorizing muscle groups, I've become quite an aficionado of the human form. John was much more fit than the average man in his late thirties. It was a pleasure for me to look down at his back and to feel the firmness of taut muscles under my hands. I pressed my thumbs deep into his lower back as the tight muscles began to ease up.

I felt like we had whole conversations without words. With so many nerve endings in our skin, it makes sense that a lot of our communication is by touch. All I knew is that as I pushed my weight into his muscles, an electric feeling I'd never known before ran into my fingers, up my hands and arms and right to my brain.

The grapefruit aromatherapy oil heightened my senses. I could hear each note of the Celtic music playing in the background, and felt as though I were outside by a brook listening to the birds singing. The softly bubbling fountain in the corner of the room became the water of life, and the glow from the Himalayan salt lamp cast the most amazing light my eyes had ever seen. Even in this state of bliss, half of my brain told me I was crazy, but I ignored such rational thoughts.

When we finished, I felt my cheeks burning with hot embarrassment that my feelings had gotten so carried away. Even though I did nothing inappropriate, I worried that just by my touch he would know my thoughts. I mostly looked at the floor as I asked him how he was feeling.

"That was incredible," he exclaimed. "What's your name again? Kristen?"

I nodded, murmuring thanks.

"I'll have to tell my wife that she was right, as usual. I feel like a new man."

After he left, I looked at his intake chart and medical history. I put his number in my phone. While my next client was getting undressed, I stood in the hall and looked him up online. This invasion of client privacy was strictly forbidden, of course, and

I should have known then that putting my job on the line over a married man I'd just met was never going to turn out well.

# 3

After driving home from John's house, I texted him to ask whether he'd slip out and meet me at my apartment for a few minutes. This was a rare thing because he tried not to arouse suspicion by leaving the house when his family was home. He didn't respond to my text. Finally my willpower broke down and I called him.

"Hello," he said, sounding irritated.

"Can you please come see me? Just for a minute? I need a hug and then I'll be okay."

"Just a minute," he said. "I'll have to go check back through my emails for that." There was a pause and I heard him telling Georgia it was one of his coworkers.

"Baby, I can't," he said a moment later, more quietly. "My wife is home, the kids are home, I can't leave right now. You know that."

I broke down in tears. I couldn't tell him I knew they were home because I had just watched them have dinner together. I had such a strong sense that if I could just see him for even one minute, things would be okay.

"Please, John. Please. I need you."

"I can't. Kristen, I didn't want to do this over the phone, but I can't see you anymore. I've made a decision to work on my marriage, for the kids' sake."

"All this time you said you were leaving her, you've been lying to me?"

"Look, this has been on my mind awhile. Please don't call anymore because I won't answer. I don't want to hurt you, but it's like ripping off a Band-Aid. It's better to get it over with quickly."

He hung up before I could even respond. I called him right back, but it went immediately to voicemail. So this was it. This was the level I'd sunk to, begging a man to leave his family and come and see me.

I didn't know what to do with myself. If it were morning, I'd go for a long run. I got in the car and found myself driving to my sister's house.

"Adrienne, John dumped me!" I cried, landing in her arms as soon as she opened the door. She usually looked annoyed when I showed up, but this time I knew I was in the right place.

"Oh, Krissy, what happened? Do you want some coffee?" she asked, leading me to her kitchen where I sat on one of the wooden stools at her counter while she dumped out the old filter and refilled it with decaf.

"He told me he was staying with his wife because of the kids," I said. "I told him he shouldn't have felt right lying to me about our future together. I invested two years in this relationship!"

Adrienne scrunched up her nose.

"When you say *invested*..." She trailed off. I knew that was the wrong word, especially in light of the fact that Adrienne was divorced because her husband cheated on her and *did* leave her and the kids for his girlfriend.

"I know, I know. He was married and I should have known better. But still! He made me feel like I had changed his life. He even said that, how his feelings were closed off and I made him realize how alive he could be again."

I suddenly understood how stupid it sounded. I believed all those words, but now saying them out loud to my sister, I saw clearly that I was being strung along all this time. I was a fool. Looking at Adrienne's situation, I had believed John would eventually make good on his promise, but who was I to believe his words when his actions said otherwise? A desperate thought occurred to me that maybe I could get John to realize he was making a mistake.

"I think I should go and talk to his wife. Maybe if I force the issue, he'll see that he's better off with me."

Adrienne grabbed me by the arms and shook me.

"No! Are you crazy?" she said, almost hysterical. "You can't do that. First of all, you were in the wrong by dating him from the outset because you knew he was married. He's only going to resent you for bringing his cheating into the open. And maybe his wife *does* know and is staying with him anyway."

"I don't think she knows," I said. "We were so careful."

"Besides," Adrienne asked, "what happened to you saying you never wanted to get married and never wanted that kind of commitment? Sure, it was exciting meeting him for lunch and sex, but do you really want to start doing his laundry and making his doctor appointments for him? Because that's the kind of stuff you'll be getting into."

"I guess the dating part is better than the commitment part," I conceded.

"And worst of all, if you two get married, you're going to have angry, resentful stepchildren who will always blame you for their parents' divorce because they don't want to blame their father."

"You sound really bitter, Adrienne. Is that why you didn't get together with George?"

"That and a lot of other reasons," she replied. "I messed up once at marriage, and I don't think I could stand to mess up again."

"You didn't mess up!" I said, leaning toward her. "It was all Drew. He cheated on you. You did all the right things."

I felt like a fraud telling her anything about cheating spouses, but she seemed to feel comforted nonetheless.

"Thanks for saying that, but I don't know. I can't help but think that if I had done some things differently, he wouldn't have cheated in the first place. I know things weren't perfect, but I felt like we could have kept it going. Didn't John always tell you that something was missing in his marriage? It's not like he was happily married and just happened to meet you and fall in love. You filled in something that was missing for him. That's what Amy did for Drew. I just wish I could have figured out what I wasn't doing."

"I don't think you could have done anything differently," I said, and I meant it. "Drew never grew up and he thinks he should have whatever he wants. Now he's the one who has to deal with stepchildren."

"Yeah, but it's not the same for men. Somehow they always get out of being blamed. You never hear a fairy tale with an evil stepfather, do you?"

"No, I guess not."

We sat side by side at the kitchen counter, sipping our decaf in silence for a few minutes. When I finished mine, I got up and put my empty mug in the sink.

"Thanks for the advice," I said, putting my arm around Adrienne's shoulder in a half hug.

Today was one of the first days I felt like my big sister talked to me without judging me. I only hoped I could keep up the willpower she had infused in me rather than trying any stunts to get John back.

# 4

A week passed, and I still hadn't heard from John. Every time I got a text or my phone rang, my heart started racing with anticipation, only to be filled with disappointment and anger that it wasn't him. I felt nauseated all of the time and had lost three pounds already.

I stood at the sink brushing my teeth, looking at the scorpion tail of my toothpaste tube and wishing John would come over and use his toothbrush again. When I finished brushing, I put my toothbrush away and picked up his, the orange one hanging next to my purple one. I had toyed with the idea of using his, but I figured that sharing mouth germs wasn't going to get me any closer to him. I had virtually no self-respect the way it was; I had to draw the line somewhere.

I threw his toothbrush in the trash, picked it up, and then threw it out again, this time burying it under a wad of toilet paper that I whipped off the roll so I wouldn't have to see it there and be reminded of him.

I walked into my room and smelled my pillows. There was a tiny trace of his cologne left on one of the pillowcases. I didn't want to do it, but I forced myself to strip the bed and wash all my sheets. After I threw them in the washer, wishing I could change my mind and smell the pillowcase one more time, I made up my bed with fresh sheets and climbed under the covers. I was erasing all the physical evidence that John was ever a part of my life, but how would I remove him from most of my waking thoughts? He was even in my dreams.

I tried to rewind the last two years of our relationship, picking apart the evidence of where it could have gone wrong. Things started to seem a little different between us a few months ago. I noticed that John was using the same patronizing trying-to-get-off-the-phone voice with me that he often did with Georgia. He'd say some bland thing about how he had to get going and have a good night. Before then, it was always me saying goodbye first. Where did the power shift happen?

I wondered if it was because he saw me pee. It is funny how you can be so intimate in bed and then want to cover up afterward. There was one night I needed to use the bathroom and I was so tired that I forgot to close the door. John got up for a glass of water and happened to see me on the toilet. It shocked me awake because it felt like such a domestic moment, like he was my husband rather than my lover. He never said anything about it. I was careful after that never to let it happen again, but maybe that moment woke him up too – we were no longer having an affair, but actually becoming a couple. The next step would be asking him to pop a zit for me or cutting hair out of his nostrils.

Who was using whom? I wanted to yell at him that he used me, but obviously I was getting something out of it too. I had grown used to receiving beautiful bunches of flowers, romantic cards with handwritten notes of how much he missed me, and gourmet meals from the best restaurants in town (even if they were always takeout to eat at my place).

It wasn't only John that I missed, but his whole family. Georgia and their kids Jack and Rachel had become like the characters on a beloved, long-running TV show. Now the series was over and I was left to wonder what had become of their lives.

I never met them in person. I wondered how Jack was doing in basketball, if Rachel was still making handmade dolls, and whether Georgia was going to follow through on her plans to go back to school for an MBA.

I checked my phone constantly for a missed call or a text that never came, but I couldn't bear to drive by their house again. Adrienne was right that no matter how painful it was for me, it was better for John's family that he and Georgia work things out. Watching Adrienne suffer through the aftermath of divorce over the past two years made me more convinced than ever that I was never getting married, no way, no how. Falling in love with someone only to realize you could lose them felt too dangerous.

Now that it was over and I could step back and really think about my part in it, I felt ashamed. It was easy to say John was the married one and it was his fault for cheating, but I let him. Yes, maybe if not me, he would have cheated with someone else, but I shouldn't have let it be me.

I was avoiding a grownup relationship where a man might actually expect a permanent commitment and children and sharing a life together. No matter how much I thought I wanted John to leave Georgia, I gave very little thought to what might happen after that. In my fantasies, he would get his own place and we'd spend nights at each other's apartments. We could go out to eat and hold hands in public and I'd finally meet his kids and we'd take them to the zoo. I did not imagine that his family would hate me, that no one could mistake Jack and Rachel as being our children together because I was so fair-haired compared to all of them. Even when he was divorced, people would always see me as the home-wrecker.

No, I didn't think of any of that. I was living in the moment, living on the adrenaline rush of getting away with something illicit. My sister and even my parents knew about John, but they found it distasteful to bring up the topic, except for the snide comments my mother made, like at holidays when he could never be with us. Of course my friends knew too, but only the single ones. It was the kind of thing I wouldn't dare tell a married friend because I knew she'd see me as a threat to her own marriage. If I'd have a relationship with someone's husband, maybe she couldn't trust me around hers.

I pulled the covers over my head and closed my eyes. Slowly and tenderly, I ran my fingers under my T-shirt and caressed my skin, remembering what it felt like when John was gentle and unhurried with me and I felt like I was his whole world.

# 5

I was still looking at John's Facebook page every chance I got between clients at work. Of course he had unfriended me, but he never set his posts to friends-only, so I could still see his pictures with his kids, and worse, the ones with his wife. How fake it all seemed... two weeks ago to the day, he had been at my place telling me how beautiful I am.

"Kristen, I have a new client for you," my co-worker Sara said, as she got off the phone at the spa's reception desk and broke me out of my self-pity spiral. "His name is Jason Schneider, and he has multiple sclerosis. I told him you can help him out. You can, right?"

I felt slightly panicky. Most of the people I worked on were there to relax or to deal with upper-middle-class lifestyle injuries like tennis elbow. We called the relaxation massages fluff-and-buffs, but I reminded myself I was trained for more than just that, so I said, "Sure. When's he coming in?"

"After lunch, at one," she said.

I had two massages in the morning, but I used my lunch to review best practices for MS, a much better use of my time than trolling Facebook. There was some encouraging information that it could help reduce anxiety and improve circulation and range of movement, but overall, massage wasn't going to alter the course of the disease.

I barely had time to eat a ham and cheese sandwich from the local gas station before Jason walked in, looking, well... not like what I expected. He was tall, skinny, and dark haired. Other than a mildly stiff gait in his walking, I wouldn't notice anything amiss. In fact, if I hadn't known he had MS, I never would have guessed anything was wrong other than aches and pains. I felt nervous and my throat tightened, making my voice sound higher than normal when I extended my hand to greet him.

"Hi, Jason. I'm Kristen. How are you today?"

"Great. How are you?" he asked, smiling so big that his eyes crinkled at the corners.

"I'm doing well, thank you. Sara told me when you booked your appointment that you'd like some help coping with your MS."

"Right. I'm not expecting miracles, but I am willing to try anything. Conventional medicine has reached its limits for me."

"What are your symptoms that you're looking for help with?" I asked, picking up my clipboard and leading him to my therapy room.

"Well, I have the R and R type – relapse and remitting," he said, walking alongside me and bumping into me a few times, as though the corridor were too narrow. "I seem to cycle every few months. I get stiff during an acute period and then spend my remission trying to regain what I lost. I'm in remission now, so I want to stretch my muscles back out so I stop walking around like an eighty-year-old man."

"I'd say more like seventy," I joked.

"I'm forty-five," he said.

I wanted to slap myself for sounding like an idiot when Jason didn't seem to find me humorous. I tried to recover. He was twelve years older, so maybe he didn't realize it was meant to be funny.

"Yes, that's a reasonable goal," I said more seriously.

"Unfortunately, there's no cure for MS," Jason said, looking at the floor. "Believe me, I've prayed for a miracle, but I don't think it's going to happen. The best I can do is keep my life as normal as possible."

"Are you employed?" I asked.

"Yes, I'm a family practice doctor," he said.

"Oh, I'm sorry, I should be calling your Doctor then," I said, feeling embarrassed for assuming he wasn't able to hold a job.

"No, no, that's fine. I have very few people in my life to call me Jason, and I'm here as your patient, so please don't call me Doctor. I have great respect for your field. I've often referred patients for massage therapy."

"Thanks," I said, brightening from the praise. "Let's get started then, okay? Have you had a massage before?"

"Yes, but it was years ago, and from a man. I know this doesn't sound very macho, but it hurt too much. I told him to lighten up a little, but he insisted he couldn't make progress if he didn't use enough pressure. I was sore for days after that, so I never went back. I specifically asked for a woman this time, and that's why I'm here at a spa instead of at a chiropractic clinic. I feel like a fish out of water," he said, looking around the room at the framed nature posters, the potted trees, and the massage table with its soft rose-colored sheets.

"Don't worry about it. Lots of people feel awkward the first time they go to a spa. It's not as clinical looking, but that's a good thing, if you ask me. I promise I'll listen to you about the pressure. I'm going to leave for a few minutes so you can undress to your comfort level and lie on your back under the sheet."

I pulled the door closed behind me and went back to the staff room to make notes on his chart while I waited. Then I knocked on the door and asked if he was ready. When I heard him respond "yes," I quietly opened the door and dimmed the lights. After washing my hands, I sat on a rolling stool behind Jason's head and put my fingertips to his temples, moving gently in circles. I moved the pads of my fingers over his cheekbones and forehead and onto his scalp and then to the back of his neck.

I could feel the tight cords of muscle running down his neck and started pressing harder.

"Is that okay?" I asked.

"Yes," he groaned, but he was breathing harder now and I could tell it hurt, so I lightened up the pressure.

"We might not be able to achieve as much as you had hoped today because you really are tight."

"Just go easy on me, please," he said. "I've been through a lot." And with that, tears pricked the corners of his closed eyes.

"I'm sorry," I said, feeling terrible. "Was I too rough on you? Or did I discourage you?"

"It's not that. This damn MS, sometimes I can't control my emotions too well. It's a side effect." He kept his eyes closed, but tears were running down the sides of his cheeks, so I rolled my stool over to the counter and put a box of tissues on my lap. I rolled back and handed him one while dabbing his cheeks with another.

"Do you want me to continue?" I asked.

"I'm so embarrassed!" Jason said, still refusing to look at me. "Yes, please continue. But do you mind if I turn over? This is too intense for me."

"Sure," I said, standing up and lifting the sheet slightly so that he could roll onto his stomach without getting tangled up in the fabric.

I placed my hands on his back gently, holding them in one place for a few seconds before beginning the lightest touch muscle manipulation I could manage. Tension flowed out of his body as I worked.

"It's been a long time since anyone has touched me like that," he said, sighing and now sounding more muffled since his head was in the face cradle. This was a line I'd heard often, but it didn't sound like a come-on when he said it.

I couldn't help but compare his back to John's. John's muscles were thick and pliable, like big slabs of steak. Jason had ropy muscles that were more defined. He was so thin that his vertebrae stuck out. Except for a little bit of tan on the back of his neck and his forearms, he was pale. He obviously didn't get outside much. I worked gently and quietly, listening to Jason sniffle a little bit while he worked to regain his composure. I had the feeling the tears had nothing to do with physical pain. The physical work often brought emotional pain to the surface too.

"My wife left me," he finally blurted out. "I think it frustrated her that I have a disease doctors can't explain."

"I'm very sorry," I said, trying to sound professional but not inviting more details.

"I need to get a grip. I really am sorry," Jason said.

"No need to apologize," I said, and we were both silent for the rest of the session. His tears stopped, his breathing slowed, and he seemed much more at peace, even smiling again when I tapped him on the shoulder and asked him how was he was feeling at the end of our time.

After Jason got dressed and I brought him a glass of water, he said he'd see me in a week and he walked over to the reception desk to pay, still looking stiff, but slightly less burdened.

Jason haunted my thoughts for the rest of the day. This was the most time I'd spent in weeks thinking about someone other than John. But this wasn't like the electric attraction I'd felt for John. John was love, or at least lust, at first sight. Jason had clearly been through a lot physically, only to have his wife leave him when he was down. I didn't know much about him yet, but he struck me kind and sincere. My general view of men was that they were untrustworthy and self-centered, yet something told me a man like Jason would never let me down. It was an odd feeling to have my perspective challenged.

# 6

Tamara and Heather texted me: *Let's go ho it up, girl!* These are my friends, who very useful for taking my mind off my troubles. It had been a rough month. Sometimes I missed John so much that my whole body hurt, but now and then I had breakthrough moments where I knew I was so much better off without him.

So here I was on a Thursday night, slipping on a silver sequined tank top over a black mini skirt and strappy high heeled sandals at 11:30 p.m. to meet Tamara and Heather in the parking lot of The Strand, the only place in our dumpy town you could fairly call a "club." No one from work would recognize me now, since I was required to wear a polo shirt with our spa's logo on the chest and khaki pants ("not tight," said the employee handbook). For practical reasons, I always had my hair in a ponytail at the spa, but tonight I wore it down.

Tamara and Heather were equally glammed up, looking like cranes picking their way through a marsh as they walked toward me in impossibly high heels to exchange air kisses and coo over my new outfit.

"Let's get our drink on," Heather declared, heading for the door. It sounded wrong the way she said it, like we were underage kids about to break the law. I followed her inside, linking arms with Tamara on the way to the bouncer at the door.

"Hey, ladies," Greg said, collecting our money and passing us through the door. He looked just like every other bouncer I had ever met. He was impossibly beefy, his neck as thick as his head and veins bulging out of his forearms under a tight V-neck shirt. He reminded me of a lobster, with wide, sloping shoulders tapering down to skinny legs. I saw him at the gym all the time, so I knew for a fact he worked for hours on his arms and chest while ignoring his back and legs, which was only going to lead to him being hunched over forward from the lack of balance in his muscle groups. Men never listened to women when they tried to give advice on lifting weights, so I kept my mouth shut. Maybe he'd be a future massage client.

As we were swept inside, I heard him greeting some girls who were twittering and tottering in behind us. Besides the fact that he called them "girls" instead of "ladies," I turned around in time to see him wave them in without collecting a cover charge from them. So my friends and I had reached *that* age already in our early thirties, where we weren't adding enough value to the club to get out of paying to be there. The expiration date was pretty young these days. Fortunately, there were still men who were happy to buy us drinks, even if we were a few years older than they were.

The Strand was the kind of place where we were among the older group looking to mix in with kids still in college who had turned twenty-one or at least had good fake IDs. The older men were there to hit on the younger women and the older women were there for the younger men. No one seemed too interested in their own age group. Older men had the currency of stable jobs and money to offer younger girlfriends, while we older women had the reputation of being indiscriminate wildcats in bed.

The music was so loud that it was hard to hear each other, but my friends and I didn't need to say much. We had our routine: We walked over to the corner of the bar and waited a few minutes to see if any guys would offer to buy us a drink. If nothing happened, we'd flag down the bartender and buy our own first round and carry our drinks to one of the tables across the room.

We bought our drinks and after we found a table I put down my Sea Breeze and motioned to my friends that I was heading for the ladies' room. Some of my mascara had gotten into my eye, and I needed to take care of it in front of a mirror. There was a line for the bathroom, and girls stood chatting with each other as we waited.

"I failed that econ test today, no question," I heard one girl telling her friend.

"I guess you go better visit the prof during his office hours and see if there's anything you can do to bring up your grade," her friend said, winking.

I felt so old here. I preferred being at work, where I usually felt young. Most of my clients were older and they were there for aches and pains.

The girl who suggested her friend seek "extra credit" turned and looked me up and down slowly.

"What are you doing here, Mom?" she asked me, sneering. Her friend playfully punched her on the arm. I could see they both were extremely drunk. They couldn't even stand up straight and they were hanging on to each other.

"That's not nice," her friend whispered, but she was starting to giggle too.

I was so shocked that I turned around and left the line, my eyes watering now. I headed back to our table as fast as I could make my way through the sweaty crowd.

"Do I have makeup under my eye?" I asked Tamara loudly.

"What?" she shouted.

"Never mind." I waved it off. She and Heather were clearly scoping out the room. I sat down and started drinking through my little cocktail straw.

Out of nowhere, a younger guy walked up to our table and said hello. Heather's face lit up and she started playing coyly with her hair, but I just sat holding my drink with both hands. He wasn't bad looking, but he didn't appeal to me.

"How are you ladies tonight?" he asked.

Heather giggled, Tamara looked back down at her phone when it pinged with a text message, and I sat quietly, looking back at him while he ignored my friend. It was too loud to have much of a conversation.

"Wanna go outside and talk?" He motioned toward the door.

I saw the girls who had made fun of me looking our way. Apparently, he had caught their attention too. Oh, what the hell, why not?

Without responding, I got up and started walking toward the door, knowing he was right behind me. I made sure I didn't look directly at the girls, but I knew they saw us because their mouths were hanging open and they were frowning. *Mom*, ha! Maybe they'd learn a lesson. I'm pretty sure I was strutting.

We walked past Greg toward the corner of the building, where it was darker and quieter. The guy pulled out a pack of cigarettes and held it toward me.

"Want one?" he asked. "By the way, my name's Kevin."

I took a cigarette, even though I'm not a smoker, and waited for him to light it. I've smoked enough that I can take a drag without coughing and looking like an idiot.

"Kristen," I said, not in the mood to talk, even though I was flattered that he singled me out.

"So, Kristen, what are you doing here tonight?" Kevin asked.

"Probably the same thing you are," I said, smiling ever so slightly.

"Well, that's interesting," he replied. "I'm here to meet a nice woman. That's what you're here for?"

"Ha, not exactly," I replied, looking down at my sandals and leaning against the wall.

"You looked lonely," Kevin said.

"I'm not sure how to respond to that."

"Lonely like you'd like someone to go home with you."

"What kind of girl do you think I am?" My heart started racing. I was dressed suggestively and trusting enough to walk away from my friends with a total stranger.

"You're not a girl, you're a woman, and I'm assuming you know what you want and how to get it," Kevin said, touching my arm. He was really creeping me out and I regretted the decision to show off in front of those girls rather than being sensible and acting my age.

"I better get back to my friends," I said. He was blocking my way, so I tried to brush against him to get back to the entrance.

"You're not going anywhere," he said, pushing me back against the wall and leaning in as though he were about to kiss me.

"Stop!" I yelled, looking to see whether Greg was paying attention. He looked our way and I shoved Kevin as hard as I could and started running toward the door. I tripped over a piece of uneven pavement and fell on my hands and knees, scraping a layer of skin off.

"Are you okay?" Greg asked, leaving his post to help me up. "What did you do to her?" he said to Kevin.

Kevin put his hands up and then turned around and walked into the parking lot.

"I'm okay," I said to Greg. "I just need to go back in and get my friends." I was limping a little now from the pain of the brush burns on my knees, but the pain was more the humiliation I felt at agreeing to go outside with some guy I didn't even know. How many times did I have to be stupid about men and their intentions before I'd figure it out?

I made my way to Heather and Tamara, in tears and wiping streaked mascara off my face with the back of my hand.

"What happened?" Tamara yelled over the music.

"I have to go," I said to them. Heather took a last long pull on her drink and we picked up our purses and left. Outside in the quiet, they huddled around me, turning over my hands to look at my scraped palms.

"Are you okay?" Heather asked, her eyes big.

"I just want to go home. Could one of you drive my car?"

Tamara offered to drive me home in my car since she had come with Heather. I hoped she was okay to drive. Tamara drinks fast and doesn't hold her liquor well, but my hands were stinging so badly I didn't think I could manage any better than she could.

Back at my apartment, Heather cleaned my hands and knees with peroxide and picked a few bits of gravel out of my wounds with tweezers while Tamara sprawled on the sofa with her head back.

"We have to stop doing this," I said to them. "We're too old for this. Everyone else our age is married with kids."

"We're young enough to go out and have fun and we don't want kids!" Tamara protested.

"And who wants to be married anyway?" Heather added.

"All I know is this is not for me. I love you guys, but I feel so fake. One of those girls in there called me Mom."

"That's disgusting!" Tamara said, rolling her head back and forth on my sofa.

I looked at my friends and thought how pathetic we seemed. I couldn't say it to them, but we were all pretending it was okay to act like we were a decade younger than we were. We'd been friends since high school, but it seemed like hanging out together was preventing all of us from growing up. We were no better than the younger girls trying to use their looks to get men to buy them drinks. We might have been poor college kids once, but now we were professional women who could buy our own drinks, or better yet, find something better to do than hanging around a lame club.

# 7

The next morning, my hands hurt so badly that I realized I was going to have to call off work. Since I unexpectedly had the time, I decided to hit the grocery store to prepare for a full-on, feeling-sorry-for-myself movie marathon at home.

I pulled on yoga pants and a T-shirt, then slid into flip flops, the only clothes I could comfortably manage while my hands were wrapped with gauze bandages. My shirt was loose enough that I hoped no one would notice I wasn't wearing a bra. I was going on a mission to buy comfort food and I planned to wrap myself into a cocoon on the couch as soon as I had some garlic bread and ice cream, the ideal combination of carbs, fat, and sugar to lull me into a stupor. Netflix was already set up for me to watch *Ghost* as soon as I got home.

As I was standing in front of the freezer doors, pondering whether to get plain garlic bread or the loaf with cheese, I heard Jason call out to me and push his cart my way. I felt embarrassed for him to see me like this, dressed for bed and buying junk food in the middle of the morning. I held up my bandaged hands.

"Whoa," he whistled. "What happened?"

"I don't really want to talk about it," I said. "I'm kind of ashamed."

His cart was filled with fresh vegetables. I doubted he was planning to buy extra-cheesy garlic bread.

"Listen, there's nothing you could tell me that would make me judge you. You know my sad story."

"I fell while trying to get away from a creepy guy in the parking lot of The Strand last night," I finally said.

"Oh," Jason replied. And then, "You go there? I thought it was all kids there."

He must have seen me wince.

"Sorry, I didn't mean to offend you, Kristen. But you know what I mean. Those really are kids there, not grown women like you. The main thing is you're okay, right? What did the guy do to you?"

"Nothing. He barely touched me. I think he figured I was drunk or something because of how I was acting, but I didn't even have a whole drink. I feel stupid."

"How does a woman like you not have a boyfriend or a husband?" Jason asked. "I mean, I know that's such a cliché question, but really, I'm asking."

"I don't want a husband," I said. "Look what happened to you. Why do you even ask that question? Marriage isn't a permanent thing anymore. Why do I want to pledge my life to some guy only to have him leave me in a few years? There's no point."

"Ah, that's where you're wrong, though," Jason said. "Marriage is supposed to be a permanent commitment. I'd still be married if there was any way my wife would have been willing to work things out. I think her family and friends talked her out of staying. I think it's because of my MS and she doesn't want to admit that."

"I don't know how you can feel optimistic about marriage," I said.

"I don't know either. I just do."

I started picking at the tape on the bandage, not knowing what to say.

"Would you be willing to meet for coffee sometime?" Jason asked.

I had been working with him as a massage client for five weeks now, and I found him intriguing, but not attractive in the overwhelming lustful way I felt about John. In all those sessions, Jason hadn't indicated having any feelings for me. John and I had a chemistry that became apparent pretty quickly when he asked for my number after our second massage session, and I stupidly gave it to him. Jason wasn't like that. He didn't seem like a man of physical desires and I was worried that by asking me out, he was just trying to take my mind off my feeling sorry for myself.

"I don't think so," I said to him. "We have a policy that we can't date clients."

"Then I'll stop being your client. You didn't say no. You said, 'I don't think so.' That means the door isn't closed all the way. It's just coffee. Something away from here?"

"I need to think about it."

"I'll call you in a few days. I promise not to bug you about it. I'll give you some time to think about it and if you say no I'll leave you alone."

"I'll meet you for coffee, but it can't be a date," I said. I wasn't sure why I was agreeing to give him my number, but I figured my instincts about men were always wrong, so maybe I'd be better off doing the opposite of what seemed to make sense to me. Jason was older, he was divorced, and he had a serious medical condition, but something about him kept him in the edge of my thoughts almost every day these past few weeks.

# 8

The following Saturday, Jason met me at the door of the coffee shop in the mall and we ordered at the counter together. As we sat down, he asked, "Do you like raisin bread?"

"Sure, I guess. Why?"

"Oh, thank God," he said. "I was afraid I would have to end this date right here and now."

"It's not a date, remember? And what, really? Raisins are that important to you?"

"They tell me everything I need to know about a woman," he said.

"Okay, I have to ask. What do raisins tell you about a woman?" The more I got to know him, the more his sense of humor caught me off guard and brought me out of my shell.

"Well, a woman who likes raisins is willing to be adventurous. I say this because kids always want everything plain, so someone who tries food with raisins in it is willing to try something new. And a raisin lover savors the sweetness in life. Raisins make everything better."

"That is about the cheesiest thing I have ever heard," I said, laughing now. "Tell me you don't really believe that."

"You'll never know," he said, winking. "It's nice to see you laugh. You have a great laugh."

I think I blushed a little. Now that we were sitting across from each other and he wasn't a massage client anymore, I felt free to look at him without the sense that I was doing something wrong. After the mistakes I'd made blurring the lines with John when we started dating, I was relieved that Jason started going to one of my co-workers for massage therapy appointments. I was flattered that he followed through on his promise that seeing me outside of work was more important to him.

It was clear from the lines around his eyes and the graying hair by his temples that he was older than I was, but he was preppy handsome. I was looking at skinny guys in a whole new way. He had those clear blue eyes that made me feel like I could see right into his soul, like he wasn't hiding anything.

"Kristen, I asked you here for something more important than to find out whether you like raisins."

"Okay," I replied, feeling curious.

"As you've noticed, I've been getting better and better physically. I've never had this long of a remission before. I know I could have a relapse, but I feel so good that I almost believe I am cured and I think you have a lot to do with that."

"I'm sorry, but everything I've read about massage and MS says otherwise. Massage can relax you, help you stretch tight muscles, but that's it."

"No, I'm not wrong. I'm sure of it. In fact, I asked God to help me. I promised I would turn my life around. Now I have to do my part."

"What's there to turn around in your life? You want me to help you get back together with your ex-wife?"

I started to think I had misread his intentions.

"No. Sadly, I've accepted that's never going to happen. And it's probably for the best. But my two daughters need the same kind of healing I've experienced. Kristen, I'm asking if you'd think about marrying me."

Okay, I wasn't misreading anything. But what was he thinking?

"You barely even know me!" I said. "And you know I don't want to get married or have kids."

"Kristen, I knew this wasn't going to be easy for you to hear. I was taking a chance even asking. But please think about it."

"We haven't even dated," I sputtered. "This is crazy."

"Sometimes you just know," he said. "You're the one for me, and you're the one for my girls."

Jason got up, took his coffee cup and napkin, and left the table without turning around to say goodbye. I was in shock. This guy is telling me I'm a healer? And I should marry him? And here I thought I was nuts; apparently there are people even crazier out there than I am.

# 9

I may have thought Jason was out of his mind, but I found myself more drawn to him than ever. What did he see in me that he'd propose on our first date? How come John never saw me as wife material? Or any of the other guys I'd ever dated? I certainly didn't envision myself married.

When he called on a Wednesday to ask me for dinner that Saturday, I didn't even try to be coy and tell him I'd have to check my calendar. I said yes.

"Good," he said. "I made reservations at La Belle Epoque." Only the nicest and most expensive restaurant anywhere within fifty miles. Whoa.

On the day of our date, I treated myself to a manicure. Then I stopped at the mall to buy a new dress. Jason was right on time picking me up at my apartment. When he knocked at the door, I counted to five slowly before answering, determined to look relaxed and not over-eager. Most of my dates were very casual or even secretive, so being taken out in a guy's car to a public place was something new for me. That was my own fault for dating the kind of men I did.

Jason smiled when I opened the door, but didn't say anything about my dress or my appearance. Unlike other men, who seemed attracted by my looks, Jason showed very little indication that my appearance was important to him. It was confusing in a way. What else did I really have to offer?

I had passed La Belle Epoque before, but had never eaten there. It was too expensive for a girls' night out. The trees lining the walkway were wrapped in tiny white lights, making a canopy above us as we walked to the front door. It was a beautiful May evening, the leaves finally fully out on the trees and the sun just setting as we were seated at a table overlooking the gardens in the back. Jason asked for a wine menu.

"Do you mind if I choose something for us?" he asked.

"I don't usually drink wine, so go ahead," I said.

"I'm sorry, do you drink at all? I should have asked you ahead of time."

"Yeah, but usually a Sea Breeze or a Bud Light Lime or something like that."

Jason smiled, but didn't respond. When the waiter came back to the table, he ordered a Bordeaux, the waiter nodding that it would be a great match with the night's specials.

"This restaurant specializes in cuisine from the southwest region of France, so we should enjoy its wine as well," he said.

I opened the menu, in a leather-bound cover as large as a desktop atlas, and started looking at my options. I'm a picky eater, used to fast food with the occasional infusion of Mom's homemade roasts, potatoes, and other bland-but-tasty all-American favorites. The whole menu was in French. Words like *duxelles*, *fromage*, and *haricots* sounded vaguely familiar, but seeing all of them together was overwhelming. "Anything you'd recommend?" I asked. "I've never been here before."

"I'm surprised," Jason said, looking amused. "Where have your dates been taking you?"

"Don't ask," I muttered. "Just tell me what to order."

"I'd suggest the *salmis de sarcelles*," he said.

"I don't even know what that is."

"It's roast duck."

"Duck? Does it taste like chicken?"

"Not at all."

"So what does duck taste like?"

"Why don't you try it and find out?"

When the waiter came back, I took Jason's advice and ordered the duck, but I noticed he ordered something else.

"Why didn't you order the duck if it's the best thing on the menu?" I asked him.

"Two people in a French restaurant ordering the same dinner? What a waste! I ordered salmon terrine so we can try each other's. You don't mind, do you?"

I shook my head no.

"Do you come here a lot?" I asked.

"Not anymore," he said. "My wife – ex-wife and I used to bring the girls here often. They've become quite the little food snobs. Would you believe they've never been to McDonald's?"

I gasped. "I don't know how I'd survive. I hit the drive-through at least three times a week."

"Maybe I can get you spoiled too. Do you cook?"

"Not really. I know how, but I don't really see the point. Do you?"

"I'm learning. My ex was a great cook, but when she left, I realized I needed to take better care of myself, especially now that I am in remission. I try to eat whole foods only, no more processed junk."

"Does that help your MS?"

"Studies don't prove it, but I believe it does."

"I seem to run just fine on McDonald's and gas station food."

"You're lucky," he said, shaking his head.

"You talk about your ex a lot."

It seemed like a bit of a red flag. Maybe I was just a rebound. Or maybe he was playing me to try to get back at her. I didn't know him well enough yet to discern his feelings about her.

"Do I? I'm sorry. I guess I'm still coming to terms with the divorce."

"Are you technically divorced?"

"Yes, we're divorced. I wouldn't have felt right to ask you on a date if I were still married. Much less ask you to marry me." He winked at me. "Have you given my proposal any more thought?"

"I didn't consider that a proposal, more like a suggestion," I said. "And I'm here getting to know you, aren't I? It's just way too soon. I don't think you're in your right mind."

"Perhaps," he agreed, although it sounded like he didn't actually agree.

"So what's your ex like? What's her name?"

"Julia."

"Jason and Julia. It sounds perfect. Jason and Kristen doesn't have quite the same ring to it, does it?"

"If only things were as perfect as two names that sound good together," he said. "Julia is perfect in many ways, but she couldn't love my imperfection. It's our profession to fix people, but they can't always be fixed. She's a doctor too."

"Wow. So she really left you because of your MS? Whatever happened to *in sickness and in health*?"

"Do you think you could stay with someone who had a disease like mine? Think about it before you answer."

"I really don't know. I was never in that circumstance. But I'd like to think that if I made a marriage vow like that, I would."

"How come you never got married, Kristen?"

I squirmed in my chair.

"I don't want to. You should see my sister. It pretty much wrecked her life."

"Ahh, but was it the getting married or getting divorced that wrecked her?"

"She didn't have much of a choice. Her husband was cheating on her."

"Could she have forgiven him?"

"I don't know. I wouldn't be able to." What if I were John's wife instead of his girlfriend and Georgia was the other woman? Would I be able to forgive him? I doubted it. I didn't believe in the permanency of relationships.

My parents were still married, but it was almost like they were assigned roommates who had made their peace by interacting with as little conversation as possible. They politely ignored each other's foibles and moved gently around each other. I never asked them if they were happy. The way I saw it, they tolerated each other. They could certainly be in a more disagreeable situation, but where was the passion?

Our meals arrived and I cut through the crispy skin of the duck. I was about to peel it off and put it to the side, but Jason stopped me.

"That's the best part," he exclaimed.

It looked like dark-meat chicken, which I usually only ate in the form of hot wings when I was slumming at the local bar, but the taste was amazing without all of the overdone flavoring of almost everything I ate. The duck tasted rich and buttery, and I smiled as I took another bite with a perfectly roasted carrot. Jason sat watching me, seeming to enjoy the duck vicariously.

"Would you like to try it?" I asked him.

"Of course I would. Do you mind?" he asked, pulling my plate closer to him. I watched him as he cut a small piece, closing his eyes as he savored it.

"Delicious," he said. "An excellent choice."

"Are you always so humble?" I asked, laughing. "And are you going to let me try yours too?"

"But of course. I'm glad you like fish." "I've only had fried fish filets, but if this is like comparing duck to chicken, it has to be amazing."

"You're quite the adventurous one. See, I was right about the raisins, wasn't I?"

"I don't know how sweet I am, but I do pride myself on trying new things," I said, smiling suggestively. He smiled back and held my gaze for a moment.

The rest of dinner was fairly quiet, as was the restaurant as a whole. The food was so good that it seemed everyone spoke in hushed voices so they could focus on the delicacies they were enjoying. Compare that to one of the large chains where everyone's talking loudly, stuffing fries and cheese-laden appetizers into their mouths and swilling down ridiculous mixed drinks. I had never experienced a meal like this, and I was afraid that Jason was right that I would become spoiled.

We shared a crème brûlée with fresh raspberries on top, cracking the caramelized sugar with our spoons, and sipped tiny cups of espresso before Jason paid the bill. I started offering to split it with him, but he waved his hand dismissively.

"If you enjoyed yourself, invite me over for dinner sometime," he said. He got up first and pulled my chair out for me, then walked me back to his car with his hand lightly on my back. The drive home was quiet, but Jason was humming and tapping on the steering wheel.

"What are you singing?" I asked.

"Oh, nothing really. I'm just happy," he replied, smiling but keeping his eyes on the road.

Back at my apartment, he jumped out of the car to open my door for me and walked me to the door.

"Do you want to come in for a few minutes?" I asked, not wanting the date to end.

"Nope. It was a beautiful night and I can't imagine a better ending than saying good night right here."

With that, he pulled me close and brushed his lips against my cheek. I thought he had been aiming for my mouth and turned toward him, so he caught me closer to the nose than the side of my face. We both laughed and pulled apart.

"Thank you. I had a very nice time tonight," I said.

"So did I. Good night, Kristen." He watched me unlock my door and then turned around and headed back down the walkway toward his car.

I closed the door behind him and then leaped around my apartment a few times in my bare feet. I don't know if it was the caffeine or the excitement of the nicest date I'd ever been on, but I was on a high. I knew it was going to be hard to sleep.

# 10

What do you wear to your boyfriend's daughters' dance recital? Correction: What do you wear to your boyfriend's daughters' dance recital when you're meeting his kids and his ex-wife for the first time? I wanted to look amazing without looking like I was trying too hard to look amazing. It was a rainy morning and I was already fighting frizzy hair and a time-of-the-month breakout on my face, plus I was feeling as bloated as a toad.

Jason's daughters both danced ballet and their June recital was apparently a major annual event for the family. Miriam was fifteen and Eleanor, otherwise known as Ellie, was nine. Jason and I had been dating for almost a month now and he asked if I would accompany him to the recital and then out for dinner to celebrate with them afterward. His ex-wife Julia would be at the recital, but it was his weekend with the girls, so we'd only see her momentarily. Still, momentarily was enough for me to stress over how I looked. I felt extra pressure knowing Jason was hoping so much that his girls would like me. He seemed really excited for me to meet them, whereas I was willing to take it slow. I liked the fact that it was just us so far. Neither of us had met our other friends or family yet, and I was happy to leave it that way a little longer because it seemed like less pressure when we were incubating our new relationship. He had laid off the marriage talk because I asked him to, but meeting his family suddenly took things to a new level of serious.

I settled on wearing a floral sleeveless shift with a yellow scarf and matching sandals. Jason picked me up exactly when he promised to be there. I looked out the window and grabbed my umbrella and ran out when he pulled up in the parking strip outside my apartment so he wouldn't have to get out in the rain. He had already dropped off the girls at the high school so they could get ready backstage.

"You look nice," he said, kissing me on the cheek as I climbed into his car, breathless from running in heels through the rain. I had stepped in a puddle and now my toes felt squishy in my sandals.

"Thanks," I said, putting on my seatbelt and consciously unclenching my hands so that I wouldn't look so nervous.

"You'll be fine, don't worry," he said, leaning over to kiss me.

"I'm okay," I said. I had spent the morning trying to think of things I'd say to his daughters when I met them, hoping I wouldn't clam up the way I usually did with my sister's boys. I hoped it would be easier to talk to girls since we should have more in common.

We parked in the high school's lot, my own alma mater, and grabbed our umbrellas to slosh through the rain to the front doors. There was a line of parents and grandparents huddling under the overhang, and before Jason even pointed her out, I spotted Julia. She might as well have been the only color in a black-and-white movie. She wore a dusky pink trench coat with its belt tied tight around her tiny waist. Below the hem of the coat and a few inches of bare leg were adorable fuchsia wellies. Jason had told me Julia is half Chinese, half Italian. She tossed her silky black hair over her shoulders so it was hanging down her back before leaning down toward a tiny woman next to her. The woman had her hand around a stout man's arm, and I guessed that these were Julia's parents. As I stared, Julia stood upright again and turned toward us, flashing her beautiful white straight teeth in an arresting smile and waving as she saw Jason and me. I forced myself to stand up taller and smile because I suddenly felt invisible.

Jason walked more quickly, almost tugging my hand, to get to Julia and her parents. He kissed Julia and her mother on the cheek and hugged his ex-father-in-law. After he stepped back, there was a momentarily silence as all three of them looked at us expectantly, until Jason said, "I'd like you to meet Kristen."

Fortunately he had prepared them all, including his daughters, for my coming with him so that it wouldn't be a shock or cause hurt feelings. Julia and her parents all shook my hand as though we were business associates. No one said anything, so I blurted out "Some weather we're having today, isn't it?" Everyone nodded. Could I sound any more stupid? Better to keep my mouth shut than try to make small talk that is so cliché I'm actually talking about the weather.

"Well, shall we go in?" Jason asked, holding his hand out as though he were a ringmaster ushering us into the big top. Julia and her parents led the way, and I followed, with Jason's hand lightly on the small of my back. I didn't know whether he expected us to sit together, so I turned to him with a questioning look.

"What?" he asked, but I couldn't really say anything out loud, so I kept following Julia, hoping Jason would detour us away. Julia went about halfway down one of the aisles, then pointed to seats in the middle of the row and motioned for her parents to go in first. Then it was a choice between me and Jason sitting next to Julia, and Jason deftly maneuvered past me so that he was sitting by her and I was on the other end. They each picked up their program bulletins and started paging through them.

"There's Miriam," Julia exclaimed, pointing at a half-page ad that they, or one of them, had purchased to help sponsor the printing for the programs. "Isn't she beautiful?" I had seen pictures of Jason's daughters that he pulled out of his wallet on our second date, but even I had to admit that Miriam looked especially lovely in the black-and-white photo, where she was silhouetted against a softly lit window in a graceful arabesque with her dark hair in a loose bun, tendrils framing her jawbone. She had the same tall willowy frame as Jason.

"And here's Ellie," Jason said, pointing in his bulletin to a photo of a younger, pudgier version of Miriam. Ellie was wearing a leotard and tutu and posing with her arms arced over her head. Unlike Miriam's more serious expression, Ellie had a huge grin.

"Hmm," said Julia, taking Jason's bulletin to look more closely at it. I sat on his left, feeling like the third wheel as he chatted with Julia about the girls, how Miriam had to help Ellie with her hair because he was hopeless at it. Finally the lights dimmed and everyone got quiet. As the curtains rose in the darkened auditorium, I hoped that Jason would take my hand, but he kept them folded together in his lap. I settled for gently resting my knee against his leg, feeling a tingle of excitement course through my body just from two square inches of our clothed bodies touching. Sometimes we held hands, and we always kissed when we said hello and goodbye, but touching his knee felt more intimate. I was used to men who were hoping to get in bed after the first date. Even though I realized Jason must find me attractive if he wanted to marry me, it made me feel insecure that he held back on physical affection.

Jason and Julia looked intensely focused on the stage, so I watched too, trying to pick out which dancer was Miriam. They all basically looked the same – tall, lithe girls with flat chests and long legs and hair scraped back tightly into buns. Each of them had long ribbons flowing from her bun and graceful dresses that fell below the knee. The only thing that differentiated them was the color of their hair and complexion.

During the intermission, Jason excused himself to the lobby and came back five minutes later with two enormous bunches of flowers wrapped in cellophane cones. I felt a little pang of jealousy that the flowers were for his daughters, especially because he had never brought me flowers in the four weeks since we had started dating. Now he had two crinkly packages covering his lap and it would have been difficult to maneuver holding my hand even if he had wanted to.

When the show ended, we walked outside, where it had finally stopped raining, and waited for Miriam and Ellie to get changed and meet us. Julia and her parents waited too, because even though the girls were coming with us, they wanted to see them first. We stood awkwardly for a few minutes of mostly silence, with a few more comments about the weather, when finally the girls came out in street clothes, duffle bags in hand. They both still had their hair in buns, but they had washed off their stage makeup. Miriam touched her head self-consciously as Ellie ran into her dad's arms, knocking him off balance.

"Ellie Bellie," he said, "these are for you!" He handed her one of the bouquets, which she immediately lifted to her nose to sniff and then held the flowers close to her chest. Miriam stood by her mother, looking at us but not approaching, so Jason moved closer to her to hand her the other bouquet.

"You did beautifully, honey," he said, kissing her on the cheek.

"Thanks, Dad."

"Only another dancer would notice the few places you were off your mark," Julia said. Miriam's head dropped ever so slightly.

"Well, shall we get going?" Jason asked. "I have hibachi reservations for us. I bet you girls have worked up an appetite after all that dancing!"

Julia had tears in her eyes as she hugged them goodbye and told them she'd see them soon. She turned to take her mother's arm and led her parents toward her car, while the girls followed us in the opposite direction to Jason's.

Miriam walked ahead of us and stood by the front passenger door. Jason started to tell her no, but wanting to be accommodating, I said, "No, it's fine. I'll sit in the back with Ellie, if that's okay with her." God, did I sound lame? I was the teensiest bit pissed off at Jason that he allowed his fifteen-year-old daughter to sit in the front, but it was her day and it was my first time meeting them.

When we walked into the restaurant, the smiling host seated us and we looked over the menu. We ended up with Jason's daughters on either side of him and me to the right of Ellie. Miriam and Jason didn't even open their menus, but Ellie and I took our time. She and I both ordered the chicken, while Jason ordered the vegetables and Miriam declined to order.

"I'll just eat a little of Dad's," she said.

"The portions are huge," he added.

"Why didn't you tell me? Maybe I should have split one with you, or with Ellie?" My insecurity was growing and I hoped my smiles didn't look fake.

"Ellie eats all of hers anyway," Miriam said, reaching behind Jason to punch her sister's arm.

"Oww!" Ellie said, but she couldn't reach as far to hit back.

"Come on, girls," Jason said, putting an arm around each of them. "How about telling Kristen what it's like up there on the stage? She's never danced before."

"It's fine," Miriam said.

"It's okay," Ellie said. And that was it. So far, conversation wasn't great. I don't spend time around kids and they always act weird. All the questions and comments I'd practiced earlier in the day seemed to fly out of my head because I was so nervous.

"You both looked so graceful up there," I ventured. "Do you get nervous before your performances?"

"No," they both said together. Great – one-word answers. I guess I was going to have to come up with better questions.

Fortunately, we were saved by the chef, who rolled out a cart full of ingredients and tools and started by slicing an onion, arranging it into a pyramid, squirting something into it and lighting it on fire. A huge *foom* and it was over, but it distracted all of us and seemed to lighten the mood. He began throwing chicken on the cooking surface, slicing and sautéing before pushing it to the side while he cooked the vegetables, artfully chopping them and incorporating all the ingredients together as he used his spatula to fill our plates.

The group at the next hibachi table was raucous and loud. They looked like a real family having a lot of fun together. I could see that Jason thought this would be a good icebreaker for meeting his daughters, but in a place like this, our quietness only seemed all the more out of place. We'd have been better off at his favorite French restaurant where it was so quiet that it felt rude to speak at an ordinary volume.

As she promised, Miriam only picked at Jason's plate, using chopsticks while he used a fork. Ellie and I both used forks and apparently we were either hungry or nervous because we were both shoveling it in. I'd definitely have to run a few extra miles the next morning to make up for this.

When we all finished, Jason paid the bill and we walked back to the car. I tried to walk a little faster to get to the front seat without being obvious about it, but Miriam got there at the same time. It felt like we were having a staring contest, but I blinked first. I stepped out of the way and let her sit in the front again. I was silently seething that Jason wasn't taking control of the situation. His girlfriend should be in the front, not his daughter. And I shouldn't have to assert myself and look bad.

Jason stopped in front of my apartment and waited while I got out. There was no practical way to kiss or hug him goodbye since he was in the front and I was in the back on the passenger side, so I just casually said "Bye, everyone" and jumped out. I didn't turn around as I walked up the walkway to my front door, but I heard him pulling away before I even unlocked the door. I slammed the door and threw myself down on the sofa to cry it out. Meeting his kids was ten times worse than I could have imagined.

# 11

Jason called the next morning. "That went well, don't you think?" he asked.

"Are you delusional? Miriam hated me!" I said, realizing after the fact that being negative about his daughters was only going to backfire.

"What evidence is there of that? I think they acted pretty normal, considering the fact that their dad was out on a date with a woman who's not their mom." He sounded so rational, but I was still hurting.

"I don't think this is for me. I'm interested in you, but this is more complicated than I bargained for." I hoped he would say he couldn't live without me, talk me back into the belief that we could work things out. He had a way of carrying us both through when I started to worry.

"How many men do you think you're going to find who don't have some baggage? I'm willing to deal with yours," he said. He had a point, but at least my baggage wasn't children I was expecting him to raise.

"Maybe I'm not ready for a real relationship." I wished we could rewind to that magical time before I met his kids, before things seemed so serious. Dating Jason was fun when it was just us and I could put it out of my mind that he had children to take up his time and his heart.

"You're thirty-three years old. If you wanted the life you had before and it was working the way you wanted, you wouldn't have given me a second glance. You wouldn't have met me for coffee that day. And you never would have agreed to see me again when I told you I want to marry you."

"I just didn't think it was going to feel like this." I paced back and forth across my living room as we talked.

"All right, Kristen. I felt from the moment I met you that we are meant to be together, but if you don't believe it too, it's not going to work out."

Whoa. From the moment we met? I had no idea. I tried to think back to how I felt when we met. I remember being nervous, but definitely no spark. No sense of destiny. I couldn't see what he saw in me. I was younger and attractive, but that didn't seem to matter to him. Why did he think we could be married and his daughters would ever come to love me?

"Are you still there?" he asked softly.

"Yes. I need to think about things."

"Take your time," he said.

I felt unsettled when we got off the phone. When I was dating John, somewhere in the back corner of my mind, I knew it was never going to go anywhere even though he constantly told me he was going to leave his wife.

On the other hand, a lifetime with Jason was a real possibility. I could go from single to married with kids, and they weren't even my kids, and they didn't like me very much and maybe never would. He was in remission now, but what would happen if he had another setback with his MS? Would I be his caretaker and a stepmom? I didn't understand why Jason felt so sure that this was the right path to take. I was caught between fearing he was using me and wanting to believe he saw a spark of good in me that no one else had ever picked up on, that I really could be a wife and a role model for two growing girls.

I hoped that going for a run would ease my mind. It was one of the few healthy habits I had for coping with stress. I laced up my sneakers and headed out the door. It was a beautiful Sunday morning, warm but not humid, blue skies with enough clouds to give a few breaks from the sun.

Maybe I have daddy issues; maybe that's why I was interested in a man who's twelve years older. There's nothing wrong with my dad, but I certainly never got the chance to be Daddy's little girl. Neither did Adrienne, for that matter. Although Mom and Dad always provided for us and we spent a lot of time together as a family, they were not in any way affectionate. We barely talked. When we ate dinner together, we were all watching TV or reading. My belief is that men may say they need you around, but that's only at their own convenience.

I ran without thinking of where I was going until I ended up at Adrienne's house. She'd given me good advice about John; maybe lightning would strike twice and she'd know what to do about Jason. I knocked on her kitchen door and she answered it wearing rubber gloves and holding a dish towel.

"Need some help?" I asked.

"You're offering to help me clean? Did you get bonked on the head?" she asked, gesturing for me to come in. I grabbed another towel from the cabinet next to the sink to help her finish drying some pans.

"You cooked?" I asked.

"I do that sometimes," she said, sounding defensive. "Want some coffee?"

"I'll just get myself a glass of water. You're busy."

"Never too busy for my little sister," she said, rolling her eyes. We both laughed. I took a long swig of water.

"I need advice."

"Uh-oh, trouble in paradise?"

"I met Jason's girls yesterday."

"Oh. Well, you didn't really expect to hit it off, did you? Didn't you learn anything from watching the way George's daughter treated me when she thought I was dating her dad?"

"They weren't *that* bad," I said. "Just... not really warm or anything. I tried to talk to them and they didn't say much."

"Look at my boys, Kristen. They've known you their whole lives and they don't say that much to you. Does that make you assume they hate you?"

"No. But they're boys."

"They're kids. Kids need some time to warm up to adults, especially adults who are dating their recently divorced parents. I can't tell you how many times Tyler and Nicky came home with stories about their stepmom. Amy tries really hard with them, but still. It's weird for them going to visit their dad in another woman's house. You have to allow for that, Kristen. It's going to take time."

"Jason is so confident everything is going to work out. I don't know how he can be so sure."

"No one is sure about anything. That's life. I would feel devastated if a man didn't want a relationship with me because I have kids and he doesn't. You could grow to love Jason's daughters."

"I never saw myself as the stepmom type."

"And I never saw myself as the divorced mom type, but here I am. Stuff happens."

"So you think I should give this more of a chance?"

"I can't make your decisions for you, but I will say that this is the first guy you've ever dated that doesn't seem like a loser. I'd like to meet him."

"Wow, thanks."

"Anytime, sis. Get back out there and finish your run. I have vacuuming to do."

I finished the glass of water, gave my sister a quick hug, and jogged back out the door. Who knew sisters could be so useful? I wish I had figured this out like maybe twenty years ago.

# 12

I wanted to try harder to get to know my nephews and give my sister a break, especially after the way she'd taken me under her wing with all my relationship problems. I told Adrienne I'd take the boys somewhere for the day so she could enjoy a date with her new boyfriend Jonathan in New York City. I also needed a major distraction from thinking about Jason and his daughters.

I realized that if Jason and I were going to stay together, I needed to learn more about kids and what to do with them. He seemed to expect that even though I had almost no previous interaction with children, I was going to get along fabulously with Miriam and Ellie. Adrienne's kids could be like my warmup.

There was no way we were going to sit around my apartment all day, so I decided to take them to the nearest amusement park. Nicky and Tyler don't usually talk to me much, so they sat in the back of the car looking out the windows while I kept changing the radio station, fidgeting and feeling nervous about being alone with them for the whole day. Usually Adrienne was with us as a buffer and she did all the talking.

We got to the park, paid twelve bucks for the privilege of parking and spending more money there all day, and spent another hundred-some dollars on admission. By the time I paid for the tickets, I realized I would not be buying any new clothes this summer. Lesson number one: Kids are expensive.

Since it was lunchtime, I figured we'd better get something before we went on the rides. When I asked them if they were hungry, they both shrugged and looked at me. "Pizza or hot dogs?" I asked, pointing in two opposite directions to the nearest food stands.

"Pizza" said Nicky at the same time as Tyler said "hot dog." I handed Nicky a five dollar bill and sent him for the pizza while I took Tyler to get a hot dog. I figured with Tyler being younger, it would be prudent to accompany him.

"Meet us right at this table," I said to Nicky, pointing to an empty one in the shade. He nodded and walked off slowly. I grabbed Tyler's hand and led him over to order hot dogs and two sodas.

"I'm not allowed to have this," he said when I handed him his drink.

"You couldn't have told me that before I ordered it?" I asked.

"You didn't give me time," he said, looking at the ground. I could see he was starting to cry now. I felt like a terrible aunt. I got back in line and bought a bottled water for three more bucks.

We took our food to the table and I started scanning the crowd, looking for Nicky. I figured he would have gotten there first because his line was shorter. After five more minutes, during which I felt too guilty to eat my hot dog, I contemplated telling Tyler to stay put while I looked for his brother, but then I realized it might be child abuse or something to leave him alone.

"We have to find Nicky," I said. "Are you almost finished?" He wasn't even halfway through his hot dog and he had ketchup all over his face, but he looked up at me and nodded. I picked up all of our food and he followed me as we pushed through the lunchtime crowd. My heart was racing and I was panicking because I realized it was not a good idea to leave an eleven-year-old alone in an unfamiliar place, even for five minutes. What was I going to do if he wasn't there?

I felt relieved to see him standing in front of the pizza stand, but then I noticed that he was crying and he didn't have any pizza.

"What happened?" I asked, lifting his chin so he'd look at me.

"I lost the money, Aunt Krissy. I'm really sorry," he choked out, before starting to really blubber. I grabbed a couple of napkins from behind him.

"Here, wipe your nose. It's okay about the money," I said, though I couldn't figure out how you could lose money that fast. I got in line to order him a piece of pizza and another bottled water, leaving Tyler to console his older brother.

"I miss Mommy," I heard him telling Nicky, which only caused him to cry more. Great. I was obviously no substitute for a mom. I thought of calling Adrienne and asking her to talk to them, but I didn't think it would be fair to her to get her worked up hearing them crying when she was trying to have one day away. Because of my own pride, I also didn't want to let her know that we just got here and I had already made them both cry. I thought of bailing out and just taking them home to watch TV, but after all the driving and the money I spent, I felt more determined than ever that we were going to enjoy this place.

Now carrying all the food and drinks, I led the boys over to another table and we sat down to have lunch. They both looked like they were calming down and I put on the brightest smile I could.

"So guys, what rides do you like? Do you go on roller coasters?"

"Nooo," Tyler said. "Tilt-a-Whirl!" Barf. This was going to be a long day. Of course they'd like the rides that make me sick and reject the only ones I felt like going on. I wondered if this was what it would be like to be a parent all the time, putting your own wishes on the back burner to make a nice time for the kids.

When we finished eating, we walked over to all the rides that spin in circles and I watched from the side as they ran to get in line and go on one after the other, seemingly oblivious to the food and water sloshing around in their bellies. Finally they asked to go on the bumper cars, and since that was something I could handle without getting nauseous, I got in line with them.

"So, what do you think of Mom's new boyfriend?" I asked, trying to make conversation, but also curious as to how they felt about Adrienne dating.

"He's all right," Nicky said.

"We liked George better," Tyler said.

"Yeah, but he wasn't really your mom's boyfriend, right?" I asked.

"Exactly," Nicky said. "He just came over and played with us sometimes. Jonathan lives in New York, so we only met him once, and he talked to our mom the whole time."

"So if she got married to Jonathan, what would you think of that?"

"I wouldn't really like it, but it's okay, I guess," Nicky said. Apparently he was the spokesman of the family.

"Our dad is married to Amy," Tyler said.

"I know. And that's okay, right?"

"They're always busy with the new baby. When we go there, we just play video games with our stepbrothers most of the time," Nicky said.

They both looked so utterly unenthused about their parents' love lives that it made me feel bad for even contemplating marrying Jason. He must be nuts to think his daughters were going to be okay with this situation. Maybe they'd like a really sweet motherly type woman, but I wasn't the right candidate for that. I had the sensitivity of a rhino when it came to kids and their confusing array of emotions.

We all seemed more lighthearted after a good round of bumper cars, slamming into each other and barely making it around the track.

"How about we try your first roller coaster?" I suggested. "Wouldn't it be fun to tell your mom and dad you went on one today?" They looked skeptical, but I led them over to the line for the least scary-looking one.

"Let's get in line. If you decide not to, we can get out of line. Look, this one doesn't go too high and it only has one loop."

"Who's going to sit with you?" Nicky asked.

"We'll flip a coin. Or you guys can sit together and I'll sit right in front of you."

"Tyler can sit by you; he's younger," Nicky said, trying to look brave.

"All right! Let's do this!" I said, taking them both by the hand. We got into the line for seats in the middle. If it were up to me, I'd sit in the front, but the middle made sense for their first time. I wanted them to enjoy it, not go home and say I was torturing them.

Tyler clung to me the best he could over the bar holding our legs down. As we climbed the hill, I turned around to look at Nicky, who had a death grip on the bar and his eyes scrunched closed.

"You're going to be fine," I said, and he nodded, keeping his eyes shut.

All of us screamed through the rest of the ride. As we got out of our seats, I looked at their faces for a reaction, but couldn't tell what they were thinking. Finally, Nicky said, "That was awesome!"

"Can we go again, Aunt Krissy?" Tyler asked, pulling my arm toward the line.

"Of course!"

The rest of the day seemed much more easygoing and I started laughing and kidding around with my nephews and patting them on the back as we waited in line.

After a couple more hours of junky food and long lines followed by adrenaline-fueling rides, we were all exhausted. The boys talked nonstop for the first half of our drive home, reviewing which rides they liked best and bragging that they couldn't wait to tell their parents and stepbrothers that they went on the roller coasters. The chatter tapered off and I realized they had both fallen asleep. I looked in the rearview mirror as their little heads were turned toward each other. I turned the radio off and felt content in the darkness and silence of the car as we drove home.

# 13

Jason made good on his word to give me time to think. We talked and met up for walks or coffee a few times, but he didn't bring up our relationship status. After about a month of our casual dates, I told him I was ready to try again to spend time with him and his daughters. Since taking Tyler and Nicky to the amusement park, I'd visited them or took them out at least once a week. Each time got better to the point that they actually looked excited to see me when I knocked on their door.

"Where are we going today, Aunt Krissy?" Nicky would ask eagerly. My bank account was pretty drained, but my heart was filling up. I felt more confident that I could be helpful with kids, even though I wasn't a mom.

On our first family night, Jason invited me over to watch *High School Musical*. Miriam and Ellie pressed against either side of Jason on his sofa while I sat on the adjacent club chair, facing them at an angle. Miriam twirled her hair with one finger, flexing her brightly pedicured toes on the coffee table as Jason and Ellie shared a huge bowl of popcorn between them, Ellie not noticing the little bits that fell to the floor as she munched. Jason gave me my own small bowl of popcorn so we wouldn't have to keep passing the big bowl back and forth between us.

So this is what family time felt like. I noticed that married parents rarely touched each other in public. There was usually one or more children between them, holding hands, demanding kisses and attention, or needing to be disciplined. I could see why the divorce rate was so high. The rumor was that kids keep a family together, but if they're always this disruptive to parental romance, no wonder everybody's giving up on marriage. I didn't want to be so cynical, but watching my sister going through the pain of divorce took its toll. I wasn't one to believe in happy endings.

Jason would periodically look over at me and wink, now and then mouthing, "Are you okay?" over Ellie's head, to which I would vigorously nod yes and give him an enthusiastic smile. Who didn't want to sit home and watch Disney movies on Saturday nights, looking longingly across the room at their significant other? A few times I caught Miriam giving me a sideways glance to see if I was paying attention before she'd pet her dad's head. It was as though she was giving me the middle finger: *See this guy you're in love with? He's mine!* The absurdity of competing with a teenage girl was getting to me. Ellie was guileless, but she was still the age to ask Jason to read her stories before bed. She was the baby and she loved it. She was in no hurry to grow up.

At the end credits of the movie, Jason stretched his arms out, pulled both girls in for a hug and announced, "It's time for bed!" Miriam allowed him to kiss her on the cheek before she unfolded her gazelle legs and padded up the stairs. Ellie pulled Jason's hand.

"It's time for the next chapter of *Harry Potter*," she said.

"You're right, Ellie Bellie. Go brush your teeth first and I'll be right up."

Ellie marched up the stairway, turning back to look at him every few steps until she disappeared from view. Once she did, Jason beckoned to me to come sit by him. I got off my chair and leaned into his open arms.

"I swear, they never pay this much attention to me when you're not here," he laughed apologetically.

"They're marking their territory," I said. "You didn't really think they were going to welcome me into your life, did you?"

"No, but I thought they'd give you a little more of a chance since I explained to them how important you are to me," he said. "They're usually so warm with other people. I'm really surprised."

*Oh, Jason, you have no idea how badly you just hurt my feelings*, I thought, but just shrugged. After what seemed like less than a minute, he nearly pushed me away, standing up and putting out his hands to pull me off the sofa after I had just gotten comfortable and touched him for the first time all evening.

"How would you like to come up and listen to a chapter of *Harry Potter*?" he asked. He looked so apologetic. I knew he was caught in the middle and it wasn't an easy place to be.

"I can stay down here until you're finished; it's no big deal," I said, ignoring his outstretched hands and folding my arms over my chest.

"I'd really like you to be part of this family," he said, putting his hands back down at his sides. "You have to understand that my girls come first right now. It's just the way it is. If you had kids, you would understand."

*Ouch*, barb number two.

"I don't understand why there has to be a rank," I said, trying not to cry. "I mean, don't you have room for all of us?"

"Daddy!" Ellie yelled from the top of the steps.

Jason looked up, and looked back at me. I could see he was torn.

"Go," I said. "I'll stay here until you're done."

He leaned forward to kiss me on the forehead and then disappeared up the stairs.

I waited about ten minutes, staring at the blank TV screen but not wanting to watch anything anyway. Finally I got up and went upstairs to hopefully catch the end of Jason's reading. Miriam's door was closed, but Ellie's was open and Jason sat on the side of her bed, brushing her hair. Ellie was smiling beatifically, her eyes closed as the brush stroked slowly through her long, dark waves. Jason and Ellie were illuminated in a small circle of light coming from a pink lamp with a frilly shade on the nightstand next to her bed. Stuffed animals overflowed off the bed and a few were scattered on the floor by Jason's feet.

After a minute, he noticed me standing in the doorway and smiled. I gave him a silent wave and smiled back. I wished I could fit somewhere into this scene, but I felt like I had walked in on something that I had no place in. I backed away from the door and went downstairs, letting myself out the front door.

I was facing reality in a way I never had with John. I felt suffocated and fenced in. I wanted to be with Jason, but I didn't want to share him. Was that so bad? He made me feel amazing when I had his attention, and the little dribs and drabs I got of his light shining on me were keeping me going, but barely.

# 14

"Why did you leave last night?" Jason asked when I answered the phone at the crack of dawn. "I was going to come back down and give you my full attention as soon as Ellie was asleep."

"I was tired," I said sleepily. I didn't want him to know how much it hurt my feelings to hear that his kids had to come first or that I'd understand that if I were a mother. "Maybe you could brush my hair like that sometime."

Jason laughed. "Wouldn't that be kind of creepy?" he asked. "You don't have a daddy complex, do you?"

"No!" I said forcefully. "I'd just like to feel like I matter to you too; that's all."

"You do matter to me. I might show it in different ways, but you matter very much. If you didn't, why would I want to marry you?"

"That's a good question. Why would you? Your girls don't like me and I have no mothering instinct."

"I have an idea," he said, changing the subject. "I'd really like it if you'd take the girls out for dinner. Maybe it will give the three of you a chance to bond."

"Take them without you?"

"Yes, I think it would be a great idea."

. . .

Even though I was nervous to take the girls for dinner without Jason, I agreed with his idea that it might help to spend some time alone with his daughters. I never fully felt comfortable with my nephews until I started taking them out without their mom, so I hoped this would be the same.

That evening, I drove to Jason's to pick up the girls for dinner. Miriam said she didn't care where we went, and Ellie asked for Red Robin. Jason gave us each a kiss on the cheek as he shooed us out the door. We seemed reluctant, and I could tell that he had worked hard to persuade them to go with me, especially Miriam. It was eerily silent in the car because I couldn't think of anything to say and apparently neither could they.

After the hostess seated us, I ordered a big drink from the fun & fruity cocktails menu as soon as possible. Ellie picked some kind of barbecue burger with fries, I chose a Garden burger, and Miriam at first told the waitress she didn't want anything, but when Ellie elbowed her in the ribs, she ended up ordering a burger and fries too.

"So, girls, I know this is awkward for all of us, but your dad thought it would be a good experience for us to spend some time getting to know each other," I said, as cheerfully as I could muster, while holding up my Mai Tai to toast them. They had either never done a toast or were declining mine because they both looked at me funny rather than raising their own glasses.

The good thing about Red Robin was it was really fast service. There was no long delay during which we had to force conversation while we waited for our food to come. The girls sat across from me in the booth and we all looked at the abundance of distracting reproduction nostalgia hanging all over the walls. We happened to be sitting under a giant picture of Jason Alexander in his George Costanza role posing in boxer shorts. I wondered if the girls had even heard of *Seinfeld*, but didn't bother asking. I tried to ask them about ballet, but got one-word answers.

When our dinners came, I took a huge bite of my veggie burger because I was feeling a little light-headed from starting my drink on an empty stomach. Ellie seemed to relish her meal, often closing her eyes and smiling as she ate. Miriam ignored her burger and at first just pushed the steak fries around, but then she poured a big blob of ketchup in the middle of her plate and started scarfing them down.

"See, you were hungry after all," I said, smiling at her, to which Miriam only glared at me.

"I'll be right back," she said, scooting out of the booth.

"She doesn't like to talk about food," Ellie said matter-of-factly.

"Why not?"

"Because she thinks she's fat. She says I am too, but I ignore her because I like to eat," Ellie replied.

"Ellie, you're beautiful. Don't worry about that," I said, looking toward the women's restroom. "Listen, I'll be right back. I want to make sure your sister is okay."

Ellie just shrugged and went back to enjoying her dinner while I walked down the short corridor and pushed open the door to the bathroom. I heard a gagging sound and then a flush.

"Miriam, are you all right?" I called out. She didn't answer. I knocked on the only stall door that was closed.

"Go away," she said. I could tell she was crying.

"What's the matter, honey?"

"Don't call me that," Miriam said. She opened the stall door suddenly and brushed past me to wash her hands. "If you must know, I'm feeling sick today, but Dad made me come anyway because he said it would hurt your feelings if I didn't. I'm doing this for him, not you."

"That makes two of us," I muttered under my breath.

"What?" Miriam asked, narrowing her eyes and glaring at me through the mirror.

"Never mind. I'll be back at the table with Ellie. I'm sorry you don't feel well. It wasn't my intention to ruin your day."

I sat back in the booth with Ellie, who had cleaned her plate. At least someone here was happy. I dabbed at my eyes a little and looked up at the ceiling to prevent tears from falling. I was losing it and one more incident today was going to push me over the edge. Miriam came and sat back down, looking hostile.

The waitress came to drop off the bill, took one look at our splotchy faces, and rebuked Miriam.

"Don't make your mom cry," she said. "She took you out to eat. You should be thanking her, not causing her grief."

"She's *not* my mom," Miriam snarled.

"Just the same, be happy. It's a much easier way to go through life."

I was surprised by this wisdom from a twenty-something. She had probably had done some hard living to come to this conclusion so early in her journey. I paid the check, giving her a hefty tip, and we rushed out of the restaurant, eager to get back to Jason's house.

The girls practically ran inside when we got there.

"So, how did it go?" he asked loudly as the girls whizzed past him and up to their rooms.

He looked at me expectantly, but between the girls ignoring him and my bedraggled appearance, his face fell. I burst into tears and he gathered me into a hug.

"I'm sorry I let you down," I cried into his shoulder. "I tried. Really."

"I know you did," he said, sighing into my hair.

# 15

"Just come in for a few minutes," I said, as Jason and I kissed good night in front of my apartment. We were just coming off the high of a great evening out at the wedding of Jason's friends. I opened the door and bent to take off my sandals. My feet were sore and I was exhausted, but I was tired of being dropped off with only a good night kiss at the door. If nothing else, Jason was going to sit on the sofa and cuddle for a little while. He didn't have his girls tonight, so there was no reason to rush home. Both of us had a few drinks at the wedding and my body felt loose and lanky and slow-moving.

Jason lay down on the sofa and I curled myself under his arm, squeezing my arms and legs around his torso and looking at his face. We looked into each other's eyes, smiling sleepily. No one in the world had ever made me feel more loved than the times that Jason looked at me like this. I could see approval and peace in his face and I knew there was nothing else he was thinking about, nowhere else he'd rather be at this moment than right here with me.

I softly moved my fingertips in small circles over his chest and shoulders, feeling his muscles under the fabric of his shirt. He felt warm. He closed his eyes and put his head back against the sofa's pillows, mimicking my motion by rubbing his hands over my hip. His fingers would creep down to the hem of my dress and then he'd stop and bring them higher again. He kept his eyes closed, but I could see the conflict on his face as I watched him. It gave me satisfaction to know he found me hard to resist. At last there was a sign that he was truly attracted to me, maybe even finding me irresistible with enough alcohol in his system.

I leaned forward and kissed him softly on the lips. He didn't move at first, but opened his eyes and looked surprised. He took his hand off my leg and held the back of my head, pulling me closer and kissing me more urgently. After weeks and weeks of pecks on the cheek and the lips, I felt crazy with desire, but I held back to see what he would do. I was so afraid that if I was aggressive, he'd stop what he was doing and leave, and I knew if he did that he'd break my heart.

He grasped my hair and started pressing his fingertips into the back of my neck, the thin chain of my necklace moving against my skin under his fingers. With his other hand, he reached into the front of my dress, breathing hard against my ear, kissing my neck. I was filled with a desire to please him, with the joy of knowing I was wanted.

He gently pushed me down on my back on the sofa, pulling my dress over my head and quickly unbuttoning his shirt. He pulled off his clothes and lay on top of me. I could feel how hard he was against my leg, but I was afraid to touch him and maybe break the spell. He kept kissing me like I was air and he was drowning and the only thought in my head was wanting more of him, all of him. With one hand, I traced the top of his shoulder, feeling the muscle on bone, while my other hand trailed down his side and over his lower back.

"Please tell me you're on birth control," he whispered.

I nodded yes.

I could feel him wedging himself between my legs and without stopping, he pressed himself inside of me. My mind exploded in a thousand stars. Finally everything I ever wanted – love, desire, and joy all at one time – all for Jason and me to enjoy together at last. He moved slowly and I wrapped my legs around him, wanting every inch of my body touching every inch of his. I moved with his rhythm, feeling him breathing into my ear as I buried my face into his neck, kissing the tiny beads of sweat and taking in his scent.

We were quiet and gentle and slow. Afterward, he lay on top of me, catching his breath. I wanted to look into his eyes, but his face was turned away from me, pressed against my shoulder. I lay still, not wanting the moment to end and our connection to be broken, but after a minute or two, he stood up and said he'd bring back a towel. He dried himself off as he was walking back from the bathroom and handed me another towel. I suddenly felt shy as I was lying naked on my sofa, watching him pull his underwear back on.

"I'll be right back," I said, and went into my room to put on a pair of pajama pants and a T-shirt. I came back out and sat with him on the sofa, and saw that Jason had tears in his eyes.

"I can't do this," he said, burying his face in his hands.

"Why not?" I asked, feeling panicky. "It felt so right. I've been dreaming of this day."

"It wasn't right. I messed up. I'm sorry, Kristen. I owe you better than this."

He started getting dressed as I sat there, stunned. How could something that felt natural and perfect to me make him feel the opposite? Didn't we share a connection? How could I be so wrong about my feelings?

"Please don't go. I can't stand the idea of us doing that and you just leaving. Couldn't you stay here tonight?"

"That's only going to make it worse," he said.

"Are you breaking up with me? Was it that bad?" I hoped he'd laugh at my joke, but he didn't.

"No, Kristen. I'll call you in the morning. I hope you sleep well." He kissed me on the forehead and left. We were both single and in love. What could be wrong with that? There was nothing to stop us from being together but his own mind. I didn't know how much longer I could take this pain and rejection, but I also didn't know how I'd ever be able to walk away from him.

# 16

We pretended after that night like it never happened. He didn't bring up the topic, so I didn't either, even though I was hurting. We spent most of our couple time with his daughters, as though Jason was still trying to push for all of us to bond as a family. I don't think they appreciated it any more than I did.

Miriam... Where do I begin? She got caught plagiarizing a paper at school and was suspended for two days. I never understood how getting to spend a day at home was considered punishment. She had just begun ninth grade a few weeks ago and it certainly wasn't off to good start.

Not being a parent, I also don't understand Jason's and Julia's irrational reactions to their kids messing things up. Isn't that what teenagers do? I sure did, but they acted like it was *impossible* that *their* daughter could have copied and pasted large chunks of stuff from the Internet in composing her freshman lit paper on Ralph Waldo Emerson.

So when Julia called Jason, he called me, to which I sympathetically said I was sorry to hear that, and hopefully it was just a mistake, and other things I thought might make him feel better. He and Julia went together for a conference with the vice principal, the English teacher, and Miriam. Jason hesitantly asked if I wanted to come, but he seemed relieved when I said no thanks; it was for her parents to deal with.

Jason told me afterward the teacher showed them printouts of a website side by side with Miriam's paper and there were clearly paragraphs of material taken directly from the site. Miriam had tried to argue that she accidentally handed in the wrong version, the one in which she had not yet put everything into her own words or cited the material, but the teacher, a grizzled veteran of teenage excuse-making, was having none of that. He said it was irresponsible of her, even if it was accidental, and pressed for the highest penalty allowed by the school, which was a failing grade in English for the marking period.

Jason said later that Julia was icy cold toward the teacher, and he felt like he was playing good cop/bad cop with her when the teacher said he was doing their daughter a favor by teaching her the consequences now, to which Julia responded, "Thanks for nothing." But Julia was like that. She felt entitled. She had worked her way to the top of the heap and she looked down from her perch on high at anyone else who hadn't made it to her level. She was the daughter of an immigrant mother and she valued hard work and economic security above all else. In turn, she had high expectations for her own daughters, but found it frustrating that American individualism was so different than the Chinese tradition of obedience she was raised in.

Julia was an orthopedic surgeon in what was still a man's field of medicine. She made far more money than Jason did in his family practice because of her specialty. It seemed that her attitude toward classes like English and history is that they were annoying obstacles to having more time to study for important courses like bio and chem.

Miriam was disdainful about her punishment, probably in part due to Julia's attitude. I'm sure Julia would have taken this more seriously had it been a science class and Miriam had fudged her lab results. I could see that Jason was caught in the middle, wanting to be reasonable and reinforce the school's punishment of her cheating, but his daughter and ex-wife were both completely haughty and felt they were above the law in such a minor transgression.

Jason wanted to ground Miriam for a month from going out, but since Julia wouldn't go along with his punishment, it only applied when the girls were with him, and once Miriam found that out, she decided to camp out at her mom's to wait out the month. Jason was in a no-win situation because if he insisted on grounding her, he'd only have to go longer without seeing his daughter.

This was the very worst thing about two divorced parents who didn't work well together. Julia's attitude made me more cautious about my relationship with Jason. If she blew off his attempts at discipline now, how might she act if we got married and the girls were staying with us?

I walked a tightrope all the time. I wanted to support Jason, but if I criticized his daughters, or even Julia, he'd get defensive. It was easier to listen and not comment at all.

Even though Jason denied that Julia ever said anything of the kind, I got the feeling she looked down on my career as a massage therapist. I believe she equated me with the immigrants who set up seedy massage parlors that were really a front for varying degrees of prostitution. I wished she could understand that my knowledge of muscles was as intricate as hers of bones, even if I didn't cut people open.

The way she looked at me made me feel as though she thought her ex was slumming, that dating me was a real step down from what he had with her. Part of me hoped she would have the indecency to make a snide comment so that I could point out that at least I wouldn't dump my husband when he became ill and didn't live up to my expectations.

I felt protective on Jason's behalf because he worked so hard to overcome the symptoms of his disease. I knew from our massage therapy sessions that he had an extremely high tolerance for pain, and I could see the many days he'd push through his exhaustion to see his patients and give them the care he promised.

I realized that my main job in helping to raise Jason's girls was to keep my mouth shut and let him handle the discipline. There was no way that anything good could come from me trying to give advice, since I wasn't even a mother. I felt like I was always going to be an outsider because I didn't have any parenting credentials. So when Miriam stayed away for a month and then breezed past me to get back to her room at Jason's house after her "grounding" was over, I just acted like everyone else did – that nothing bad ever happened.

# 17

"Come to church with me," Jason asked, taking my hands. It was Saturday night, and I was hoping we could stay up late watching movies and maybe he'd even stay over this time.

"I'm not the church-going type," I said, making my best apologetic face as I shrugged my shoulders.

"Come on, give it a try. It'll be fun."

"I don't think anyone equates church with fun," I said, laughing. "I went every year on Christmas Eve when I was a kid, and it was boring as could be, as I remember it. The only thing that helped me get through it was fantasizing about what Santa might bring later that night."

But as usual, what Jason wanted, Jason ended up persuading me to do. I was very nervous about what people would think of Jason going with a date to church, but he kept telling me not to worry. Unfortunately, all of my "dress up" clothes were meant for going out with my friends, so I needed to make an emergency trip to my sister's closet. Everything Adrienne owns looks like something you could wear to church. I might screw up in some other way, but it wouldn't be from showing cleavage or too much thigh.

The next morning, Jason knocked on my door early, presenting me with coffee and an oatmeal banana muffin, then nudging me toward the shower. I procrastinated as long as I could and flashed him a little bit, hoping he'd change his mind, but he seemed determined to be a holy roller.

I ended up rushing through my routine and we hustled out the door to get to church by eight. Who leaves the house at eight on Sunday morning, I wondered, but apparently people do because the parking lot was full.

Jason grabbed my hand as we walked through the front doors and immediately started greeting people left and right by name, hugging some, kissing women on the cheek, and shaking hands with the men. I hung back a little behind him so he wouldn't feel obligated to start introducing me to everyone.

He placed his hand on my lower back and propelled me toward a pew in the middle of the church when I would have preferred the back. I don't know what I was expecting, but so far everything seemed pretty normal. I looked through the program, or whatever you're supposed to call it, and was relieved to find that everything we had to say and do was spelled out. The worst part about the Catholic masses my parents took us to for Easter and Christmas was that they expected everyone there to already know the procedures. I found myself feeling confused and out of place the whole time. Adrienne and I would just look at each other and shrug when everyone was chanting or singing or making strange hand gestures.

I listened to announcements about bake sales and wedding anniversaries before it was time for the show to get started. I felt like the woman at the lectern was warming up the crowd for the main event, the pastor.

We had to stand up and sing a lot and then read some prayers. My mind wandered a little during the sermon. Just like when I was in school, when I wasn't sitting in the front, I got distract-ed by watching everyone in front of me. Jason looked utterly relaxed and in the zone. I felt envious that he could come here and get something out of this. Maybe it was something you had to keep practicing at for a while, but to me, it just felt rote.

"I believe in God, the Father Almighty, Creator of heaven and earth..." Everything I recited was a jumble of words with no clear meaning to me. I shook hands with the people in front of and behind us, saying "Peace be with you" as they said it to me.

When the service was over, it seemed that people flocked over to talk to Jason. I didn't know if this was a regular occur-rence or if they were curious about me, but he introduced me to at least a dozen people, all of whom he seemed to know well, as he asked questions about their children and their afternoon plans.

Jason was beaming as we walked back to his car. It was nice to see him so happy and relaxed. It made me feel more positive about the whole church thing, even though it was still pretty uncomfortable.

"So what did you think?" he asked once we were in the car and on the way back to his house.

"It was nice. You sure know a lot of people there."

"I joined this church after Julia left," he said. "When we were married, we didn't belong to a church."

"Oh."

"Is it the kind of thing you'd consider doing regularly?" he asked, glancing over at me to see how I reacted.

"Uh, I don't know. I guess I'd think about it. I didn't really get any religious feeling, though, you know what I mean? Maybe it's just something you have to grow up with."

"Maybe," he conceded, looking disappointed.

Not wanting to let him down, I said, "I really will think about it. I'm not blowing you off. It would be a big change in my life, so I want to take my time on this."

"Makes sense." Now he smiled and looked more relaxed again. "Want to go home, make popcorn, and watch a movie?"

"Sounds good to me." I tried to imagine myself thinking of Jason's house as *home*.

He chased me up the walkway and playfully patted me on the rear as he opened the door.

# 18

I sat on one of the playground benches, coffee in hand, but even with the quintessential mom prop, I still felt out of place. The other mothers at the park had the same haircut, short and ruffled in the back, longer on the sides, lots of highlights. They all wore yoga pants and shirts with zip-up puffy vests over top. They wore scarves, even though it was early September, loosely draped around their necks. They stood in a circle, looking at their phones and comparing their to-do lists and all the activities they had to drive their kids to, while I sat on the periphery. If I married Jason, I'd have to try harder to fit in.

I divided my time between eavesdropping on the moms to try to learn their language and watching Ellie climb around the jungle gym alone. She looked as out of place as I did, a giant at age nine in the domain of preschoolers. Jason had to take Miriam shopping for a laptop and Ellie asked him if I could take her to the playground so she didn't have to follow them while they spent two hours deliberating over how much RAM the computer would need. I didn't blame her; those two could be intense when they got together. I wondered where Ellie got her playful, free-spirited side, because Jason was so earnest and it sure didn't seem like Julia was the fun type either.

Ellie climbed around aimlessly on the jungle gym, looking over at me every few minutes to see whether I was watching. Finally, she climbed off and wandered away to a balance platform.

I meandered over to watch since she had moved out of my field of vision. Ellie walked heel to toe with light steps to the middle, stepping forward until the platform would fall to the ground on one side, then she'd turn around and walk to the other end.

"Do you want to come on this with me?" she asked in a small voice, probably fearing I'd say no.

"Sure, why not," I answered, and stepped onto one end.

"Let's try to get it to balance," she said, tugging at my arm to steady herself. We both stood in the middle with one foot on each side, bending our knees a bit and swaying our weight side to side until the beam seemed level. Ellie looked at me in triumph, then stepped abruptly to one side. I almost fell and some of the coffee sloshed out the top of the cup and dribbled down my hand. She froze, looking sheepish and nervous, but I laughed.

"If you want to play like that, let me put this cup down first."

I jumped backwards off the platform, letting one side fall down and knocking her off balance too. I put down the cup and then stepped back onto the platform. We darted from side to side, getting the platform to topple to one side and then the other like a see-saw. I could feel the muscles in my legs working as I shifted my weight back and forth. I had to keep my knees slightly bent to keep from falling as Ellie jumped and leaped around on the platform, laughing and clapping her hands.

I could see some of the other moms looking at us and I wondered what they thought of my actually playing on the equipment, but I wasn't feeling self-conscious anymore because I was having so much fun.

I took one big step back to throw Ellie's balance off, but before I knew it, she fell forward off the side. I was still laughing for a second before I realized she was crouched forward and not getting up. I jumped off the platform and knelt down beside her.

"Ellie, are you all right?"

"No," she whimpered softly. She had tears in her eyes. I could see she was holding her right wrist with her left hand.

"Can you move your hand?" I asked, reaching gingerly toward her, but she cradled her arm and pulled it back toward herself protectively. Ellie's wrist looked broken rather than sprained to me. It was already swelling, turning discolored, and her hand was bent at an odd angle.

"No," she cried. "I need Daddy."

"Okay, we'll get him," I said, rubbing her back softly. I pulled out my phone and called, but he didn't answer. Of course not; he was probably deep in discussion with a salesperson by now.

"Listen, I'll take you to the hospital to get checked out and I'll call him again to tell him to meet us there. Do you know your mom's number?"

Ellie shook her head no and started crying harder. I realized how crazy it was that I was spending time with Julia's daughter and didn't even know how to get in touch in an emergency.

"I don't want to go to the hospital," she bawled.

By now, all the moms were looking over toward us curiously, but none of them came to see if we were okay. I helped Ellie up and started walking her slowly toward the car, calling Jason again to leave him a voicemail.

"Hi Jason, I don't want you to be alarmed, but Ellie fell at the playground and we're going to the hospital to get her wrist checked out. I'm hoping it's just a sprain, but it would be great if you could meet us there as soon as possible. Ellie doesn't know her mom's number, and we're going to need an insurance card."

I tried not to sound panicked, but I couldn't imagine there being much more cause for panic than realizing you caused someone else's kid to get hurt.

I helped Ellie into the front seat of the car and put her seatbelt on for her. She was crying so much that her nose was running, but she wouldn't let go of her arm, so I grabbed some fast food napkins from the glove box and dabbed at her face the best I could without getting her snot on my hands. A little too late, I realized I was probably supposed to put a nine-year-old in the back seat, but I wasn't going to risk moving her now that I got her in.

I drove faster than I should have, worrying I'd make things worse by getting into a car accident. Why did this have to happen? Why did I start fooling around with her? An endless script of self-recrimination played through my head even as I spoke soothingly in my massage therapist voice to try to calm Ellie.

"I don't want... to go... to the hospital... without my dad..." she blubbered, her shoulders shaking from crying so hard. It was that kind of crying where you periodically need to take a huge breath to keep up with it.

"He'll be there soon, honey," I repeated for the tenth time, lightly patting her leg as I kept my eyes on the road and my left hand on the wheel.

I couldn't very well send her in alone, so I had to park and walk her in very slowly. I'm sure the nurses were accustomed to seeing crying children walk through the ER doors every day.

I sat Ellie down in one of the waiting room chairs while I went to sign her in. There was only one other person in the waiting room, a young woman holding a bright blue sand bucket and looking extremely nauseated. She was bent forward in a defeated posture, clammy and clutching the plastic pail in a death grip.

Even as Ellie cried and held her wrist, the sight of the woman made her stare.

We didn't wait long before we were called in, and Jason still hadn't arrived yet or returned my call.

"So what brings you here today?" the nurse asked cheerfully once she closed the exam room door behind her. Ellie stopped crying instantly and sat up straight.

"I hurt my wrist at the playground."

"And how did that happen?"

"I was on the balance platform with her, and she made me fall off," Ellie said, pointing at me. Traitor! It was an accident!

The nurse looked over at me, narrowing her eyes slightly.

"Are you her mother?" she asked, looking skeptical.

"Umm, no. I'm her dad's girlfriend."

"You know I can't release any medical information to anyone but her parents," the nurse said.

"I know. I called her dad and left him a message. I don't know her mom's number. Her parents and Jason and Julia Schneider. They're both doctors, so maybe you know how to reach her? Jason should be here soon, I hope." I think Ellie could tell by my breathless rambling that I was nervous. She started crying again, but the nurse stopped her.

"Young lady, I need you to focus now on telling me exactly how you fell," she said, leaning forward and looking at Ellie intently. It was awe-inspiring to watch how this nurse's professional demeanor had the effect of turning off Ellie's tears like a faucet. Either she was hurting a little less than she professed to be, or she was so focused on telling her story that the pain became secondary.

After the nurse gave her a cursory exam, she told us an X-ray technician would be in shortly. She pulled the door closed behind her and we sat in the examination room looking around at the bare walls to avoid conversation. Now and then, Ellie would make a sort of shuddering noise that sounded like more tears were coming, but she managed to hold it in.

Ten minutes later, Ellie hitched a ride in a wheelchair to the X-ray room, while I waited in the exam room. Shortly after she left, the door flew open and I jumped when I saw Jason looking wild-eyed in the doorway, Miriam standing behind him and peering over his shoulder.

"Where is she?" he asked, only glancing at me and looking around the room as though Ellie might be hiding somewhere.

"She just went for an X-ray. The technician said she'd be right back. We're not allowed to go in with her anyway."

Jason turned around and looked down the hallway. Without saying anything else to me, he pulled out his phone. I knew he was calling Julia.

"Hi," he said, when she answered. "How are you?" And after a short pause, "I'm okay. Sorry to be the bearer of bad news, but Ellie had a little playground accident. She's getting her wrist X-rayed now." He started pacing back and forth in front of the open door. "No, she was with Kristen. It was just while I took Miriam to pick out her laptop. No. I'm sorry, Jules. Can you come down now? Okay. See you in a few."

One of the most uncomfortable conversations to have to overhear is your boyfriend talking to his ex-wife. They have a shorthand way of talking that takes years and years of intimacy to develop. They had seen each other at their worst and at their best and there was no way to fast-track your way into that way of talking that people who were married had. Even though she was his ex-wife, they still had nicknames for each other. They still went immediately into partner mode when there was anything involving the girls. And I felt shut out.

Things felt even weirder for me fifteen minutes later when Julia showed up, still wearing a lab coat and looking authoritative. The hospital staff immediately deferred to her, the orthopedic surgeon. I faded into the background. I felt like I should leave, but I also felt like I needed to stay in case anyone else needed yet another account of how exactly this had happened. People were acting like it was a shockingly unusual thing for a kid to fall and get hurt at a playground.

I was stuck sitting on the bed in the exam room with Miriam tapping her foot standing in the corner and Jason and Julia having a hushed conversation in the hallway. It was something like, "Why did you leave Ellie alone with *her*?" And "I'm sorry. It was only for a few minutes. Obviously, I didn't expect anything like this to happen." *Way to stick up for me, Jason*, I thought. I wished I could tell Julia that Ellie hadn't asked for her even once.

While they were still in the hallway, the emergency room doctor told them that Ellie had in fact fractured her wrist. She was going to get a cast put on and had the honor of choosing what color she wanted. Of course, she chose fluorescent pink. Julia knew the orthopedic doctor and oversaw the whole procedure. I was surprised she didn't do it herself.

Once I was sure Ellie was okay and I wasn't needed anymore as a witness, I slipped out of the emergency department and practically ran to my car. I couldn't wait to get away from that family and from feeling like such an outsider. Jason must have been smoking something if he thought there was a place for me in his perfect little family. The only thing that wasn't perfect about it was that he and Julia weren't still together.

# 19

The next week felt strained when Jason and I spent time together. If he even noticed I left the ER alone, he never mentioned it. And even though he denied it, I know he couldn't help but blame me a little. I realized from watching Adrienne and her boys that nothing comes between parents and their protective instinct for their children. No matter how much he said he loved me and that I would become part of his family, I was never going to be fully on the inside.

Up until Ellie's accident, he was the one reassuring me that things would work out with us becoming a family, and I was starting to believe it because he did. It seemed like the accident made him step back a bit and start thinking more rationally, but I missed his optimism and big dreams, especially when I worried so much that it would never seem easy for us.

Out of the blue, Jason asked me if I'd like to spend a weekend away and enjoy some time alone together. I was surprised because he never asked me to spend even one night with him before, and it meant he was giving up time with his girls.

I was curious to know what we would be like away from the constraints of home. Besides that, it was rare that I got to travel anywhere and I was excited to see anyplace new. Jason made reservations for us at a bed and breakfast in New Hope. It sounded like the place we needed to go.

I spent a lot of time packing and unpacking my overnight bag because I wasn't sure of our plans since Jason said he wanted to surprise me. I wondered whether we'd be outside hiking, shopping in quaint little stores, eating at fabulous restaurants, or (fingers crossed) spending some quality time in bed. I had just finished packing and zipping my bag when he knocked at the door.

"Ready to go?" he asked, looking handsome and preppy. I loved the way Jason dressed. I felt like such a grownup handing him my bag and looking around my apartment one last time to make sure the lights were off before I locked my door.

I pulled on my seatbelt and leaned over to kiss Jason after he put my bag in the trunk and got in on the driver's side.

"I am so excited for this weekend. Thank you," I said.

"I am too. It's nice to have a lovely lady and somewhere to take her," he said, winking at me.

The drive was about two hours and we alternated talking with listening to the radio. It was a beautiful day, just beginning to hint at fall with some of the leaves on the trees turning orange or red. Whatever the weekend brought, I was excited to have a boyfriend who could devote two whole days just to me. Jason only mentioned his daughters once or twice and it felt like such an escape to be away from everyone else in our lives.

He pulled into the driveway of a bed and breakfast, a light yellow wooden Victorian rambling house with rocking chairs and large ferns on the wraparound porch.

"It's perfect!" I exclaimed.

"Wait until you see the inside before you say perfect," Jason answered. "Sometimes the rooms can be pretty old-fashioned. I did make sure we have our own bathroom. It's a little different from a hotel."

"Whatever you picked, I know I'll love it."

The innkeepers were an older married couple, and the wife led me upstairs to our room as Jason greeted the husband and checked in.

"You're on the third floor. It's nice and quiet and private up there," she told me. The carpeted stairs creaked as we walked up and she opened the door to a canopied four-poster bed with a frilly comforter and mounds of odd-shaped pillows. There was a little table and mirror with a padded stool in one corner and a cushioned window seat on the other side of the room.

"The bathroom is this way," the innkeeper said, as I followed her down the hall to a bathroom with an old iron claw-footed tub. I was speechless as she brought me back to the bedroom before heading back down the steps. I felt like a school girl, giddy with excitement and no words to express myself. I heard Jason coming up the steps and I ran and pulled him into a big hug.

"Oh, thank you, thank you, thank you!" I exclaimed.

"That's what I love about you, Kristen. You don't take anything for granted. Julia wouldn't stay anywhere that doesn't have Wi-Fi access and a fitness center on site. I've always loved these old houses. If I had more energy and any ability to fix things, I'd love to own a big old rambling house like this."

"I wouldn't want to own one, but I'm very happy to visit," I said, basking in the comparison with Julia. In some ways, her perfectionism came across more like snobbery, even to Jason. I was glad for that because I could never match up to her in that department.

"I'll give you a few minutes to get settled in while I see about a dinner reservation," Jason said.

"Sounds great," I replied, unzipping my bag. As soon as he left, I closed the door behind him and pulled out a creamy pink chemise and white thigh high stockings with lacy strips of elastic at the tops. I changed quickly, zipped up my bag again and sat nervously on the edge of the bed. He had never seen me in lingerie before and I wasn't sure how he'd react. What if he expected to go hiking or something? I'd just have to wait and see.

I sat looking out the window and listening for him to come back to the room. A few minutes later, I heard his distinctive footsteps and held my breath as he knocked at the door.

"Are you decent?" he asked through the door before turning the knob.

"I hope so!" I called back, starting to blush already.

He stopped right in the doorway and looked me up and down.

"Well, this is an unexpected surprise," he said. "And here I thought I was the one with all the surprises this weekend."

"Do you like it?" I asked, peeking up at him shyly.

"What a question. Of course I do! You look so sweet and innocent and sexy all at the same time." He closed the door behind him, made a point of locking it, then came to stand in front of me, running his fingers through my hair. "I don't think I say it to you enough, but you are so beautiful, Kristen, inside and out." He lifted my chin and looked steadily into my eyes. I wanted to look down, but I didn't want to miss the intensity of the moment. He bent forward and kissed my forehead before his lips touched mine, softly but intently.

I leaned forward to press myself against him, and then he pressed me back on the bed and lay down next to me, tracing his finger down my side and back up my belly and between my breasts. I felt like my breathing had stopped and I shivered at the pleasure of his touch.

"Are you okay with this?" he asked softly, and I could only nod yes. "Because I've been thinking about us, and it seems like waiting isn't making sense anymore. We are in this together, aren't we?"

I nodded again, afraid my voice would crack if I tried to talk, as he traced the lace at the tops of my thigh highs before gently running his hand up underneath my chemise.

This time, everything was just right. He didn't get up right afterward and he didn't tell me it was a mistake. We lay for a long time in each other's arms, just smiling. This time, I was the one closing my eyes and drifting off. I knew Jason wasn't going anywhere. I didn't worry I'd never have a moment like this again. I trusted the universe would provide for us.

I didn't know how much time had gone by when I woke up, but I could see the light had changed outside. Jason sat up on one elbow when he saw I was stirring.

"Shall we get ready for dinner?" he asked. "I found a place just a few blocks away that looks really promising."

"That sounds great," I said, clearing my throat. "I'm glad you've never been here before either, so that we can explore it together."

We got dressed and walked hand in hand down a tree-lined street, each brightly painted building advertising art and antiques on wooden signs outside their open front doors. I felt completely relaxed and at ease with Jason; this was the best date I'd ever had.

As we sat down for dinner, he pushed my chair in for me and then sat across our table for two, looking into my eyes and smiling. He shook his head once, as though he felt like he was dreaming. I was glad it wasn't just me.

After dinner, he fumbled in his pocket, and I started to wonder if he was about to propose to me. My heart raced and my cheeks felt hot. But then he pulled out his wallet to pay the bill. It surprised me that I felt a tiny quiver of disappointment. Could it be that I was starting to believe that we could make a marriage work?

# 20

"Can I tell you a secret?" Ellie asked me, leaning forward as I sat with her in the orthopedic office waiting room to get her cast removed. Julia had several surgeries on her schedule and Jason had patient hours, so he asked me whether I'd mind taking Ellie. I was surprised that they trusted me with their daughter again after I caused her to break her wrist in the first place, but it seemed fitting that since I was there for the beginning, I should also be there for the end.

"Of course you can," I told her, patting her on the knee.

"I want to keep my cast on because I hate dancing, and my mom let me skip it while I had the cast."

"Oh. Why is that a secret?" I think I knew the answer to that, but I wanted to hear it from her.

"Because my mom won't let me quit. She said I need to stick with it and it's good for me. I hate it."

"Well, she's right. It's exercise and it's nice to have an artistic outlet, but maybe if you really don't like it, we could find something else for you to do instead."

"Miriam is so good at ballet. I'm never going to be like her," Ellie said, putting her head down. "She's so skinny and perfect. I'm fat and clumsy."

"You are not!" She was a little chunky, but I was sure she'd grow out of her puppy fat into a beautiful young woman. She was unfortunately entering the most awkward stage of being a girl: those years of going through puberty. My nephew Nicky was in the midst of it too: the cracking voice, suddenly seeming so self-conscious about his changing body.

"My mom says I'm just going through a phase, but when I look at old pictures of Miriam, she never looked like me. She was always skinny, even though she says she's fat. If she's fat, I'm whale blubber!"

"Ellie, you're a beautiful young woman. Miriam is very thin, but that's not better than what you are." The truth was, Miriam was too thin. I had many reasons to believe she might be anorexic. Every time Miriam refused food, Jason looked the other way – parenting denial at its best. She rarely ate more than a few bites of anything, and her elbows were wider than her upper arms.

"I wish I could look like her, but I like food too much."

"Ellie, it's natural to love food. I love eating! It's one of my favorite things," I said, trying to reassure her.

"If you love eating, why are you thin?"

"Well, I'm careful about how much I eat most of the time, and I work out a lot. That's probably why your mom says dancing is a good thing. It's great exercise. A lot of it is probably genetics too."

"Would you tell her I want to quit?"

"I think we better talk to your dad first. It's not my place to step in between you and your parents," I said, hoping she'd understand. I felt so amazed that Ellie was opening up to me in a way she couldn't with her parents.

"If you want, I'll sit with you while you tell him how you feel about dance," I reassured her.

"He'll agree with me, but he won't tell Mom," Ellie said. "He knows I don't like dance anymore."

"We'll talk to him tonight; I promise."

The nurse called Ellie in from the waiting room, and she pulled my hand to come with her.

"Is this going to hurt?" she asked the nurse, looking fearful.

"Nah, it doesn't hurt, honeybun. Your arm is going to feel funny for a few days after you get the cast off, though, because your muscles haven't had a chance to do any work for the past six weeks."

Ellie laid her arm on the table as the nurse buzzed through the cast with a saw. She squeezed my hand with her other hand, cutting off the circulation in my fingers and scrunching her eyes closed tightly.

"Now wiggle your fingers for me," the nurse said. Ellie opened her eyes and looked down to see her pale arm. "I bet it was itchy in there, wasn't it?"

Ellie nodded and started wiggling her fingers. The nurse wiped her arm down with a damp cloth and patted it dry.

"Your mom can take you out for some ice cream," the nurse told Ellie. I could see Ellie getting tears in her eyes, but she didn't say anything. After the nurse tossed her cast into the trash and left the room, Ellie started full-on blubbering. I was still having trouble figuring out how kids' moods changed so quickly.

"What's the matter? Does your arm hurt?" I asked her.

"No. I miss my cast," Ellie cried, wiping her nose on her arm.

"Well, I guess you could keep it if you really wanted to, but isn't it kind of smelly?"

"No, I mean, I want it back on my arm!"

"Oh, the dance thing? I told you, we'll talk to your dad tonight."

"I want ice cream, but I don't."

"You can have ice cream now and then. You are a beautiful girl, Ellie. Don't talk about yourself like that." I looked around the room for a tissue, and when I found the box, I pulled a bunch out, handing Ellie one and saving the rest for the car. "I'll tell you what. How about if we ask your dad tonight if he and your mom would let you join the gym with me? Would you like to come and work out with me?" I couldn't believe I was volunteering to let her in on my gym time, but I was desperate to get her to stop crying. Ellie looked up at me and nodded enthusiastically, wiping her nose with her forearm again.

When dinner was finished, Miriam immediately jumped up from the table after mostly pushing her food around her plate and only eating three bites (I watched her as surreptitiously as I could and actually counted). Ellie and I stayed behind so we could talk to Jason without her older sister around.

"Jason, Ellie has something she'd like to tell you," I said, looking at her encouragingly. She didn't say anything, so I nudged her leg with my foot under the table.

"I don't want to do dance anymore," she said, looking at me rather than Jason.

"Oh? Why is that? You're so good at it."

"I don't like it, and I don't like the clothes I have to wear. I look all lumpy in the leotards."

"Ellie! You look beautiful when you dance!" Jason exclaimed. "There are all different body types and yours is just as good as anyone else's."

"I don't like it. I want to quit, but Mom won't let me."

"Have you talked to her about it like you're talking to me now?"

"I tried to tell her, but she said if I don't like how I look, she would take me to a dietician. I don't want to go to a dietician. I just want to quit dance."

"Well, maybe we can talk to her together when she picks you up tomorrow," Jason said, pushing his chair back from the table to start clearing plates.

I kept my mouth shut in front of Ellie, but she looked discouraged. When she went up to her room, I followed Jason into the kitchen to start putting away the leftovers while he loaded the dishwasher.

"Jason, I don't think you're taking her seriously enough," I finally said.

"You don't need to get involved," he said. "This is between Julia and me."

"Yeah, but if you want me to marry you, there's stuff with your girls that I'm going to have to get involved in. I would never be critical of you or Julia in front of the girls, but I think making her do something she doesn't enjoy is only going to backfire later."

"You don't have kids. How do you know what's best for her?" Jason asked, glaring at me. I tried to avoid feeling defensive. I know it's only natural for a parent to find it hard to hear advice or criticism.

"I don't know what's best for her. I have no idea," I said, after thinking about it for a few seconds. "But you should know that I offered to start taking her to the gym with me, if it's okay with you and Julia."

"Oh, boy, you really opened a can of worms, didn't you?" he said.

"I thought you wanted me to be part of your family. I was trying to help."

"I know you are, but it puts Julia in a bad position. She tells me she already feels like the bad cop, and now with you taking a bigger role with Ellie, I think she's a little jealous, to be honest."

"Please talk to her. If your goal is for Ellie to be happy and healthy, forcing her to do something she hates is not going to help."

"I'll talk to her," Jason said, turning his back to me to wash a pot.

"And while we're talking, I think Miriam has an eating disorder," I said. It felt like my words hung in the air for a few moments, as the only sound was the water splashing into the pot that Jason was rinsing.

"She's never been a big eater," he said.

"Jason, she ate *three* bites at dinner. I counted! Can't you see and feel how thin she is?"

"She's going to be thin. Look at Julia; look at me. We're both skinny. If you ask me, the only one that's not normal in this family is Ellie. I don't know where she gets it from."

"Jason! Come on. Ellie is a normal little girl. If you're comparing her to Miriam, anyone would look heavy. I know it's hard to think about, but please, please, give it some consideration. You and Julia are both doctors, and neither of you is looking objectively at your own daughter."

"Let's say she is too thin. It's a phase. She'll grow out of it."

"That's not true! There are eating disorder clinics! She can go to a psychologist. The worst thing is to pretend there's nothing wrong and go along with her crazy diet."

"I'll talk to Julia," he said, sighing.

"Thank you. I should go now. Your girls could use some time alone with you. I feel like I've been here too much lately, and I don't want to meddle." I stepped behind him and wrapped my arms around his waist as he washed the last pot. He didn't even turn around, so I kissed him on the cheek.

"I love you," I said. "Have a good night, Jason."

"You too," he said.

It felt like a step backward whenever I said anything negative about the girls, but I knew that if Jason wasn't going to see me as an equal partner in this family, neither would anyone else. I was relieved to go home and have a quiet night to myself after how coldly he had said good night.

# 21

A couple of days later, I went into Jason's downstairs bathroom in socks and stepped in a puddle of water. I blew up. I really couldn't take it anymore.

"Miriam!" I yelled up the stairs. "Miriam, you left the floor all wet after your shower *again*!" I cursed to myself and peeled my socks off. I stomped up the steps and knocked on her bedroom door.

"I'm getting dressed!" she yelled over the blaring music in her room.

"You need to show some consideration. You always leave wet towels all over the floor and toothpaste blobs in the sink and puddles of water on the floor and your hair in the drain. Why do you expect your dad and me to clean up after you? Who do you think you are, a princess?"

The door flew open and Miriam stood eye to eye with me, glaring.

"Who do you think *you* are, my mom?"

She shoved past me, ran down the steps and slammed the bathroom door. By this time, Jason had heard the commotion and emerged from the upstairs bathroom, shaving cream still on half of his cheek.

"Kristen, it's really my job to be the boss of them, not yours," he said, looking exasperated. He sighed a lot these days.

"You can't let them walk all over you like this," I said. "They're slobs. It's not fair that we should be cleaning up after them. You need to teach them to clean up after themselves."

"I'll hire a housekeeper if it bothers you so much."

"That's not the point! Yes, my feet get wet every time I go in the bathroom, but the point is, you need to teach the girls this stuff. How are they going to take care of themselves if they are used to their dad doing everything for them? My mom never would have put up with this."

"You lived with your mom and your dad," he said. "It's hard for them going back and forth between houses. Neither one feels like home to them. That's why they don't take better care of things."

"You're making excuses for them. If we were staying in a hotel, I'd leave it cleaner than this! Why should a maid or anyone have to deal with this mess?"

"I don't know what you want me to say. I can't instantly change them."

"You could support me, instead of making me look like the bad guy. You want me to marry you and be a secondary parent to them, but then you won't let me do anything. They know that any time I don't approve of something they do, they can just appeal to you and the problem goes away. They need discipline!"

"Fine, Kristen. Do what you want. I have to finish shaving." I could see Ellie peeping out from her bedroom. I went back downstairs and knocked on the bathroom door again. Silence.

"Open up, Miriam. I'm sorry I yelled."

The door stayed closed.

"I'm not going to give up," I said, pressing my forehead to the door. "I'm going to treat you like I'd want my own daughter to be raised. You might not get it now, but it would be a lot easier for me to keep my mouth shut and let you girls do whatever your mom and dad let you do. I say this stuff because I care."

"You sound like such a bitch when you do," she said, on the other side of the door.

"I sound like my mother," I said, laughing. "Do you know how many times I got yelled at for the same stuff?"

Miriam unlocked the door and opened it a crack.

"Come on, I'll help you wipe up the water this time," I said. "Next time, please take care of it before you leave the bathroom. I'm running out of dry socks!"

We wiped the floor together, and I neatly folded each towel in half before hanging them. She grabbed a paper towel from under the sink and cleaned up the toothpaste.

"Isn't this much better?" I asked. "Can I give you a hug?"

"Now you're really pushing it," Miriam grumbled, but she let me give her a half hug.

We were watching TV together when Jason came down a few minutes later, looking hesitant. I guess he was in shock that we had resolved things so quickly. I was still annoyed at him that he didn't back me up, but at least he didn't interfere on the girls' behalf, like he sometimes had in the past. A few months ago, he would have been at the bathroom door himself, coaxing Miriam to come out and making the whole thing worse between her and me. Maybe he'd start to trust me that I could figure this out on my own, even though I wasn't technically a mom. He sat on the sofa with us, and this time I was the one sitting in the middle.

# 22

The next Saturday morning, sitting with Jason in his kitchen, I put the next step of my plan with the girls into action.

"I really think this will help," I cajoled, making big puppy dog eyes at Jason. He was always skeptical of my ideas until I could somehow convince him to try them. Then he seemed like it was a natural choice and pretended like he had never resisted in the first place.

"We could just hire a decorator. That's what Julia did," he replied.

"That's the point. We want to do something *different* from what Julia always does. Please? I think it would help me bond with the girls."

Bringing the girls into it usually swayed him, but he still seemed doubtful.

"You really want to spend the whole day on *this*?" he asked.

"Sure. I love to paint. I'm not allowed to in my apartment. I'm tired of boring white walls."

"All right. Well, if you can get them out of bed, we'll go."

"Thank you," I said, kissing him on the cheek as though he were doing me a favor. In reality, I felt it was the other way around. I was trying so hard to make inroads with Ellie – and Miriam, especially. While Ellie seemed to like me from the get-go, Miriam was still standoffish most of the time. We needed to find a way to bond, and it wasn't going to be from me constantly telling them what they were doing wrong.

I bounded up the steps and opened their bedroom doors, singing, "Wake up, sunshine! We're going shopping today!" I heard groans, and saw Miriam put a pillow over her head to block me out, while Ellie pulled her feet under the covers.

"Guess what," I said, popping my head in one doorway, then the other. "Your dad gave us his credit card and we're going to redecorate the downstairs bathroom. It's going to be girl heaven!"

I was hoping that if they had a hand in redoing the plain, utilitarian bathroom to their own taste, they'd take more of an interest in keeping it clean. Neither of them moved.

"I'm going to make us French toast," I called out. "I didn't have breakfast yet either and I'm starving. We're going to need a good breakfast to get us going for today!" I hoped my cheerfulness would mask the fear I felt over wanting this day to go well.

I went back downstairs and pulled out the mixing bowl from the cabinet, and the milk and eggs from the fridge. Jason sat at the counter, sipping coffee and reading the paper.

"Julia never lets them decide anything," I said. "I might be stricter in some ways, but I also treat them with more respect to make adult decisions."

Part of me thought that Miriam's anorexic eating behavior was an attempt to control at least one aspect of her life. Between her parents' divorce and her demanding dance schedule, she probably felt she had very little say in anything. Maybe leaving messes everywhere was also a way to assert herself. I'm sure it wasn't easy having me in the house when she was used to having her dad to herself.

A lot of this I couldn't say to Jason because he'd always get so defensive, but my sister and I pondered over these situations all the time. Now that Adrienne was dating, she was having some of the same issues with bringing a man around her boys, although it didn't seem quite as intense. She and Jonathan were not talking about marriage.

I flipped the French toast and then called up the steps, "Almost ready!"

The girls came down a minute later in their pajamas, hair sticking up all over the place. They sat on either side of their dad and waited to be served. I poured juice and put a plate in front of each of them.

"Eat well. We're going to need lots of energy if we want this to be a one-day project. And we do want it to be a one-day project. Nothing's worse than a bathroom in the middle of a remodel."

Ellie dug in, Miriam cut hers into tiny bites and pushed it around the plate, and Jason ignored his and continued reading the paper.

"Don't you like French toast?" I asked him. These were the kinds of things I'd need to know if we were going to be married. I wondered if we could work all of these differences out and live in harmony, or whether it would always be a lot of hard work to cohabitate with these people. Would I ever feel like one of the family instead of an interloper who came in and shook things up, even if I was invited to do just that by Jason?

"Yes, I like it. I just don't like breakfast."

"Don't like breakfast? What kind of role model are you?" I asked, rolling my eyes. I left his plate in front of him and took the last two pieces out of the pan for myself. I ate standing up on the other side of the counter.

After breakfast, I rinsed the dishes and put them into the dishwasher, putting most of Miriam's and all of Jason's French toast down the drain. I sat on the sofa, alternating between playing games on my phone, reading bits of the newspaper, and tapping my feet impatiently while Jason and the girls took their showers and got dressed.

Finally, everyone was ready and seemed somewhat awake. We piled into Jason's car to head for Lowe's, where I'd hoped they'd have everything from paint to a new light fixture, and of course, towel bars. I led the way into the store, grabbing a shopping cart from the entrance and looking at the sign headings above us for paint. I figured that would be the first step, deciding what color the bathroom would be.

Jason was clearly not a frequent shopper at home improvement stores and did not look like the other men here, who seemed purposeful, focused, and dressed to get right to work on whatever it was they were building or fixing. Jason looked like he was heading to a matinee on Broadway in his crisp khaki pants, brown loafers with tassels, a button-down shirt, and sweater vest. I loved the man, but he's not someone I'd call in a plumbing emergency. Even though I couldn't paint the walls in my apartment, at least I didn't have to worry about fixing anything either. My landlord came in with a giant, well-worn canvas tool pouch anytime something went wrong.

We stood in front of the brightly lit paint display. The choices were so numerous, it was overwhelming.

"So what color are you thinking, girls?" I asked, hoping they could come to a reasonable agreement and it wouldn't take forever. I guessed Jason was hoping they wouldn't say pink.

"Purple," Ellie said at the same time as Miriam said, "Blue."

"We can work with that," I said, rubbing my hands together. "How about something kind of in between?"

The two of them starting pulling out cards they liked, while Jason checked his phone, looking bored. Suddenly, my ex-married-boyfriend John and his family came around the corner. My heart felt like it dropped two feet. He didn't notice me at first because Rachel was tugging his sleeve, saying, "I know what color I want, Daddy." If I could have run away, I would have.

John finally noticed me, but made no reaction to indicate we knew each other. I backed up a step so I was standing next to Jason, who was oblivious. Couldn't he at least have looked more interested in me?

Georgia was even more gorgeous in person than in the pictures I had seen of her. She had her hand hooked around one of John's arms while his daughter held his hand on his other side. I may have been his lover at one time, but I was never the woman in his life the way these two were. I rarely felt like Jason needed me. I hated myself for measuring my relationship with Jason, which was real and legitimate, against a fling I'd had with a married man.

"Let's go look at this side first," John said, turning around to the display behind them. "Let these people finish here."

Now I was "these people." I felt so low, so utterly unimportant. I couldn't focus at all anymore on what the girls were doing, but they managed to find a color they liked. They took it to the paint-mixing counter and waited for their can of blue hyacinth paint. Jason finally looked up from his phone once he realized a decision had been made.

"Where now, hon?" he asked.

"I don't know. I guess over there," I said, pointing vaguely. I went to stand at the counter with the girls until the woman who mixed the paint handed the can to Miriam. I followed behind Jason and the girls as they started looking at towel bars. Every single one of them looked the same to my blurred vision. I wiped my eyes with a tissue.

"What's the matter?" Jason asked. "You were so into this trip. What happened?"

"Nothing. Low blood sugar, I guess."

"You had the biggest breakfast of all of us!" he said, poking me in the ribs.

"I'll be fine. Let's just get out of here and get started on the project."

Once we were out of the store and in the car, my heartbeat slowed down again. Seeing John was a shock, but it was normal to feel this way, or at least that's what I told myself. We never really had the all-important closure. There was no goodbye and I was forced to move on only because he cut off all communication with me.

Meeting Jason shortly afterward helped because I had another man to think about, but the flame I felt for John was rekindled the moment I saw his brown eyes looking back at me, even though they seemed vacant. I missed so much the way John would look deep into my eyes and smile and look so utterly content. I loved it when his attention was on nothing but me, but those moments were rare because his cell phone was never more than a foot away from his body. It was as though his guilt kept him even more tethered to his wife when he was away from her.

By the time we got to Jason's house, I had managed to put John in the back of my thoughts, to be saved for later when I had time to be alone. We sent Jason to his den so he could be surprised when we were finished. I focused on the task at hand, first removing everything from the bathroom, then wiping down the walls, putting up tape, and helping the girls stir the paint gently so it didn't get bubbles in it. They argued over who got to paint first, but I mediated by giving the Miriam the top half and Ellie the lower part of the walls. The color actually looked great. The girls had picked a shade that blended well with the rest of the house. I wondered if they'd want to show the finished bathroom to Julia, and what she'd say about it.

I felt my phone vibrating in my back pocket as the girls ran to get their dad to show them their newly painted bathroom. I looked at the screen and my heart jumped again: It was John.

# 23

*Baby, who's the new guy?*

That's *all* he wrote? Did this mean he was jealous? Curious? Just making conversation? But why would he want to make conversation if he didn't want to start something again? I was panicking, not knowing how to respond, or whether I should respond at all. The logical, rational side of me said, *Don't you dare, girl!*

I knew it would seem desperate if I texted him back right away. How long would be a decent amount of time to seem casual? I needed to know what John was thinking. I didn't notice Jason come up behind me as I stared at the screen until he wrapped his arms around my waist.

"What's the matter, hon? You were so into the bathroom project and then it's like you dropped out. The girls are so proud that they want to call their mom and show her."

I slid my phone into my back pocket and shrugged my shoulders.

"Sorry. I'm just not feeling so good this morning. Maybe the paint fumes got to me."

"It's okay. Let's get back and make the girls feel good about their work."

I followed Jason back to the bathroom and oohed and ahhed over the new bathroom, thinking of what I could say so that I could go home and call my friends for their advice on John. Julia gave me the perfect out when she agreed to stop over and see the bathroom.

"I'll give you guys some time together as a family," I said to Jason. "It's uncomfortable when I'm always hanging around and the girls want to be with their mom."

"They're going to have to get used to it," Jason said, smoothing my hair down in the front where it was always sticking up. "We're going to be a family, and when you're living here, you're not going to be leaving just because Julia stops over."

"I know, but we're not there yet," I said, reaching for my coat.

Julia was already coming in the door before I could get out. I said hi, trying to look casual, but feeling guilty for some inexplicable reason. I had nothing to do with her and Jason not being together. For once, I wasn't the third party in a relationship. It was a novel experience and perhaps I still wasn't used to the concept of a legitimate relationship.

"Hello, Kristen," Julia said, giving me the once over. I prided myself on how put together I looked, so it was rare that another woman made me feel inadequate, but as usual, I was blown away by her natural beauty and perfect clothes. She always wore bright colors, like lime green or fuchsia, and every shade she chose perfectly highlighted her buttery complexion. I felt so drab in my sweatpants, Adrienne's old college sweatshirt, and my ratty sneakers that were no longer good enough for workouts. But hey, I was here to paint, and I spent more time with her daughters than she did. I doubted Julia had anything in her closet that she could have worn to paint a bathroom.

"You have a drip of paint on your cheek," she said, leaning forward as though to make sure it was paint and not a pimple.

"I know," I said, fruitlessly wiping my face. "I'm going home to take a shower now. I know you'll be proud of the girls; they did a great job."

"I'm always proud of my girls," she said, turning toward the bathroom. Don't think I didn't notice the "my girls." I followed her down the hall, said goodbye to the girls from behind her, and gave Jason a quick kiss. Julia had grabbed his arm, so he stayed with his family while I practically ran for my car.

I started the car and then texted Tamara and Heather, *Emergency girl talk at my place. Coffee's on me.*

Before I even pulled away from the curb, Tamara had texted back *Be right there.*

I stopped at the Starbucks drive-through and ordered everyone's favorites, because that's what friends are for, knowing how they like their coffee, their cocktails, and their men, and that they'll be there for you when you need them.

By the time I had scrubbed the paint off my cheek in front of my bathroom mirror, Heather was walking in.

"What's up?" she asked, flopping down on the sofa.

"We'll wait until Tamara gets here. This is *big*."

She looked at my hand and when she didn't see an engagement ring, she asked, "Did you and Jason break up?" *Big* in single lady world meant either getting engaged or breaking up. Not much else required emergency girl time.

"No, we didn't break up! Things aren't that unstable," I said. "Besides, if we did break up, you'd know about it before Jason. I don't think he'd break up with me."

"Wow, someone's full of herself this morning!" Heather said, but she was winking, so I know she didn't mean it.

Tamara walked in, grabbed her coffee, and sat down by Heather, tucking her legs underneath her and wrapping herself up in my favorite blanket.

"The reason I asked you over is this," I said, pulling out my phone to show them the text from John.

They both gasped.

"He didn't!" Tamara exclaimed.

"What balls!" Heather joined in.

"So what do I do?" I asked. "Do I write back and tell him I have a much better boyfriend who wants to marry me? Do I ignore him?"

"We need to discuss all the options," Tamara said wisely. Thank God for girlfriends. This is exactly what I needed. I hate to say it, but if I asked Adrienne, there'd only be one option in her mind and it would be "Don't you dare answer that text!" She was such a Jiminy Cricket. Even when I didn't call her, sometimes I thought my conscience was really my sister's voice in my head. My friends would go over all the options and they wouldn't judge me no matter what I decided to do. That's why I could tell them everything when I was dating John, but I couldn't talk to Adrienne about it.

"If you ignore him, you'll stay out of trouble," Heather said.

"But you won't know why he was texting you in the first place," Tamara chimed in. "It might eat at you. He might be trying to get back with you."

"*Or* he might have just been embarrassed he couldn't say hi to you in the store, so he was awkwardly trying to acknowledge almost literally running into you," Heather said.

My head swiveled back and forth as though I were watching a tennis match. I listened to and evaluated everything they were saying. My heart wanted to get in touch because I hated the way we ended with no chance to say goodbye. I wanted John to know I moved on, although I guess he could see that for himself by the fact that I was out shopping with another man and his daughters.

"What does it mean that he called me *Baby*?"

"Habit," Tamara said.

"Fishing around to see how you feel about him," Heather said.

"Well, that's decisive," I laughed.

My phone chimed with another text and it surprised me so much I almost dropped it.

"It's him again!" I yelled.

*Happy to see you looking good. I always thought it would be us shopping for paint.*

What?! He's the one who broke up with me. I had many fantasies of doing just that. We could have been doing that.

"What an ass," Tamara said. She knew every detail, the whole history of our sordid two-year relationship, so she was definitely allowed to call him an ass.

"Okay, that's it. I have to write something. But what?"

"Why don't you tell him you're obviously in a relationship and go away. Serves him right for the way he dumped you," Heather said.

"You're right. I can't let him know in any way that I still miss him." I started texting.

*Thanks for the compliment. Things are going well for me; hope they are for you too.*

"There. That sounds completely neutral, right? Like he could respond if he wants to, but it's not asking for a response."

Tamara nodded her head and I sent the message. Before I even put my phone back down on the coffee table, it was chiming again.

*Things were better with you in my life.*

"Oh, my God. He's killing me," I said. I was secretly thrilled for the attention, but also feeling guilty that I still wanted to hear from him when I was with Jason, and fearful that I was going to screw up the first normal relationship I ever had.

"Be careful, Kristen," Tamara said. "He's a narcissist. He thinks all the attention should be on him. I know you don't want to hear this, but if he didn't see you with Jason today, I don't think he would have gotten in touch. He only wants to be with you now because the tables are turned and it's a challenge again. If he knows he can get you, it's over. Do you really want to risk what you have for a married guy who dumped you already and is clearly *not* going to leave his wife?"

"No. That would make me an idiot."

"Right," said Heather. "Jason might not be as exciting, but at least you know he's not going to mess with your head."

"True," I said. "Why am I even considering this?"

"Because the grass is *always* greener," Tamara said. "I think you're scared of getting married. I would be too. In the back of your head, I think you realized you never had to worry about that with John."

"You're probably right," I conceded. "So what, just ignore this message?"

"I'd delete him from my phone completely," Tamara said. "Block him. Whatever."

"Okay. Will you do it for me? I can't. It feels too mean."

"I would be more than happy to block that jerk. Then you won't even know if he's trying to get in touch." Tamara grabbed my phone, and seconds later, handed it back, saying, "Done. You are done with him. Got it?"

"Got it," I said. "How about we watch some Netflix now?"

We pulled the blanket over our laps and I tried not to look at my phone as it sat silent on the coffee table. I couldn't even get into the chick flick Heather picked because my mind kept wandering back to John. What if he was sending me more texts and letting me know what his feelings were and he wouldn't even know he was blocked, so he'd just think I was being rude for not answering? Why did I care if he thought I was rude after what he did to me?

I started to plot how I could get rid of my friends. I felt like an addict. They were here to be my minders and I was scheming to get my fix behind their backs. Tamara noticed me staring at my phone and mouthed, "Are you okay?" over Heather's head. *Yes*, I nodded back to her. I tried harder to focus on the movie, but it was one of those ones where you knew the girl would get her guy in the end.

Did I already have my guy and I didn't realize how lucky I was? Did I already have my happy ending? I wished so much I could be content thinking about Jason, or wishing it was him I was hoping to get a text from.

After the movie, Heather got up and stretched, yawning loudly.

"I gotta go or I'll end up crashing here the whole rest of the day," she said.

Tamara stood too, but she looked hesitant about leaving.

"Are you sure you're going to be all right?" she asked, grabbing my shoulders and looking deeply into my eyes.

"Yes, I'll be fine," I said, looking at the floor.

"No Facebook stalking, no Googling him, no unblocking his number. Got it?"

"Got it."

"Promise?"

"I promise," I laughed, pushing her toward the door. "I'm going for a run soon. That'll clear my head. And I have plans with Jason later."

"Good. Call me if you need anything," Tamara said, following Heather out the door.

As soon as they left, I broke my promise.

*My life was better with you in it too*, I texted, as soon as I had unblocked John's number.

# 24

"Jules, remember when you grabbed that kid's hockey stick and broke it in half?" Jason said, laughing and slapping his knee. This was just a barrel of laughs... me sitting in Jason's living room while he and "Jules" relived all their best memories together with the girls. Sometimes the man had the emotional sensitivity of a goat. Unfortunately, it was something I had to get used to, because Julia often stayed for a while when she dropped off the girls. I tried to tell Jason it bothered me, but I felt like he brushed me off, saying that it was healthier for the girls to have some "transition time" from one parent to the other. Apparently, my sister and her ex didn't know that, because Drew never went farther in her house than the front door.

"Oh, wait! I almost forgot to show you this," Julia said, as Jason and the girls huddled over her phone.

"What is it?" I asked mildly, but they were all too busy giggling over some video. All I could make out was something about a kitten in a crib. I laid my head against the back of the sofa, my hands in my lap and my feet propped up on the coffee table.

"I guess I should get going," Julia said, sounding reluctant.

"No, Mom, stay!" Ellie begged. "I want you to put me to bed tonight."

Julia turned toward Jason, silently asking for approval. He looked sheepishly over at me, then back at her.

"I think it would be better for the girls to stick to our normal schedule," he said. "I'll put her to bed here and you will at your house. Besides, we're at a very important part in *Edward Tulane*. I need to know what's going to happen next."

"Mommy could read it to me and I'll tell you," Ellie offered.

"No, Ellie Bellie, Mommy has to go now," Julia said. She leaned over and kissed Ellie on top of the head, blew an air kiss to Miriam, and buttoned her coat. She didn't even acknowledge me. Jason jumped up to walk her to the door. I appreciated what a gentleman he was, but did he always have to be such a gentleman toward his ex-wife? I guess he did if he wanted his daughters to see how they should be expect to be treated by a man. I wondered if Miriam picked up on the coldness between her mother and me. I was pretty sure it went right over Ellie's head.

While we waited for Jason to come back, the girls got preoccupied with something on TV. I decided I'd go out to the entranceway to give Jason a secret kiss, but he and Julia were still standing at the door talking. They were laughing together again, and it really looked like they were flirting. If I had seen them together like this at a bar, I would assume they were two people who just met and were getting to know whether there was substance to back up the chemistry they were feeling. My sister and her ex never acted like this. They were cordial with each other, but it was all business with Adrienne and Drew. Whenever I heard them talking, it was just to figure out the schedule with the boys.

Julia looked up and saw me watching them. She touched Jason on the arm and said again how she should get going. He closed the door behind her and turned around to see me standing there with my arms crossed. I tried not to furrow my brow because I didn't want to turn into one of those perpetually angry-looking women, even if that's how I felt on the inside right now.

"Hey, hon, how are you? Sorry for all the talk about old stuff. I know that was rude in front of you. We just got carried away," he said, trying to pull me into a hug.

I rigidly kept my arms crossed, not letting myself melt into his hug. I was trying to decide whether it was good or bad that he *knew* he was doing jerky things but did them anyway. Was that really better than not even being aware of it? He backed up a step and looked at me.

"What's the matter? You're not really mad, are you?" he asked.

"I don't know what I am," I said, rubbing my arms. "I never thought I'd have to be jealous of your attention to your ex-wife. It's hard enough. She's so beautiful, she's the mother... I don't fit in here."

"You have nothing to be jealous of," he said, sighing. "Don't turn into one of those insecure women who gets jealous over every little thing. I've never given you a reason not to trust me. And we're divorced. There are a lot of good reasons for that."

"Yeah, but she left you. I have a feeling you'd still be together if you could."

I often worried that he wished he was still married to Julia, but this was the first time I had the nerve to say it out loud for fear that he would agree.

"Not true. She was the one who left, but I understand now that we didn't work together married. She couldn't deal with my imperfections. She couldn't handle the fact that she couldn't fix me. One of the things I appreciate about you is that you never asked me or expected me to be anything other than I am."

"But if she wanted to get back together, you would, wouldn't you?" I asked, holding my breath to wait for his answer.

"That's not on the table. I don't know what you expect me to say."

"You could say no," I said, bursting into tears. "You could say, 'I have you now and I wouldn't take her back'."

Now I wanted the hug he offered before, but as I stepped toward him, he leaned back.

"Kristen, why don't you take some time to cool off. I don't think you're thinking straight right now."

"This is what I hate about us! Every time I get upset, you're so rational about it. I want you to get emotional too! I want to see your passion! I don't even know why you love me."

I was sniffling pathetically and I hated that it seemed like he always had the upper hand. How come I was always the one feeling insecure?

"I love you because you're a good person. You're honest, and I can trust you."

"I slept with a married man," I blurted out. "How trustworthy and honest is that?"

Jason looked taken aback, but he recovered quickly.

"You won't do it again, though. I know you and you've turned a corner," he said. "When I met you, I fell for you because I could see you wanted to change your life, and so do I. I know you will be my wife and you will stand by me. And you know I'll stand by you. You say this crazy stuff about Julia, but I think in your heart you know it's not true."

"I don't know what I believe. I'm confused."

I didn't think he'd cheat on me, but maybe John's wife never thought he would either. I was just as scared that I'd let Jason down. Maybe his trust in me wasn't deserved.

When it came down to it, I was probably picking a fight with him because I felt guilty about the texting back and forth I'd been doing with John. We hadn't actually met up again, but some of the things we said were suggestive and I'd be very ashamed if Jason found out.

He stepped toward me again and this time I let him hug me and kept my mouth shut.

# 25

I used to believe everything was random. The universe seemed like a bunch of haphazard coincidences. Lately, though, I'm starting to wonder if God or the universal creator or whatever does things for a reason.

John was texting me, pressuring me to meet up with him. I answered his texts, but I kept putting off the actual getting together. A few months ago, I would have jumped at the chance to be with him, married or not. I would've taken back a man who cheated on his wife with me and then dumped me. I still missed the excitement of being filled with anticipation for him to knock on my door, opening it to find him holding a bouquet of flowers, putting them down to jump into his arms and kiss him so hard.

But then I got a new client, and she changed everything. Brooke swept in one windy day, curled up leaves blowing in around her ankles, with no appointment, requesting a massage. I happened to have a block open between other clients. The way she walked in like she owned the place reminded me of Julia, but everything else about her appearance was different. She had my petite and muscular build, but curvier and more feminine, and her wispy blonde hair was cut in loose layers. I could be wrong, but I think she was *actually* a blonde, unlike me. She was wearing a white button-down shirt tucked into a fabulous pair of black trouser pants that flowed over her curves perfectly.

We shook hands and I walked backwards toward my room, feeling like a tour guide. She never stopped talking, but I had a feeling she'd be talking whether anyone was listening or not. She talked so fast and changed topics so often that I couldn't follow, so I just nodded when it seemed appropriate. She certainly was wound tight. I was going to have my work cut out for me.

"So what brings you here today?" I asked, when she paused for a breath.

"What brings me here today? Well, I'll tell you. What brings me here today is my husband is cheating on me."

*Oh boy.* Not only was she going to be impossible to calm down physically, but I was going to be providing therapy too. Little did she know she was talking to the *wrong* person for dealing with a cheating husband.

"Okay," I said neutrally. "So this would be a relaxation massage, or do you have specific areas you want me to work on?"

"I want you to hurt me. I want you to pummel the pain out of me," Brooke said, nearly growling.

"It's not my policy to hurt people, but I'll do my best to get you feeling better."

"I mean it, hurt me. It's the only thing that takes the pain away."

I didn't respond to that, but told her she could undress to her comfort level and lie face down on the table.

"You don't have to leave," she said, as I started to exit the room. "I'm not shy."

"Umm, I do have to leave because it's our policy here," I said, trying to look calm. She was unbuttoning her blouse before I backed out of the doorway. "I'll be back in a few minutes."

I closed the door and pressed my forehead against the metal frame for a few seconds, trying to gather my thoughts. This was going to be dreadful, and I still had three clients left to get through. When it sounded quiet in the room again, I knocked softly at the door as I opened it a crack, asking, "Are you ready?"

"Sure am," she said, sounding muffled with her face in the head cradle.

"If you would like to relax, my clients find it best to be as quiet as possible," I said gently, hoping she'd get the hint to shut up. She didn't.

"I'm not here to relax, sister. I'm here to get the shit pummeled out of me so I don't *kill* that lying, cheating bastard. Wait – do I get attorney-client privilege, or is that only for actual attorneys? If I tell you stuff, are you bound by law to keep your mouth shut?"

"No, I don't have that, whatever you called it, but I am discreet because it's my job to work on your *muscles*, not give you legal advice." I wondered if I could gag her and tell her that was part of our procedure here.

I let her ramble for a while, trying to tune her out but finding it more and more impossible as she told me the steps leading up to finding out about the infidelity. I had always wondered about that – what it's like to be on the other side. With John, I wavered between living in fear that Georgia would find out about me and wishing it would happen so he'd be forced to make a decision. I didn't like the limbo he kept me in. He didn't seem to realize how dangerous I was – I could have told Georgia, but the only thing that stopped me was I loved him and I knew he might be angry enough to leave me if I exposed our relationship.

Just as I expected, Brooke's whole back was tight as a drum. I was pressing my elbows into her back and barely getting the muscles to release.

"So what do *you* think I should do?" she demanded.

"What?" I had lost track of where we were in the conversation.

"Should I file for divorce?"

"I have no idea. I've never been married, so I couldn't tell you. But my sister got divorced, and it was pretty awful for a while. Same thing as you, her husband was cheating."

"Do *any* men stay faithful?" Brooke asked, and I told her I didn't know. But I thought of Jason and I realized that every fiber of my being told me he'd never cheat on me. With some men, you just knew. If I was jealous of Julia, that was my own insecurity. What was I thinking, even taking a chance of losing him to fool around with John again?

I tried harder to listen to Brooke. The hour flew by, even though I was sweating and sore from the exertion of trying to wrangle my new client into a state of relaxation.

When I finished, she sat up, pulling the sheet around herself and standing up.

"We need to be friends," she said. "When can we meet up for lunch?"

"It's our policy here that we can't socialize with clients," I answered.

"That's ridiculous. This place has way too many policies," she huffed. "I won't tell if you don't. How about tomorrow?"

"I guess that would work." I didn't know why I was agreeing to this, but I didn't feel like I had much choice. And besides, Brooke clearly needed a friend and something about her seemed to be unlocking answers to some of the questions in my own heart.

"Great! See you tomorrow. Noon. Pasquale's."

By the time she walked back out the door, I was completely smitten with her bossiness and self-assurance. Now *that* was my kind of woman. I blocked John's number from my phone again with a renewed sense of appreciation for Jason and the near-miss I'd avoided.

# 26

"Couldn't we just stay in bed today? It's raining, it's yucky, I don't wanna get up!" I said in my best pleading voice, pulling Jason's hand so his head flopped back onto the pillow next to me.

"Nope, not today, sunshine. I am a communion assistant," he said, prying my fingers off his wrist.

"It doesn't say that on the schedule."

"Jim got sick and I have to fill in for him."

"Oh. Well, couldn't I stay in bed and you just go, and then bring me home some breakfast?"

Jason swatted me on the rear end through the covers.

"Get up, slug-a-muffin. Rise and shine. It's a beautiful day and we're going to church."

"You must be delusional. It is not a beautiful day." But sensing Jason's persistence, I rolled out of bed and headed into the bathroom for a shower. He seemed extra fidgety as I got ready, looking at the clock every few minutes and pacing around.

"Easy, cowboy. I'll be ready on time. You know I always am."

"Yeah, and every time it's down to the wire. Couldn't you maybe be a little early instead of just on time?"

"Sorry, but on time is good enough for me."

"What are you going to wear today?"

"I don't know. Anything special you'd like to see me in?"

"You look beautiful in anything. How about that pink sweater?"

"Sure. How about you giving me a little privacy. I promise I'll get ready faster without you mooning around looking at your watch constantly. I won't let you down."

"I know you won't," Jason said, wrapping his arms around me from behind and kissing my cheek. "See you in eleven minutes?"

"Eleven minutes, you got it." I winked at him and pushed him out the door.

I dried my hair, put on makeup, and pulled on the sweater, a black pencil skirt, and knee-high boots. No time for jewelry today. I grabbed my purse and ran down the steps, just as Jason came around the corner standing at the bottom of the staircase, looking like he was about to yell up the steps for me. Instead, he got tears in his eyes.

"What? I'm on time, aren't I?"

"You are, and you look absolutely amazing. Come on, let's go," he said, pulling me into a tight hug and then spinning me toward the front door.

I didn't know why he was acting so weird, but getting emotional was nothing that unusual for Jason. After all, he cried the first time he met me. Corny commercials on TV could set him off. And if his girls gave him a gift they had made, that was guaranteed to open the floodgates.

When we got to church, we sat in the usual spot and I leafed through the bulletin while we waited for the service to start. I nudged Jason.

"See, we were *more* than on time," I said. He smiled, but looked distracted and kept looking all around, as though he was waiting for someone. "What's the matter?"

"Nothing, I'm fine," he said, patting my hand.

We listened to the announcements – birthdays, who was in the hospital, who was home from the hospital, a new grandchild, a family moving – and then Pastor Dawn said, "We have one more special announcement this morning."

She looked in our direction, and I looked behind me, wondering who she was talking about, until Jason stood up, turned sideways so he could look around the church and said, "I asked for a moment this morning to share something with all of you, since you are all my family."

Then he took my hands.

"Kristen, you know that since the day I met you, I've known you are the one for me. I asked you to marry me on our first date. I don't know how seriously you took me, but as I stand here today, I know more than ever that you were meant to be my wife. I only hope that you agree, or I'm going to look really silly in front of all these people."

He knelt down between the pews, fumbling in his pocket and then pulling out a jewelry box. He opened it to show me a stunning ring and asked, "Kristen, will you be my wife?"

"Oh, my God. Oh, my God, Jason. I'm in shock."

"Well, it's kind of a yes or no question. Obviously, I'm really hoping it's a yes."

"Yes."

"Ladies and gentlemen, she said yes!" Pastor Dawn announced from the front of the church. The whole congregation erupted into applause, with a few whistles thrown in. Jason slipped the ring on my finger, and of course, it fit perfectly. Knowing Jason, he had somehow found out my ring size ahead of time.

"I love you," he whispered in my ear.

"Love you too," I whispered back, smiling. I was in shock, but I realized also, very, very happy. It was hard to focus on the rest of the church service that morning. As soon as the last hymn was over, people started milling around us to offer congratulations.

"It's 'best wishes' to the woman," one woman rebuked her husband. "You only offer congratulations to the man, because he's lucky to have found his bride."

"I am lucky indeed that this woman will take me," Jason said, squeezing my hand.

I couldn't think of anything to say, but at least it seemed no one expected me to say anything other than "thank you."

When we finally got out to the car, Jason pulled me towards him for a sweet kiss.

"I'm so glad you said yes. I don't know what I'd have done if you said no. I'd probably have to start going to another church."

"Is that why you asked me in front of so many people, to make sure I'd say yes?" He looked hurt for a second, until he realized I was joking.

"I asked you here because I want us to get married here. Is that okay with you?"

"Of course it is. You've given this some thought, haven't you?"

"Only for the past eight months," Jason said, laughing. "I can't wait to call you my wife." He hugged me again and I rested my head against his chest, the word *wife* making me smile.

# 27

Ever since Jason and I got engaged, I felt this unfamiliar sense of domesticity. I suddenly wanted everything to be orderly and neat. I stopped eating fast food sandwiches and throwing the balled-up wrappers on the passenger seat of my car. I didn't leave empty coffee cups lying around on the counters. I spent a lot more time at Jason's, thinking about where I fit in there, physically and emotionally.

When I thought about us being married, some of the things I looked forward to the most were washing the dishes together and getting to go to bed together each night. I enjoyed folding the laundry and putting the neat stacks into everyone's bedrooms. When I lived at home, my mom went as far as to put my clothes into my drawers and closet for me. Jason usually tossed the piles of clean clothes on each girl's bed with the intention that they'd put them away. Instead, the hangers in their closets were half unused and they did most of their dressing from clothes that were strewn about on the floor. I'm not sure how they could tell what was clean from what needed to be washed.

I thought I'd do the girls a favor by putting their clothes away for them while they were visiting their mom and Jason was wrapped up in a documentary about an expedition to find a sunken pirate ship. I started in Ellie's room, which was the messier of the two. She collected stuffed animals, which were wrapped up in the tangles of her sheets and blankets, along with socks, books, and a Nintendo Switch. I made her bed, which probably hadn't been made since the last time the sheets got washed.

Jason and I differed on how much was expected of his daughters as far as keeping the house neat. He let them have free reign to make a mess, knowing that he'd eventually clean up after them. They were better about the bathroom, just as I'd predicted, now that they had painted it and made it their own space. Sometimes I heard Miriam telling Ellie to wipe out the bathroom sink or pick up her wet bath towel from the floor.

After I made the bed, I put Ellie's clothes away and brought the basket with Miriam's clothes into her room. She was slightly neater, but I think it was mainly because she had less stuff. Her mess was mostly clothes and school papers. I stacked them up, pausing to look at a lab report for which she'd earned a B-. I gave up trying to understand what the experiment had been about and what the results were. I couldn't read the teacher's red scrawled comments at all. I wondered if Miriam could, or if she had disregarded whatever the teacher had to say about her report once she saw the grade.

As I opened her dresser to start putting clothes away, I gasped. The top drawer had probably a dozen empty cookie and cupcake packages stuffed into the back. The middle drawer held crumpled bags from several different flavors of potato chips. And the bottom drawer was overflowing with empty candy bar wrappers peeking out from under the clothes. I left everything as is, as though I had stumbled upon a crime scene, and called to Jason from the top of the steps.

"What is it?" he said, grumbling, but also sounding a little worried. The tone of my voice must have told him there was trouble, or he would never have left a TV show halfway through to come see anything upstairs.

"Look at Miriam's dresser," I said, pointing, but staying at the doorway. I didn't want to go back in her room and have to look at the dresser up close.

"Just some wrappers in her drawers; what's the big deal?" he asked.

"Have you noticed how skinny your daughter is? How she never eats anything at the dinner table? She has to be binging and purging."

"She couldn't be. She wouldn't be able to keep up her dancing schedule if there was anything like that going on. She wouldn't have the energy."

"Jason, you don't want to see it because it's your daughter. I don't blame you. But I will blame you if you don't do something about this. She's very sick. It's only going to get worse."

He sighed. His shoulders seemed to sink as I watched the air go out of him. I had a feeling he was trying to figure out how to approach this. Miriam would surely be angry at the invasion of her privacy. Julia would be infuriated that I was implying her daughter wasn't perfect. I didn't want to be caught in the middle of this.

"Please, Jason. Don't tell them it was me who found this. Don't tell them I'm the one pushing her to get help. Miriam and Julia will both accept things much better coming from you. I'm the evil stepmother-to-be."

"I won't. I just need to think about what I'm going to say. Are you sure? I mean, are you really sure it's not just a teenager's bad eating habits? Maybe she's not hungry for dinner because she's eating chips in her room after school. Kids have notoriously bad eating habits. I think we would have noticed more."

"Jason, I caught her throwing up. She told me she was just sick, but it was right after dinner that night I took them to Red Robin. Don't think about this like it's your daughter. Think about it like you would think of a patient. She has an eating disorder and you need to send her for help. You need to stand up to Julia and make sure she's on board with it too, or Miriam will just go to her and stay there until she feels like it has blown over. She'll try to punish you by not talking to you."

Jason pushed the dresser drawers closed and went to his room, sitting on his bed and putting his head between his hands.

"You don't think about this stuff happening when you're having babies," he said. "No one tells you how hard it's going to be."

"I know. Well, I mean, I know it's hard from watching my sister raise her kids. I don't think I could handle it. I mean, I'm going to be handling it with you, but when it comes down to it, it's still your responsibility." I couldn't think of what to say that would help.

Jason pulled me into a hug and rested his head on my shoulder. I ran my fingers over his head to soothe him, wishing I could fix this somehow and knowing I couldn't.

# 28

After a day of wrangling, Miriam was in an inpatient treatment center for adolescent girls with eating disorders, Julia was enraged at me, Jason was avoiding me, and Ellie was walking around her dad's house in circles, crying and clutching her favorite stuffed bunny. I felt guilty, like it was all my fault for blowing up this family.

Because they are doctors, Jason and Julia were able to find a hospital unit with a bed very quickly, before their resolve would weaken. They didn't give Miriam much choice in the matter. At first she said the wrappers were Ellie's and she was hiding them for Ellie, but when Ellie protested loudly and vehemently that she never got any of those cookies or chips, and it was unfair that she didn't, Miriam's next excuse was that they had been piling up in her drawers for months and she just never bothered to throw them out. No one could be sure of that because it had been months since anyone put clothes away, but the doctor evaluating her observed that she was seriously underweight, and whether she was binging and purging or not, she was certainly suffering from malnutrition.

Finally, Miriam admitted that she had thrown up "once or twice," but it was something that all the girls she danced with did to keep their weight down. She said she learned how to do it from the older girls. I was horrified to think of Ellie maybe coming across the same information and thinking she should starve herself or throw up. Maybe that was why she so fiercely wanted to quit dance. Ellie has a very strong sense of right and wrong.

Julia angrily called Miriam's dance center, demanding to know why no one red-flagged Miriam's weight. The owner's only explanation was that a lot of the teenaged girls were thin, and it was just a "natural phase" they were going through.

Jason made good on his promise never to connect me in any way with the wrappers, but Julia still seemed to hone in on me as a scapegoat.

"Everything was fine with the girls until you came on the scene," she said venomously in the waiting room outside the locked unit where they had taken Miriam.

Jason was in the bathroom, and Julia saw her chance to say what was on her mind. What could I say in my defense? I didn't know if it was true that the girls were better off before Jason met me because I wasn't there. All I could go by was the dozens of times he had told me that they were happier now with the stability and routine I brought into the household, that even if they weren't overtly affectionate toward me, they were happy for him being happy.

"I've only done things I thought were in the best interest of the girls," I said, wishing Jason would hurry up.

"Oh, you mean like encouraging Ellie to quit dance? That was really helpful," Julia snarled.

"That wasn't my idea. She told me she didn't like it anymore and asked if I would talk to her dad. I told her how important it is to be active. I started taking her to the gym!"

"No one asked for your interference, Kristen. Jason and I were doing just fine."

"All I can say is he asked me to marry him. He asked me to help with the girls, so he must value what I have to say."

Julia whipped her hair around and clicked out of the room in her high-heeled boots, pushing past Jason as he came back in.

"What's with her?" he asked.

"I think she's just stressed because her daughter's locked up in here," I said. Part of me wanted to give her the benefit of the doubt, and I didn't want to go running to Jason every time his ex-wife made a crack at me.

"Are you ready to go?" he asked. "They said we can't see her again until Thursday. They said it's easier for patients to acclimate without their family around."

"How's she doing?"

"They didn't say much. She just got here. I'm sure it's going to be difficult. Look, I know you did the right thing. Julia is probably mad, but you were right that we need to face this head-on. I only hope that my little girl comes out of here better off. I don't want her learning new tricks from the other inmates."

"They're not inmates; they're patients!" I protested.

"That's a matter of semantics. I doubt any of them volunteered to stay here."

"Try to be more positive, okay? I think this is going to work out for her. What she was doing could have killed her."

"You're right," Jason said, kissing me on the top of the head. "Come on, let's go home."

# 29

I cradled a bouquet of flowers in one arm as I pushed the buzzer outside the unit Miriam was staying in. Neither Jason nor Julia could go because of patient appointments and they wanted her to have a visitor every day, so I volunteered. I had more school assignments for her to work on. Once the nurse at the desk checked my ID against the visitors' list, she led me to Miriam's room. Miriam was sitting on her bed reading *To Kill a Mockingbird*, an open notebook beside her and pen in hand.

"Keeping up with your homework okay?" I asked, knocking at the door.

"Yeah, it's actually easier in here because there's nothing to distract me."

"Well, that's good because I have more."

"Lovely," she said, rolling her eyes.

"So how's it going? Do you like your roommate?"

"She's all right. She's going home in a few days. She's been here almost a month already. She gained eight pounds since she got here."

"Wow, that's good, right?"

"I guess so. I hope I don't have to gain eight pounds to go home."

"Miriam, you're awfully thin."

"I'm not, really. You should see some of the other girls I dance with. You can see every bone in their backs. They look like their bones are going to pop out of their skin."

"Is that what you want to look like?"

"Not really, but they do look so graceful up on the stage, at a distance."

"More people see you up close than at a distance. And you don't want a guy to hug you and say you feel sharp."

"I'm never going to have a boyfriend anyway. It doesn't matter."

"You don't want one?"

"It's too complicated. I see what it's been like for Mom and Dad and I don't want to deal with that. What's the point?"

"Well, there must be something special about love if people keep trying," I said, hoping to sound light-hearted. This was the longest conversation Miriam and I had ever had. A nurse padded in, pulling a blood pressure monitor on a rolling cart.

"Time for your vitals check," she said cheerfully. I started to get up. "Your mom can stay; it's fine."

I noticed Miriam didn't correct her. I wondered if it got tiring to always tell people I wasn't their mom. To me, it would have been obvious with how different we looked. Maybe they thought her dad was Asian, or that she was adopted.

"Everything's great," the nurse said a minute later, patting Miriam on the arm and pulling her cart out of the room with her.

"Do you feel like it's helping you to be here?"

"I don't know. I guess so. I still think I'm fat, but I've learned a lot about why I do what I do."

"Like what?"

"Like I binge when I feel angry. I do it to like stuff down my feelings with food and go numb."

"What makes you angry?"

"Girls at school. Dad. Mom. Ellie. Dance class. Anything. I get angry a lot."

"Do I make you angry?"

"Sometimes. But don't take it personally. You're okay. You make Dad happy."

"I know it's hard having him be with someone other than Mom –"

"The thing is, though, it's not that hard. They were horrible together. Mom was always mad at him and he was never home. The year before they got divorced is when I started binging. It helped me feel better. Ellie was doing it too, but she never caught on to the purging part, thank God. That's why I'm thin and she's not."

"Where did you guys get all the junk food? Your mom seems pretty strict."

"We'd go shopping with Dad. He'd let us put anything in the cart that we wanted. And you know, just walk to the store and get stuff. It's not that hard. Ellie told me one time she snuck into her friend's kitchen in the middle of the night when she was sleeping over and ate a whole box of cheese crackers. She hid the box under her friend's bed."

"Oh, my gosh, Miriam. I'm sorry. I don't know what to say. I never really thought about food that much. I've done other stupid things, though, believe me."

"It's okay. I realized I have to get better so I can help my sister. She's so unhappy. She doesn't remember Mom and Dad fighting as much. Little kids don't get divorce."

"I don't think anyone gets divorce."

"Probably not. Anyway, thanks for stopping by. Who sent you? Dad?"

"Your dad, yes. He couldn't get away from his office hours today because there's another virus going around that everyone seems to be getting."

"Well, thanks for the homework and the flowers. I do have to get back to work. I have group meeting in a few minutes."

We stood up together and awkwardly hugged. I left the unit and sighed with relief. I hadn't realized how I had been practically holding my breath the whole time, hoping the visit would go well. I wanted to be able to tell Jason that Miriam was looking good, and that she was happy to see me. She definitely seemed healthier, and I was pretty sure she was glad to have me visit. I hoped that her getting better was also a new start to our relationship.

# 30

"Don't you think it's time I meet him, now that you're engaged?" my sister asked. "I mean, it's not like your other boyfriends. He's actually single!"

"I'm used to keeping my relationships separate because of how judgmental Mom is, but I guess you're right," I replied.

"You can't really blame Mom for that. It was kind of scandalous."

"I know. I was an idiot. What can I say?"

"Put it in the past and let's get together with Jason. I can't wait to meet him. Maybe we could have a double-date. Or wait, how about Christmas dinner?"

"I don't know. I'd have to see..."

"Kristen, you're going to marry the man. We have to meet him. What, are you afraid we won't like him? Or he won't like us?"

"No, it's not that. I just don't know what his family's plans are."

"You have a family too, and now that you're getting married, you have to take both families into account."

"I never realized how complicated things were going to get."

"I guess not," Adrienne said, laughing. "It's one of those things you kind of have to be in it to understand."

Later that evening, I texted Jason to see if he had time to talk. When he called, I took a deep breath before answering. I don't know why I was so nervous.

"What's the matter?" he asked. "I can always tell when you have something on your mind because you get that funny high voice. What is it?"

"I was wondering if you'd spend Christmas with my family," I blurted out in one quick burst.

"Oh. I hadn't thought of that. I figured you'd be spending it with us because of the girls."

"I know, it's just that Adrienne wants me to be there, and I should see my nephews. I always do. And my family wants to meet you and it just seems like a good time for that, right?"

"Give me some time to work things out with Julia," he said, which unfairly made me feel resentful. I wished he could just say yes. This was the first time I could bring a boyfriend – no, a fiancé – home, and it was still so damned complicated. I know I sounded irritated when we said good night and I half appreciated and half felt infuriated that he ignored the tone of my voice. It seemed like he jumped to do whatever he could to make Julia happy anytime she was upset, but me, I had to just deal with it, alone. I brought this up one time and he seemed surprised.

"You're so different than Julia," he said. "She's demanding and you're not. It's one of the reasons I love you. You're so understanding."

But I wasn't always. Sometimes I wanted him to reassure me and tell me I came first. I didn't have the ace in the hole that she did – their children.

After a few days of negotiating, Jason worked out with Julia that he and the girls would come with me to my sister's house for dinner on Christmas Day. I would spend Christmas morning with Jason (and Julia) while the girls opened their presents, but on Christmas Eve he was going to his in-laws' for their special dinner and I wasn't invited, obviously.

I usually spent Christmas Eve at home alone anyway, but I was bummed about it this year. There was never anyone else I rightfully should have been with on Christmas Eve before. Adrienne was visiting Jonathan in New York City for the day while her kids spent Christmas Eve with their dad, and our mom and dad weren't coming until the next day either. I guess I could have made the drive to their place, but sitting at home with them seemed like a gloomy prospect. I'd have to do what I usually did on Christmas Eve: sleep in, watch Netflix all day, give myself a mani/pedi, and order Chinese food for dinner.

When I asked Jason how we'd handle the holidays when we were married and he had new in-laws, he just told me we'd work that out when we had to and there was no sense worrying about it now. But I did worry about it. I worried that we would be married and I'd still be sitting at home alone on Christmas Eve while he spent the evening with his ex-wife and her family. I was afraid there was never going to be a time that he was fully mine.

My sister and my mom made me feel like a freak that I was bringing someone home for the first holiday ever. They kept asking me what Jason would eat and the girls would eat and was it obvious he had MS and should they ask him about it or not. And of course they wanted to know what to do about Miriam's eating disorder. I told them to ignore it and don't be insulted if she didn't eat much, and not to push her to eat, just let Jason handle that. Ugh. I did my best to ignore them or reassure them, depending on my mood.

As it did for everyone, the days leading up to Christmas flew past. I never enjoyed shopping and it was extra stressful trying to think of gifts for Jason and the girls on top of my parents, Adrienne, and her boys.

Miriam was home from her inpatient treatment, but still had to be driven back and forth for outpatient sessions. Now and then, I took her when neither Jason nor Julia could get away from work. Ellie was in school, so it felt a little awkward without the cheerful buffer that she always provided, but Miriam and I settled into a routine of listening to whatever music she was in the mood for during our car rides. I was fine with it; I liked most of her music and when I didn't, I tuned it out and let my mind wander. She played it just loud enough that it would have been hard to talk over. I read or went shopping while she was in her sessions, so even though the Christmas shopping was stressful, I had plenty of time to get it done.

Christmas Eve was dreadful and lonely. Jason texted me a few times, but he was busy participating in the large Italian feast of the seven fishes with Julia's father's side of the family. I thought it ironic that I was eating food from the other side of her family heritage, digging into a carton of so-so Chinese food. I got through it by spending the day in a semi-comatose state, brought on by a nonstop marathon of *Sleepless in Seattle* and other hopelessly romantic comedies that made me cry. I camped out on the sofa with a box of tissues and my takeout boxes. Eating with Jason and cooking more made me spoiled. All the staples I used to live on were no longer satisfying. The salt and grease made me feel bloated, which added to the dramatic effect that I would die alone on my sofa. I didn't even have a cat or a dog to sit by my rotting corpse.

# 31

By Christmas morning, I was an emotional wreck, ready to cry but holding it in because I knew I had to appear carefree and happy to Julia. I knocked on Jason's door, feeling silly because this would soon be my house too. No one answered, so after a minute I let myself in with my key. I toted my gift bags into Jason's den to find the family in what seemed like swaths of gift wrap, tissue paper, and bows. There were piles of new clothes strewn about on the chairs and the girls were opening boxes that held laptops. The house smelled like cinnamon buns and bacon.

"Merry Christmas!" Jason called out from the sofa. Julia gave me a half smile and then turned back toward her daughters, who didn't seem to notice yet that I was there. I felt like I was intruding on someone else's holiday and I could feel my throat closing up and tears filling the corners of my eyes.

"Merry Christmas," I said back to him. "Am I late?" I thought they were going to wait for me to open gifts.

"No, no, not at all," he said, motioning for me to come sit by him. "The girls got up earlier than usual and they didn't want to wait to start opening presents, so we let them."

I sat down next to him on the sofa, wishing he'd give me a hug or a kiss, but then berating myself. I was his fiancée after all; why did he have to prove he loved me? Wasn't his intention to marry me enough?

Then I noticed there were *more* piles of presents; he was right when he said they had just started. I had never seen such excess, and I tucked my bags on the side of the sofa, feeling like my modest gifts were so meager compared to everything else they were opening. I had heard that children of divorced parents often end up with more presents because both parents are shopping separately, but this was way above and beyond what Adrienne and Drew gave their boys. It was certainly different than the Christmases I grew up with, where we all took turns opening gifts and spending a few minutes looking over each one because there weren't that many and we wanted to savor the unwrapping.

Jason put his arm around me and I let out a big breath. He suddenly seemed to notice I was there, looking me in the eyes and smiling in his big, eye-crinkling way, and I forced myself to feel happy, to realize this was the first of many Christmases we'd be spending together, and even though it wasn't exactly what I had envisioned, it was still good. I could see how happy he was, how much he was enjoying watching his daughters' delight, and I thought how, especially after all they'd been through the past few months, it was wonderful to be here. Miriam was home again and seemed to be doing well with her eating. Ellie was starting to feel like a real daughter to me. Julia, even though she wasn't what I'd call warm, had seemed to accept me as a permanent fixture in her daughters' and ex-husband's life. And they'd be meeting my family later in the day. I had one of those rare moments of feeling completely content, and I held on to it, knowing there were plenty of times that having these moments stored up would have to carry me through the challenges ahead.

I stayed at Jason's until the girls had opened all of their gifts, then went home to unwind. I still needed downtime to myself, even after the misery of spending the entire previous day alone. He and the girls were going to be picking me up around five to head over to Adrienne's house.

When I got into his car a few hours later, there were more presents from Jason to my family. I felt like the outfit and journal I had gotten each of his girls wasn't enough. He and I hadn't had time to exchange our gifts for each other yet, but I was hoping we'd have a few moments to slip away sometime at my sister's house and have a little bit of private time together. I realized our couple time when we got married would be limited to when Miriam and Ellie were at their mom's, and now that we were engaged, we didn't go on dates very often. Instead, we spent more time in his house rearranging and sorting through his stuff to make room for mine.

"You girls look beautiful," I said, turning around from the front seat. They were each wearing new dresses from Julia, and Miriam had wrapped a silky watercolor scarf around her neck and put her hair up in a loose bun.

Ellie smiled and said thanks, while Miriam looked out the window as though she hadn't heard me.

When we got to Adrienne's, I led the way in, not bothering to knock. All at once, there was a flurry of greetings thrown back and forth as I introduced Jason and his daughters to my mom and dad, Adrienne, her sons, and her boyfriend, Jonathan.

"Merry Christmas! Come in, make yourselves at home," Adrienne said, gesturing for everyone to follow her into the living room. I veered off into the kitchen to get myself a glass of wine and Jason a glass of water. I would go back and ask Miriam and Ellie what they wanted once they got settled in.

There wasn't enough furniture for everyone to sit without being squished, so Jason and I stood, Miriam standing on his other side. Ellie looked furtively at Adrienne's sons, quickly turning away if she thought one of them was going to make eye contact with her. It was cute to see her at the age where she was noticing boys but not yet knowing what to do about it. I hoped she wouldn't get too interested for a long time – Miriam's teenage years were enough stress.

"Are you okay to be standing like that?" my mom asked Jason. "Why don't you come take this chair?"

"No, I'm fine, Mary-Grace."

Ellie may have been checking out the boys, but they were checking out the presents Jason brought. He noticed.

"Would you boys like to open these now?" he asked.

"We usually wait until after dinner," my mom piped in.

"Okay, then. You'll just have to guess what's inside and be patient," he said, winking.

With the group of us and Adrienne's boyfriend joining us too, it was almost overwhelming for my reclusive parents. Fortunately, Jonathan was an outgoing conversationalist who kept the ball rolling.

"So what's it like to be a doctor today dealing with all these health insurance companies?" Jonathan asked Jason.

"I pay my office staff very well to handle that for me, but as I've been cutting back my hours, I had to let one office assistant go and I have to pick up the slack," he said. "The paperwork is the worst part."

"Tell me about it," Jonathan laughed. "Ninety percent of my job is paperwork. Same with you, right, babe?" he asked Adrienne, who nodded, and looked like she was blushing. Whoa...someone was calling *my* sister babe? I could see our dad shift uncomfortably in his chair, but as usual, he didn't say much unless you asked him a direct question, and even then, he'd keep it as brief as humanly possible. That was better than our mom, who had a real knack for saying the wrong thing and not even realizing it. I silently prayed that she wouldn't bring up MS or anorexia.

After what seemed like a painfully long period of chitchat, mostly led by Jason and Jonathan while everyone else watched them, Adrienne announced that dinner was ready.

"Do you need some help putting it out?" I asked, uncharacteristically.

"Sure," she said, also uncharacteristically. I was happy to get some time alone in the kitchen with her to see what she thought of Jason. I'm sure she wanted the same lowdown on Jonathan. "Can you believe we both have boyfriends for Christmas?" she asked.

"It's pretty surreal. Not just a boyfriend, either. He's my fiancé. And those girls are going to be my stepdaughters."

"It's so crazy to think of you as a mom. An instant mom. The last I heard, you were never having kids."

"Love does funny things, doesn't it? Sometimes I'm freaking out at the amount of responsibility it feels like I am taking on, but other times, I feel like this is perfect. Ellie's such a sweetheart, and even Miriam is really wonderful. She has her moments, but she's a teenage girl. I had my moments."

"Nooo," Adrienne laughed, swatting me with a potholder. "You were just an angel, twenty-four-seven."

"Haha. And so were you. Hey, you know, Jonathan seems really great. Do Tyler and Nicky like him?"

"I think they actually do. We'll have to talk later. We better get this food out there." We started carrying in platters and bowls of potatoes and vegetables and baked ham. I wondered when

Adrienne had gotten so domestic, but she swore she made the whole dinner herself.

After we sat down, Jason asked if he could say grace, and my dad looked vastly relieved. He was brief and solemn, and then began a toast by holding his glass up and touching it to mine.

"Merry Christmas, wife-to-be," he said. "And Merry Christmas to you, Adrienne. Thank you for having us all in your lovely home."

Even the kids joined in, clinking together their glasses of water, juice, and soda. I started to relax when I realized how happy and comfortable Jason looked with my family, how they seemed to like him, and that my mom was apparently going to make good on her promise not to bring up taboo topics.

I saw Miriam pushing food around on her plate, but then she noticed me watching and started to eat a few bites. Ellie, as usual, dug in and matched Adrienne's boys on seconds of everything. It was hard for me to really taste my food in social situations because I was so focused on what everyone was saying, but I had to give Adrienne credit for making a delicious meal in her welcoming home.

After dinner, the boys opened their gifts from Jason and thankfully, they were much more modest presents because Adrienne did not buy gifts for Miriam and Ellie. "Was I supposed to?" she whispered to me, and I shook my head no. Jason was out of control with Christmas. He had selected a few vintage comic books of *Teenage Mutant Ninja Turtles* and *Superman* for Tyler and Nicky. They both looked pleased, in their quiet way, and started reading them immediately. Jonathan had managed to crack Miriam's shell and got the two girls talking about funny things that happened at school. Jason and I finally had the chance to slip outside to the little deck off the kitchen.

There was no snow, but it was cold enough that we were exhaling white steamy puffs as we hugged and kissed.

"Merry Christmas, Kristen. I love you," Jason said, handing me a small, beautifully wrapped box. I opened it to find a necklace, a delicate chain with four silver heart charms, two larger and two smaller. "It's to signify our new family. I hope you like it."

"I love it," I said back, hugging him tightly and almost pulling him off balance. "I couldn't imagine a better gift. Thank you."

I handed him a larger package. It was a photo album I had made that included pictures of us, Miriam and Ellie, and the four of us together.

"This is perfect," he said softly. "I can see we were thinking alike."

We stood for a few more minutes, side by side with his arm around me, enjoying the quiet private moment before returning back inside to our family.

# 32

New year, new me. Brooke and I had started running together. I found myself spending less time with Heather and Tamara, who were champions at partying but not so much at running, and more time with Brooke, who matched me step for step. Our strides were effortlessly compatible. I tried introducing her to Adrienne, since they had the cheating husband thing in common, but they didn't take to each other. Brooke secretly told me she thought Adrienne was boring, and my sister said Brooke was too high maintenance.

The thing Brooke and I had in common was no kids and no desire for kids. Now that people knew I was getting married, there was the expectation and the question in their minds, would Jason and I have children? It was something he and I had discussed, and thankfully, he seemed accepting that, although I would do my best to be a bonus mom for his girls, I didn't want any of my own. His girls were halfway grown, and having spent time with my sister's boys as babies was the perfect reinforcement I needed to realize that childbearing was not for me.

After we ran, we'd often grab coffees and sit and talk for a little bit on a park bench while we were cooling down. Brooke didn't seem to mind telling me anything and everything about her life. I wondered if she held back at all. It seemed like the little sensor in her head that tells you when to shut up was broken.

She even told me she didn't like my hair because it looked too fake. At first I was really taken aback and insulted and I think she could see how hurt I was, but gradually I came around to her way of thinking. A friend is someone who doesn't lie to you and sugarcoat things. You always know where you stand with a friend. You don't have to wonder if she means what she says.

With this in mind, I felt like I needed to finally confess my dating background. She asked me a lot of questions about Jason and who I'd dated before meeting him.

"There's something I need to tell you," I said, as casually as I could muster, while we sprawled across a bench with iced coffees in hand, enjoying the cool morning air.

"It's about time! You're closed up tighter than a clam," she laughed. "Go ahead. You know my whole life story and it ain't pretty. There's nothing I could judge you on."

"My last boyfriend was married."

Silence. She stared at me, starting to look angry.

"Don't even tell me it was my rat-bastard cheating-ass hus-band!"

"No, no. I don't even know your husband. Ex-husband, whatever you call him. I've been feeling guilty since the day I met you about this whole adultery stuff because I guess I played a role in that too."

"You *guess* you played a role? Honey, you were the star of the show. What the hell is wrong with you? There aren't enough single men out there?"

"Brooke, I'm sorry. I don't feel good about it. Obviously. But I think the one who's married is the one to blame."

"You've never been married," she said and I shook my head no. "Because if you had been married, you would have realized it's no walk in the park. Marriage is not for the faint of heart. No matter what kind of wife you are, your husband is going to have a wandering eye now and then. Men are visual creatures. They get tired of looking at the same face and the same body, day after day, year after year. Most of them aren't going to cheat, though, unless it's really easy for them. Women like you make it easy for them. Women like you are a traitor to the rest of us women."

I didn't even know how to respond. What happened to not judging me?

"I'm sorry," was all I could manage to stammer out, before getting up from the bench and walking away. I threw my coffee out in the nearest trash can and started running again. Brooke made me realize what a bad person I really had been.

My sister had never been so hard on me, even though she was the victim of "the other woman" too. I knew she deserved an apology too. I wondered how people like Adrienne and Jason could look at me and see me as a fundamentally good person. Were they dishonest with me in a way that Brooke couldn't be?

I took out my cell phone and called Adrienne. When she answered, I started blubbering full force. "I'm sorry I'm sorry I'm so sorry," I cried into the phone.

She sounded alarmed. "Are the boys okay? Mom and Dad?"

"Yes, they're fine. Well, as far as I know. I'm sorry I had an affair," I said, and then lost it again in a fit of tears.

"Did you cheat on Jason?"

"No! I mean John. I don't know what I was thinking."

"You scared me. What brought this on? You're not one to cry over the past."

"I told Brooke. And she told me I'm a bad person."

"Even if you were a bad person, you aren't a bad person now. And even if what you did was wrong, you weren't a bad person."

"She said husbands wouldn't cheat if it weren't for women like me."

"That's ridiculous. No matter what, you're my sister. Don't worry about her. I told you she's a drama queen."

"She's the only one who tells me the truth," I said, starting to cry again. "She said my blonde hair looks fake!"

"What are you really crying about now, your past or your hair? Come on, Krissy, let it go. She's still in the middle of a divorce. Of course she wants to blame someone other than her husband, because if she blames him it's like blaming herself for picking a guy who would cheat. I think the healthiest thing I did was accept that it wasn't my fault Drew cheated. You know how many months – no, years – I spent berating myself and wondering what I could have done differently? The answer is nothing; there was nothing I could have done differently."

"Okay. I am sorry, though, for what I did in the past."

"Let it go. You've learned and now you are marrying a wonderful man with two nice daughters and he knows and accepts your past. That means you should too."

"Thank you. I know I have to do that if I'm going to have a future."

# 33

I spent the next day cocooned in my apartment with chips, candy, and Netflix before I realized I was going to have to snap out of it and go on with my life, even if Brooke never talked to me again. Adrienne was right; I had changed. Maybe I *was* a cheater, but I wasn't going to cheat on Jason. I had the chance to see John again and this time I made the right decision.

Exercise would be my stress antidote. Instead of thinking about my own troubles, I asked Jason if I could spend a day with Ellie, taking her to the gym and making dinner together. I wanted to spend time alone with Miriam too, but I figured it would be easier to start with Ellie because she'd be more receptive to the idea. Jason seemed pleased and said we were making strides toward becoming a family.

I drove over to Jason's house bright and early to make sure Ellie ate a healthy breakfast and found something to wear to the gym that she'd be comfortable in so she could concentrate on exercising, not tugging down her shirt hem or pulling at her shorts. She had a lot of mannerisms that I guess were typical of preteen girls. Their self-consciousness only highlighted how insecure they felt about their changing bodies. I thanked God for making that phase of my life pretty short and uneventful.

I grew several inches and gained about twenty pounds when I was twelve, but it felt like my body adjusted quickly to its new dimensions. It was harder for Ellie, but she had an older sister who was beyond graceful, while my older sister was still seemingly growing out of her awkward phase.

Ellie looked adorable with her hair pulled back in a messy ponytail, a bright green t-shirt with a sparkly unicorn on the front, pink shorts and striped knee socks.

"Do you want to maybe wear shorter socks?" I asked. "You might get pretty sweaty in those."

"I have to cover my hairy legs since my mom won't let me shave them," she said plaintively. "Do you think I should start shaving yet?"

I did think she should shave if she was old enough that it was bothering her, but I wasn't going to get involved in that mess. I'd tell Jason later and he could deal with Julia. I really didn't know how old girls were supposed to be to shave their legs and I don't remember how old I was. I just remember battling it out with my mom that *all* the other girls were doing it and then going behind her back to do it anyway when she said no. These are exactly the kinds of things that make me relieved not to be a mom.

"You're fine; don't worry," I said, hoping the non-answer would work for now. I changed the subject and said, "Ready to go? You have your water bottle?"

She held it up and nodded, her ponytail bobbing up and down with enthusiasm. I hoped she'd still feel this way after we got through a workout together. I wasn't going to go easy on her just because she was a kid.

As we entered the gym, Ellie started looking a little nervous and pulled on my shirt hem.

"It's going to be fine," I reassured her, taking her by the hand. "It looks intimidating at first with all the machines here, but I'm going to teach you how to use them, and once you know your way around, it's a lot of fun."

"Okay."

"I started going to a gym when I was fifteen. I wish now I had started even earlier. How about we try the treadmill first? I'll teach you how to use it."

We stepped onto side-by-side machines and I leaned over to show her the settings, starting off really slow.

"It feels weird!" she laughed. I had been using treadmills for so long that I forgot what it was like to step onto one for the first time.

"It does at first, but the treadmills are awesome when you can't go outside. The coolest thing is when you get off and you feel like you're still walking on the treadmill and your feet feel all light and funny."

Ellie walked slowly and then picked up to a moderate pace while I did a quick thirty-minute run, not even breaking a sweat until I was fifteen minutes in.

"You need to get sweaty, Ellie. How about trying to walk a little faster?"

She did, but didn't look thrilled. "I don't like to get sweaty," she said. "That's one of the reasons I wanted to quit dance."

"What are the other reasons? I know you told me you didn't like what they made you wear. What else?"

"I didn't like that the older girls were always talking about being on a diet, trying to eat five hundred calories a day. I tried to follow it and I felt all dizzy. I almost passed out at school one day."

"No wonder. That's not enough."

"I'm jealous of how skinny Miriam is. She could stick to that diet. I'm weak. I like food too much."

"You're not weak, Ellie. You're a very strong and determined girl and I'm proud of you for sticking up for yourself. Miriam had to go to an eating disorder clinic. Even if it looked like she had everything under control, she really didn't. She wasn't healthy, and she's always going to have to be careful about taking care of her body now. You don't really want to be like her, at least not in that way, do you?"

"No, I guess not. But I want my mom and dad to be proud of me."

"Oh, sweetie, they are! They couldn't be more proud of you. And I know it doesn't count quite as much, but I'm so proud of you too. You're perfect the way you are."

Ellie smiled a little then and walked with more pep. When I saw that she was getting tired, I told her to slow down and cool off before we tried the weight machines. She seemed to enjoy the machines more with the slower pace and the deliberate breaks between sets. She liked adjusting the seats and setting the weights. I had bought her a little pink notebook and a pen with a feather on the top to keep track of her workout.

"If you keep coming regularly, eventually you probably won't need to write it down because it will all be in your head, but for now this is a big help."

I tried to enjoy the slower pace rather than getting frustrated that I wasn't speeding through my workout as I usually did. I was learning what it was like to have the patience of a parent. Everything took longer now, but seeing Ellie look confident and happy was worth it. Now she had something of her own, something her sister didn't know how to do, and I could tell that meant a lot to her.

When we finally finished, we headed over to the grocery store. The next step was showing Ellie what was healthy to eat. I had read that kids are more likely to try new foods if they get to help select them, and I hoped this would be the case with her. I noticed she had an alarming fondness for chicken fingers, French fries, and not much else. She always came back from Julia's feeling hungry because she didn't get those foods there, and Jason indulged her by letting her eat whatever she wanted. I felt like the back and forth on what the kids ate was not healthy for either of them, and I wanted our households to be more synchronized.

Grocery stores are a devil's den of temptation. We had to pass the bakery to get to the produce and Ellie asked, "Could we get cupcakes for dessert since we worked out today?"

"I hate to tell you this, but we didn't even burn enough calories to work off one of those cupcakes. Unfortunately, what you eat is the main factor for how healthy you are going to be."

"Then why did we go to the gym?"

"Don't you feel a little better? Happier? Stronger?"

"I don't know; I guess so."

"You're probably going to have to get used to it, but trust me, it's worth it." I thought about all of the things I had been doing – running every day so I could eat cheeseburgers without gaining weight, stopping for fast food instead of preparing a meal with vegetables, not sleeping regular hours – and how they were the opposite of what I was trying to teach Ellie.

What kind of role model could I be if I didn't practice what I preached? And Jason had made so many changes in his own lifestyle to try to keep his MS at bay. I needed to be healthy for him and with him, and I needed him to see that it was great he was making changes, but he had to include his daughters as well.

Our household would never be in harmony if it continued to be a free-for-all.

# 34

Since Ellie's favorite meal was chicken fingers, we were going to have chicken fingers. But it wasn't the packaged frozen junk she was used to. We bought chicken breasts and cut them into strips to sauté in lemon juice, a little olive oil, and some salt and pepper. I wasn't much of a cook, but I was impressed with myself. We also made smashed potatoes and roasted asparagus. Ellie picked out a carton of raspberries for dessert since I had vetoed the cupcakes.

"Mmm, what smells so good?" Jason asked, as he walked in the door from work. Ellie beamed.

"We made dinner!" she said, running to pull him into a hug and knocking him off balance.

"That's great, Ellie Bellie!" he said, putting his arms around her and kissing her on the top of the head. "Run up and get your sister for dinner."

As she skipped out of the kitchen, Jason kissed me.

"And how did *your* day go?" he asked. "Was Ellie good at the gym?"

"She was awesome. She tried everything I asked her to and I really think she liked lifting weights. I know Julia would rather her be dancing, but maybe this will be a good activity for her."

"I hope so. Let me go wash up. I can't wait to try what you made."

"Don't get your expectations too high," I said. "You know I'm no chef."

"True. But who knows, maybe Ellie is." I gave him a little swat on the back with the dishtowel I was holding as he scooted out of the way.

Ten minutes later, we were all seated. Ellie and I had lit candles and put out cloth napkins to make dinner more special.

"We should do it like this every day," Jason said.

Miriam looked unhappy. "I like it better when we can eat in the TV room," she grumbled.

"That's nice for snacks and movie time, but I think we should have dinners at the table," I said. "This is how my sister and I had dinner every night."

"Well, you were eating with *both* of your parents. It's not the same."

"I know it's not the same, but your dad and I are trying to make the best of it. We're still a family. You have a family with us and a family with your mom."

"This is not my family. My mom and dad are my family. And by the way, I'm not eating this. Yuck," she said, pushing her plate forward and getting up from her chair at the table. Ellie burst into tears.

"But I made it! You have to at least try it," Ellie said.

"Sorry, Ellie. I'm not hungry. And *she* can't make me eat it," Miriam scowled, pointing at me.

"But *I* can," Jason said. I was surprised because he rarely spoke up when Miriam got upset with me. "You know what your counselor said about not skipping meals. Ellie and Kristen worked very hard on this dinner and you *are* going to eat it."

"Fine," Miriam said. "But I'm getting the measuring cups." In a family session, her counselor told us that it would help ease Miriam's anxiety about eating normal portions to use measuring cups to show she wasn't eating more than a serving at a time. It looked kind of ridiculous to see her cutting up chicken and putting it in one measuring cup, and trying to figure out how to measure the asparagus spears, but finally she did start eating.

"How much fat is in this?" she asked accusingly.

"It's very low fat," I said. "We just misted on the olive oil."

"It's hard to trust you. You can eat anything and not gain a pound."

"It's true, I was blessed with a good metabolism, but I wasn't eating healthfully, and now I'm really trying. I wouldn't ask you and Ellie to do something that I wouldn't do too. And your dad has been a good influence."

"I don't want the potatoes. Too many carbs."

"One bite of potatoes, Miriam," Jason commanded, and she rolled her eyes but ate a bite.

"Let's enjoy this," he said, when it looked like things were settling down. "Ellie, tell us about the gym."

Ellie recounted each part of our workout, looking proud. Even Miriam paid attention for once. Then Miriam had her turn to talk about her day. I definitely gave Jason credit for getting his daughters to converse with us more. I liked his gentle way of soothing ruffled feathers. I was thrilled that he had finally stood up for me and it worked; Miriam grew cheerful and didn't harass me any further about the meal. It seemed like he was finally getting it.

# 35

As the girls grew more comfortable, I started having dinner with them almost every night they were with Jason. I finished work early enough to cook most nights. I fumbled with the keys, still getting used to opening Jason's front door. I knew I needed to stop thinking of it as his door and starting remembering that it's our door, or at least, it would be soon. The house was supposed to be empty, but I heard footsteps quickly shuffling out of the den and poked my head inside. I did exactly what every girl in the horror movie does: go straight for the source of the noise to see what it is. Luckily, it wasn't an axe murderer. Unfortunately, I feared Jason would turn into one when he discovered what I did find.

A pile of clothes, including a pink bra, was strewn over the sofa. Two sweating bottles of cold beer sat on the coffee table, and I quickly realized that Miriam and someone else were hiding in the closet.

"I know you're in here," I called out. No response. I pulled the closet doors open with a flourish to find Miriam covering her chest and a random guy covering his you-know-what.

"Miriam! Wait until your parents hear about this!"

"Oh, please, please, please don't tell them. Oh, no. They will *kill* me."

I turned around and grabbed her bra from the sofa, dangling it from my finger.

"Put this back on. And neither of your parents is going to literally kill you. That would defeat the purpose of giving birth to and raising you, wouldn't it? And you," I said, pointing to the boyfriend – I hoped he was at least a boyfriend rather than a hookup – "I am not picking up your clothes, so you're going to have to come out here and get them. And then get out of this house."

He scuttled out sideways like a crab, but not before Miriam grabbed his hand and gave him a meaningful look.

"Later," she mouthed to him.

"Don't bother," I said, glaring at both of them. "I will have her phone as soon as she gets her clothes on."

As I watched him quickly pull on his shorts and leave, I realized he was just a boy, probably Miriam's age. He looked terrified. Not that it made this okay, but at least he wasn't some older man preying on an innocent teenage girl. It looked like they hadn't taken more than a sip or two of the beer. They probably didn't like it.

I hoped it was the first drink Miriam ever had, and hopefully the last for a long, long time. I was a little surprised she would even try it. Normally she wouldn't drink anything with calories because she said it was a waste of her daily limit, which I believed was now up to fifteen-hundred a day, still maybe about half of what I ate a lot of days.

"Sit down, Miriam. We need to talk. First of all, who was that?"

"Do I have to tell you? I don't want him to get in trouble."

"Yes, you have to tell me. It's going to be worse if you're not honest."

"His name is Billy. He's my boyfriend."

*Whew.*

"For how long? How serious is this? And what happened to you never wanting to have a boyfriend?"

"For a couple of months. We were friends since last year, but then when I came back to school after... you know... the clinic... he was asking me a lot about why I was gone so long and told me he missed me."

"How far were you planning to go if I didn't walk in on your little assignation?"

"I don't know what an ass-ig-whatever is, and that's really none of your business."

"Would you like to make it your father's business?"

"No, I would not. I don't think you have any place telling him either."

"First of all, Miriam, this is going to be my house too in a few months, and secondly, even if I am not biologically your mother, I have a role to play with your parents in raising you. The sooner you accept that, the easier things will be for all of us. Ellie is fine with that; why can't you be?"

"Ellie likes anybody, so that doesn't count. And I am fifteen. I'm not some little kid who needs *three* parents telling her what to do all the time. I don't even need two of them bossing me around."

"Fine, if you want two parents, I will call Jason and Julia right now to handle this and I will stay out of it. This is not my problem to deal with anyway." I pulled out my phone, but Miriam grabbed my hand.

"Please don't," she pleaded. "I'm sorry. If you and I talk about this more, can we please leave Mom and Dad out of this? I promise you I will never do something like this again."

I was torn. On one hand, I tried to put myself in Adrienne's place: How would she feel if I kept information from her about one of her sons? But I also knew that opportunities to bond with Miriam were rare. We had made a little headway when she was hospitalized for her anorexia, but things seemed back to normal after she got home. If Jason and I were going to be successful, my relationship with his daughters needed to be secure too. I think she could see the indecision on my face and hoped to take advantage of it.

"Please, Kristen? If I make *any* more trouble, I promise you can tell my dad. Let this be a one-time free pass."

"What about birth control? What about the birds and the bees talk? Is anyone handling that?"

"I don't need any of that. We were just fooling around. It would never go that far."

"Miriam, don't be naïve. It could go that far. When you love someone and you feel attracted to them like that, it's hard to say what you'll do. We need to talk."

I took a deep breath, and launched into the sex talk I'd thought I'd never have to give. Miriam looked embarrassed, but she listened to everything.

"I get it, okay?" Miriam said. "Could we please keep this between us?"

"I don't think I should keep something like this from your parents. It's not right."

"But you said yourself you're going to be one of my parents, and you handled it really well and I promise you I won't do anything I shouldn't. Please, Kristen?"

I couldn't believe I was falling for the clichéd look she was giving me, head down, mouth in a quivering pout, eyes looking up hopefully to me. But she did have a point. I handled this exactly the way I would've if she were my own daughter. I felt like such a cool mom. I could imagine Miriam and her friends wanting to hang out at our house on weekends because she had the best stepmom ever.

"I promise," I replied, breaking out of my daydream. She jumped off the sofa and ran up to her room, slamming the door behind her before I realized she'd grabbed her phone off the coffee table on the way.

# 36

"What is this?" Jason asked me accusatorily, holding up my phone. I grabbed it from him to read a text from my sister: *You HAVE to tell him. He may be mad that you kept this from him for weeks, but better late than never. If Jonathan did that to me, I don't know that I could forgive him.*

I could feel my adrenaline response kick in. I was angry and terrified at the same time. I shoved the phone into my back pocket and stormed out of the kitchen. I wanted to go in my room and slam the door, but oh yeah, I didn't have my own room because I was in his house. I settled for stomping outside, the front door rattling behind me because I closed it so hard. I wanted to run, but I was wearing flip flops, so I started walking down the sidewalk. Jason came rushing out behind me, yelling now.

"You owe me an explanation! You can't just walk away!" I turned around to face him. He was still ten steps away from me, which made me talk more bravely than I felt.

"You owe *me* an explanation. What are you doing looking at my phone?" I demanded. "And are we really going to have this conversation outside in public?"

"I don't know. Are we? You're the one who ran away when I asked you a question. Are you trying to buy time to make up some excuse?"

Neither of us moved, so now we were talking loudly at each other from a distance of two sidewalk squares. Out of the corner of my eye, I thought I saw a neighbor peeping through the blinds.

"How can you violate my trust like that, reading my texts? I would never in a million years pick up your phone, Jason."

"I saw it was from your sister, and I was just going to write a goofy response. I was playing around. How was I supposed to know I was going to see a message like that? And I'm still waiting for you to tell me what she meant. What is it that you should be telling me?"

"There's probably no point trying to explain it. If you don't trust me, then why would you believe anything I had to say?"

"That's no excuse not to try. What I would like to hear is the truth. Did you cheat on me? Did you get some terrible medical diagnosis that you're not telling me?"

"No, no, nothing like that. Look, I had an incident with Miriam. She asked me not to tell you and Julia about it. I mentioned it to Adrienne after the fact. Obviously, she thinks I should tell you, but the problem is, I promised Miriam I wouldn't. So now I'm in a bind."

Jason walked up to me, took my arm and steered me back toward the house.

"We have to talk," he said. I never saw him so mad. I don't think I had ever seen him angry, period. I wished to God I had never walked in on Miriam and Billy. I never wanted to be part of the messiness of parenting. Jason practically pushed me down on the sofa and sat beside me. "You have no right to keep information from me about my daughter, not if it's something that could bring her harm. I know you made a promise to her, but I need to know what happened."

"I caught her with a boy, here in your house."

"Doing what?"

"Drinking beer, making out. I had a long talk with her about safe sex and I told her if there were any more incidents I'd have to tell you and Julia."

"So not only did you withhold information, but you talked to her about something that should have been a conversation with her mother and me? What if I didn't like what you said to her about sex? Did you ever think it's not your place?" I started to cry now, sniffling pathetically.

"I did the best I could, Jason. I'm sorry. I'm so confused. You want me to be their mom, you don't. I don't know where I fit into this family!" I put my head in my hands, dripping tears onto my lap.

"You put me into a difficult position with Julia. She was angry enough about the eating disorder clinic, and now this."

"She needed help! She needs help now. She needs parents who are addressing who she is and what she's doing. You guys put your heads in the sand and pretend like she's not growing up. Maybe my talking to her is preventing a teen pregnancy."

"How dare you," Jason seethed. "You're not even a parent, so where do you get off telling me I'm not raising my kids right?"

"I can't do this anymore, Jason. I'm sorry," I said, twisting the engagement off my finger and gently placing it on the coffee table in front of us. He didn't try to stop me when I got up and once again left the house, this time closing the door so quietly that it felt like I was sneaking out.

# 37

I woke up with burning, puffy eyes. My cheeks stung from all the tears running down my face and the tissues I used to wipe them away. My lungs ached. Even in my destroyed mental state, I thought how crazy it was that you could cry so much that your lungs hurt. My chest felt like it was collapsing... heartbreak is real.

I forced myself to put my feet on the floor, to get up at my normal time and to function. If I got moving, I'd still have time for a run before work. I thought of calling off, but I realized I'd go crazy if I sat home all day. I needed the physical release of work, and even though I didn't intend to tell anyone yet what happened, I wanted to be around other people, having a sense of normalcy.

Two days ago, I took off my engagement ring, and since then I couldn't stop rubbing my finger where the ring should have been. Jason was all I thought about. No, that's not completely true. Jason and Ellie and Miriam were all I thought about. This was so much more terrible than John's rejection. I knew a future with John was tenuous and that our whole relationship was wrong, but Jason and I planned to be together forever. How could one mistake unravel everything so easily? And the thing was, I still didn't know if it was a mistake.

I understood why he was angry, but was what I did really so wrong? I handled a situation like a parent would. He asked me to be a parent, and even though I was uncertain sometimes about what to do, I was stepping up to the plate. I had months, not years, of experience. How could he be so unforgiving? All this stuff he said about knowing I was meant to be his wife and a mother to his girls – didn't it mean anything?

Yesterday I texted Jason to ask if we could talk things over. He waited six hours to respond and then all he wrote was *I need more time*. I called him, but he didn't answer. How were we supposed to work things out if he was going to just block me out? I was desperate to stop feeling so alone. I knew my sister was away for the weekend with Jonathan and I didn't want to spoil the little time she had alone with him. I couldn't tell my mom because she criticized everything I did and I knew I'd fall even lower if she told me Jason was right. Tamara and Heather would only offer to go out drinking and look for a new guy. I don't think either of them had ever truly been in love, and they both thought I was crazy for agreeing to marry a man with two daughters anyway.

I texted Brooke: *I need you. Jason and I broke up. Please, can we go for a run?* The way we had left things, I figured we might never talk again. How did I get into this pattern of pissing people off so much that they cut me off? It was ironic because when I didn't care what anyone thought, nobody seemed to get that mad at me. Now that I was trying to do the right thing, it seemed like it was always backfiring.

I had spent two days in bed and besides my face and chest hurting, so did my back and legs from lying around. With or without Brooke, I was going for a run, taking a shower, and getting to work.

I was pulling my hair into a ponytail when I got a message back from Brooke: *Meet me at the usual spot*. I couldn't tell by her terse response whether she was still angry, but I felt so relieved that she was willing to see me again. I was beginning to wonder if I was an irredeemably bad person. I laced up my sneakers and jogged out the door, picking up the pace slowly as I headed toward the bench in the local park where we started and ended our runs. Our falling out caused me to change my route so that I wouldn't accidentally see her, and I'm guessing she did the same. People are creatures of habit, and besides the loss of my running buddy and confidante, I had also lost a part of my morning routine, passing the same landmarks, the same houses, the same other runners every day.

She was already there, her foot up on the bench, leaning forward to stretch her hamstrings. All her stretching seemed to have no effect whatsoever on her muscle tightness, whereas I barely ever bothered to stretch. I'd have to do that now to be a good role model for Ellie, I thought, but then I realized, wait a minute, it doesn't matter because I might never see her again.

"Hey," I said to Brooke.

"Hey," she said back. "Are you ready to go?" She remembered that I didn't need to stretch before we started. Without looking back, she took off at a faster-than-usual pace and I took a few longer strides to catch up with her. For a few minutes, we didn't say anything. Normally she kept up a nonstop stream of chatter, punctuated only by deep breaths here and there to keep herself going. Maybe she was waiting for me to talk since I was the one who asked, but I was so used to being the quiet one that it was hard to know where to begin. I could usually express myself pretty well when I needed to, but I felt like the pain had taken away my ability to communicate and isolated me in a glass cube where I could see the world around me but not reach it.

"You're going to get over this," she finally said. "I know you don't believe it now, but you will. Hold your head up high."

This was all it took to launch me into a fresh round of tears. She let me cry without explaining what happened and giving me time to wordlessly process the thoughts in my head. She didn't ask questions or offer stupid platitudes about plenty of fish in the sea or try to figure out what part of this was my fault. She was exactly what I needed.

We ran, we made our way back to our bench, and I awkwardly hugged her goodbye, hoping it wasn't going to be the last time we saw each other.

"Thank you," was all I could manage. "I needed that."

I walked the rest of the way home, not knowing what I was going to do and how I would make it, but feeling at least a little bit lighter knowing that even if I didn't have Jason, I had friends.

# 38

I lay flat on my back, splaying my arms and legs out like a starfish. There was road construction going on a block away and I felt like the grading machine with its deep bass thrum was a jackhammer directly behind my eyes. The room seemed to be spinning, even though I was lying perfectly still. My forehead was sweating. I just hoped I wouldn't have to throw up, because I didn't know whether I could get myself out of bed on time.

I vowed right then that I was done with drinking forever. It wasn't my idea to get smashed. I have only myself to blame, because I should have been way beyond peer pressure, but I will say that Heather and Tamara, while well meaning, pushed me into something I never wanted to do.

It was Friday night, and as usual, I was wrapped in a blanket on my sofa, watching *Dirty Dancing* and crying, crumpled tissues balled up in a little wastebasket nearby, a half-eaten bag of Cheetos lying on the coffee table. My friends showed up, banging at the door.

"This is an intervention," Tamara said.

"A much-needed one, apparently," said Heather, looking at my orange-stained fingers. "Let's get over to the kitchen and wash you off." I let her lead me to the sink, my blanket trailing on the floor behind me like slug slime.

"Look at you; this is pathetic. You need to take a shower and we're going out," Tamara said, from my other side. It was like having a devil on each shoulder instead of only on the one. My inner angel (always in Adrienne's voice) told me they were wrong; this was a healthier way to grieve, even if it wasn't perfect, than trying to drink my troubles away. A woman trying to get over rejection should stay away from alcohol and especially from men drinking alcohol. Everyone's judgment was impaired and regretful things could happen.

I was too tired to resist. I had been feeling so poorly that maybe they were right. I wished we were doing something that didn't involve alcohol, but my friends didn't believe it was possible to have fun without a drink in hand. I couldn't blame them; they were the same as when I met them; it was I who had changed.

Tamara pushed me toward the bathroom, promising to pick out something for me to wear. Judging by what they had on, at least they weren't planning to go to The Strand. I hadn't been there since the night that disgusting guy cornered me outside. I still felt dirty and guilty every time I thought about that creep. It was a sad state of affairs for women when we are the ones feeling bad about men's behavior, but it always ran through my head that maybe if I had acted differently, he would have been more respectful.

I had to admit, the shower felt good. I hadn't taken one all day because I didn't go for a run or to work. I sat around for hours, telling myself I'd get off the couch and clean my apartment and go grocery shopping and cook something healthful, but that never happened. Thus the Cheetos for dinner.

Tamara had laid out a tight pair of jeans, some wedge sandals, and a black snug-fitting V-neck t-shirt. I nixed the thong she threw on top in exchange for some more comfortable bikini bottoms. Visibly panty lines be damned, I just couldn't take the constant wedgie tonight. Putting on form-fitting clothes felt like an extreme transition from being wrapped in a blanket. I felt raw and exposed, but as I put on makeup I began to see a woman in the mirror who looked like she had her act together. It was amazing how makeup could cover up not only the blemishes on your skin, but the ones inside as well.

I was hopeful that a night out with my girls would be just what I needed. We'd have a few drinks, sit somewhere quiet, and laugh about all the things we used to do, back when we were wild and crazy twenty-somethings. By the time we left my apartment, I was feeling buoyed with hopefulness.

Heather offered to drive and took us to The Lucky Mug, the local hole in the wall. It was the kind of place that looked tiny from the outside, marked only by a small hanging sign above the door and a neon Budweiser light in the tiny window. When you walked in, everyone at the bar swiveled their head to see who it was, and they were rarely surprised. People had their routines, and it was usually the same old-same old. We weren't regulars there, by any means, but we had been there often enough that we only got the cursory "who's that" look before the barflies realized we weren't really new.

This was an older crowd, mostly male, with a few rough-looking women mixed in. They all sat hunched forward, nursing various beers and the rum and Coke or Jack and ginger – nothing fancy. If you even tried to order something like a Cosmo, the barmaid would glare at you until you changed your order – two ingredients max; no mixing or shaking allowed. Most of patrons looked blankly at the small TV overhead, watching the local eleven o'clock news with the sound off and the closed captioning on. Few of them talked.

Tamara stopped at the bar to order three beers and Heather and I settled in at one of the little tables in a dark corner. The night began well. We had a few beers, talked about all kinds of stuff, but nothing heavy. When I brought up Jason, which I probably did numerous times, they gently steered the conversation in another direction. Part of me was resentful that they didn't want to talk about him, but even in my buzzed state, I realized that a break from obsessing about Jason was exactly what I needed.

"Let's shoot some pool," Tamara offered, when we had run out of things to talk about.

"I'm ready to go home, get to bed," I said.

"Come on," Heather said. "It's early, barely past midnight. What else do you have to do?"

"Go to sleep."

"You can do that later. We're here to have fun. Get off your well-toned little ass and play pool with us," she said, pulling my hand. I reluctantly got up with them. We all carried our beer bottles over to the table. Three attractive, youngish women playing pool got the guys' attention. I felt more comfortable sitting in the corner because the last thing I wanted was male attention, but Tamara and Heather were basking in the compliments and stares.

I wondered how this could be enough for them. I had recently heard the word "objectification" for the first time and it made me feel resentful. I had never realized that most of my interactions with men weren't honorable. It wasn't until Jason that any man had truly treated me with respect and saw me for who I was on the inside rather than on the outside.

I couldn't believe that it used to be so important to me that a guy whistled or made some remark about any part of my body. Usually they'd start with "you're pretty," but they were looking at my boobs or my butt or my legs as they said it. I was so used to this that I thought Jason wasn't attracted to me because he never mentioned those assets. Instead he said "You're honest" or "you're a good person." I was confident that I did, indeed, have a nice ass, but I wasn't sure what to do with "You're a good person" because I didn't know if that was true. I hadn't thought much about it before Jason.

A couple of men started circling around the table, checking us out.

"You ladies mind if we watch?" one said, lighting a cigarette that dangled between his lips as he spoke.

"Of course not," Heather said, smiling, while I felt more like we were Jell-O wrestling than playing pool judging by the leering looks of the men standing around us. I felt cornered and caged and my heart was beating fast.

"Shots on them," the barmaid said, carrying a tray with sticky liquid dribbled on its surface and several glasses full of amber liquid.

"No thanks," I said, but Tamara nudged me, saying "Come on, Kristen, be nice." I knew I shouldn't, but I didn't have it in me to fight. The easiest thing was to give in, and I threw my head back and downed a whiskey, feeling the fire go down my throat all the way to my belly. Instantly my cheeks grew red and I realized I was feeling a little unsteady on my feet. The whiskey also made me care less about the looks I was getting. I'm pretty sure I was swaggering around the pool table by that point, or maybe sashaying was the better word. None of the guys caught my eye. They wore Levi's jeans and work boots and faded T-shirts. They had nice bodies and one of them was model handsome with chiseled cheeks and two-day stubble, but they weren't Jason.

I'd take skinny, dignified Jason over a beefcake any day. We played pool, getting worse and worse with each game, but caring less with each drink. One of the guys asked if I'd leave with him and I shook my head no. Tamara whispered in my ear that he would be one way to get Jason out of my system, and if I wasn't going to leave with him, she would. Go ahead, I told her, as long as I still have a ride home with Heather.

Finally, it was closing time and we had to go. Heather looked more sober than I was, but I still worried about her driving. I called a cab while I still had some sliver of common sense, and we convinced Tamara that she needed to come with us too. Forget the guys; we'd hate ourselves in the morning. The three of us pooled our money, pulling out sweaty, crumbled ones to make sure we had enough to pay the driver, and then stumbled into the cab.

"We can't keep doing this," I slurred to Heather and Tamara, but they seemed oblivious.

My stop was first and I sloppily said good night to my friends and walked unsteadily up to my door, collapsing on my bed and knowing I'd done a bad thing, but thanking God it wasn't a whole lot worse.

# 39

I forced myself to swing my legs to the side of the bed and put my feet on the floor. My memories of the previous night were hazy, but I do strongly remember feeling that this was the breaking point. I liked my life so much better when I woke up with a clear head every morning, ready to go for a run alone or with Brooke. I liked when I didn't feel vaguely sick after every meal I ate, because I was no longer putting junk in my body. I liked going to bed and getting up at the same time every day. I missed my life with Jason, but just because he wasn't in it didn't mean I couldn't continue all of the positive changes I'd made. I hadn't realized before I met him just how *tired* I was: tired all the time and masking it with caffeine and sugar and alcohol and forcing myself to stay up long after I wanted to get to bed. I was tired of irregular schedules and loneliness and rushing out the door, late for work.

There was no way I was going to make it for a run with this kind of a hangover, but I remembered a stack of business cards for a yoga center sitting on the reception desk at the spa and I tried to recall the name of the place. I remembered basically where it was located and felt pretty certain I could find it.

An hour later, after a cup of tea and a piece of dry toast and part of a banana, my stomach was settled enough to try my first yoga class. I arrived early, not wanting to come in late and be disruptive. There were two women sitting on mats, talking quietly and looking relaxed. The teacher was in the front, lighting a candle and arranging pillows around herself. When she saw me, she got up and came over to me.

"Welcome. I'm Mindy. Is this your first yoga class?"

"Yes, can you tell by how nervous I look? I'm Kristen."

"Nothing to be nervous about. Grab a mat from the back and you might want one of those little blocks as well. It helps for some of the poses when you are a beginner."

"Thank you. I run almost every day, so hopefully I'm in shape for this."

"Yoga fitness is its own kind of fitness. But you will find with daily practice that your body is quick to learn."

I unrolled a mat near but not directly next to the women who had already arrived, and tried to set up as close to the wall as I could manage. I wanted to be out of sight of the other people in the class but in a position to see what the teacher was doing, since I had no idea.

Within a few minutes, the room was filled with about fifteen women of all ages and sizes. This was a beginner class, but some of the women there had amazing, lithe bodies. I was kind of in the middle.

The first poses were simple, on our hands and knees doing cat and cow, although I felt self-conscious. I tried to look around surreptitiously, and I noticed right away that unlike at the gym, where everyone is either looking in the mirror or checking out everyone else, the women here seemed to be in a different state of mind. Most of them had their eyes closed; the few that didn't were focused solely on Mindy. There were no mirrors here. I couldn't tell whether the cow pose made my belly hang down unflatteringly.

The next pose, downward dog, was much harder. I realized that the lack of stretching after my runs had left my hamstrings very tight. Mindy's heels were nearly touching the ground, while I looked like I was standing on my toes.

By the end of class, I had worked up a sweat without even doing anything aerobic. I hadn't picked up a weight or used a machine, yet my muscles were quivering and sore. I felt so clear-headed, and for once I was thinking about what my body could do rather than what it looked like.

Mindy came up to me as I was rolling up the mat.

"What did you think of your first class?" she asked.

"Honestly? I think I'm in love," I answered, smiling. "This is the first time I've felt really good in quite a while. I will definitely be back."

"Great to hear! We get that a lot. Make sure you pick up a schedule on the way out. You can buy classes in blocks if you want a discount. Or you can continue to pay by the class, to make sure you like it."

"Thank you so much."

I didn't talk to anyone else in the class, but I smiled at them as we put our shoes back on in the back of the room. I grabbed a schedule and headed home. I hoped it wasn't just post-drinking haze, but I was pretty sure yoga was going to change my life.

# 40

*I have a strange request for you...*

I hadn't heard a peep from Jason in weeks and weeks, and this is what he texts me? Okay, I'll take the bait. Play it cool, Kristen. Don't let him know you're dying a little bit inside each day that passes and he doesn't beg you to come back.

*What's the request?*

*Can I call you?*

*Yes.*

Now my heart was beating a million miles an hour. This was it. He was going to tell me what a mistake he made and ask for my forgiveness. But if that's why he wanted to talk, why would he call it a "strange request"? Before I had much time to obsess over it, my phone rang.

"Hello?"

"Hi, Kristen. How are you?"

"I'm okay," I said, warily. "How are you?"

"Fine, thanks. I'm sure you're wondering why I'm calling."

"Yeah, kind of," I said, trying to sound like it was no big deal, even though my heart was pounding.

"It's about Miriam." Oh. "She wondered if you would teach her to drive."

"What? Why me?"

"Because Julia is spastic in the car and Miriam says I make her nervous. She specifically asked for you."

"Oh, Jason, I don't know. Wouldn't it be kind of weird, with – you know – the way things are? And how can Julia possibly approve of this idea?"

"Julia and I got into a blowout fight about this, and she finally agreed to it. I trust you completely with the girls and it would be good for Miriam."

"I don't know how you can say that. Our relationship ended *because* you didn't trust me."

"I don't want to get into this right now. Could you please think about it and let me know one way or another? We got a driver's ed teacher, but she has to practice on her own too and she needs an adult in the car while she still has her learner's permit."

"I'll do it. I don't have to think about it. Jason, I miss you, but I miss the girls too."

"I know. I'm sorry, Kristen. I'll tell her you said yes and she can text you to set up a time. Sound good?"

"That's fine. Bye." I hung up before he had a chance to say anything else and I would say something I regretted or burst into tears.

The next day, I drove over to Jason's house to meet Miriam. She looked kind of happy to see me and came out the front door before I had a chance to knock, swinging a set of keys around her finger.

"I figured you wouldn't want me to use your car," she said. "I got my dad's."

"My beat-up ride? I wouldn't mind, but it'd probably be better for you to practice with the car you're going to use for your driving test."

She jumped in the driver's seat while I climbed in the passenger side, pulling on my seatbelt immediately.

"Is your dad home?" I asked, trying to sound casual.

"Yeah, but I thought maybe it would be easier for you not to see him," Miriam said.

"Oh. I guess that makes sense. And I'm sure he wouldn't want to see me."

"I didn't ask him. Kristen, the thing is, I need to focus on driving right now, okay? I'm not even at the phase where I can have the radio on while I'm driving yet, because I'm so nervous. Look at my hands shaking," she said, holding them up.

"Got it. I'm not here to interrogate you about your dad. I'm sorry. It's just hard sometimes."

"I get it, believe me. And we can talk after. But right now, let's only talk about driving, okay?"

"Absolutely. Now the first thing is, relax. You've driven a little bit before, right?"

"Umm, well... if you count being in the instructor's car, but she had brakes on her side too, so I don't know if that counts. Just don't yell at me, okay? I couldn't even get out of the driveway with Mom freaking out. And then I tried with Dad, and I don't think I even went a block before I quit. He was analyzing every single move I made. It was too intense."

"So ideally, I will be quiet and let you figure it out, right?"

"Exactly. I hope you won't *have* to say anything."

I mentally zipped my lips as she put the car into drive and headed at maybe one mile per hour toward the road, stopping at the mailbox to look both ways a few times. I saw that it was clear, but since I promised to be quiet unless we were in danger,

I waited quietly. This was an extreme test of my patience, a trait I don't have in abundance.

Miriam put on the right turn signal at the end of the driveway, looked both ways again and sloooowly pulled out of the driveway. An old lady with a walker could have crossed in front of us without getting hit.

We drove a couple of blocks, after which Miriam made another four right turns, bringing us back into the driveway. She put the car in park, shut off the ignition and took the keys out, and sighed with relief.

"That's it?" I asked. "You didn't even make a left-hand turn, drive in any traffic, practice parking."

"That's all I could handle today," she said. "Maybe we could make this a regular thing, though? Baby steps?"

"Sure. I can do that. I remember how stressful it was getting started. I'm happy to help, if you really do like going with me."

"Oh, I do! You're the calmest person I know."

"Thanks," I said, smiling at the unexpected compliment. First of all, that Miriam thinks I'm calm, and secondly, that she'd say it. "So I guess I'll be going then. You have my number; get in touch when you want to drive again." I said goodbye without actually leaving, hoping she'd invite me in.

Miriam glanced back at the front door and then looked at me.

"Do you want to come in a minute? Have a glass of water or whatever?"

"Sure," I said, hoping I didn't look as desperate to her as I felt. "Maybe I could say hi to Ellie?"

"Yeah, she'd like that," Miriam said, leading the way. I followed her in, heading toward the kitchen, and stood at the counter while she got me some water. I asked her about school and dance and she answered politely, but looked like she was itching to go, so I reluctantly put down my glass.

"I'll let myself out," I said. "Thanks for the water."

"Thanks for the driving lesson! See you soon."

"Miriam, I –" I was going to tell her I loved her, but I realized how awkward that would be, considering her dad and I were no longer engaged and it was never something I had said to her before. She looked at me expectantly. "Never mind."

I turned around, heading for the front door. I walked slowly to my car and looked back toward the house as I started it up, but no Jason. Was he avoiding me? He was home and he knew I was there; why didn't he even want to see me? Why did I want to see him? Clearly, if we were destined to be together, like he always used to say, one little hiccup in our relationship wouldn't have caused it to fall apart. I wished I could go back to the person I was before I met him, but unfortunately, I had changed. I had to figure out how to live my old life as my new self.

# 41

I came home from work to a message on my answering machine letting me know that my bridal gown was in and could I please set up an appointment for a fitting. That's just great. The universe was telling me what a loser I was.

Adrienne and my mom and had gone shopping in Philadelphia for a gown a few months ago, expecting maybe to find something, maybe not. As girlie as I am, I was not one of those women who fantasized about her wedding. I had gone through it all with my big sister, only to see her marriage crash and burn, and perhaps it was for that reason I was a little jaded about weddings. I had flipped through a few bridal magazines hoping the perfect gown would stand out, but nothing really caught my eye. They were all too much – too much lace, too much beading, too much train.

We were walking down South Broad when I saw it in the window. I pulled my mom and sister into the shop, even though we didn't have an appointment there, and asked to try it on. This one was me. There was no lace or beading anywhere on the dress. The train was extremely short. It was a sleeveless sheath in one gorgeous piece of ivory satin. All I could think about as I looked at myself in the mirror was the expression on Jason's face when he saw me walk down the aisle. We cancelled all the appointments and went out for lunch to celebrate.

I dreaded the thought of calling the bridal shop to tell them the wedding was cancelled. I wasn't even sure what would happen to the gown. Did I still have to pay the full amount? I realized they must deal with this situation now and then. Maybe it was the first time for me, but I bet whoever answered the phone received more than one call from a tearful bride whose wedding was called off. Maybe they could recommend a support group for ex-brides.

I wondered if I might actually die of loneliness. I spent my days with people, talking and acting like everything was normal, but the nights were awful. As much as I had loved having my own apartment, it was beginning to feel like a prison. I looked around and saw nothing that felt like home. The walls were white, the windows were shaded only by vertical blinds, and the whole place looked like a temporary home for someone who was waiting to move on. I had sorted through my belongings and gotten rid of everything unnecessary in preparation for moving in with Jason. A lot of my stuff was already at his house. The idea of having to go back and get it was too terrible to contemplate.

I alternated between crying and feeling numb. The long nights finally broke me, and one evening after tossing and turning until my sheets and blankets were twisted into a useless heap, I propped the pillows up in front of my headboard and sat with my laptop composing an email to my ex-boyfriend John, telling him the whole story of breaking up with Jason.

I didn't even expect John to write back. It had been months since I blocked his number from my phone. Even if he did write back, I didn't know what kind of response to hope for. Even though we had an affair, for a while, we were friends too. We had talked in the intimate way of two people who knew their secrets would never be shared. The process of thinking over how to explain the whole situation to John and write it succinctly gave me some much-needed clarity and a sense of release. For the first time in weeks, I slept soundly the rest of the night and woke up in a more optimistic state of mind.

I got up a little later than usual the next morning, opening my laptop hopefully. John had responded! I started to read, smiling as I felt the concern in his words, even after all these months.

*Kristen, I'm so sorry to hear you're going through this pain. You have a good heart. Here is what I would tell you: move on. Maybe he will realize he was wrong to let you go; maybe he won't. Either way, sitting around waiting for him to come back isn't going to help you. Trying to beg him to come back never works. Let his kids go too. There is nothing you can do to fix this. You apologized and explained why you didn't tell him. I know we haven't kept in touch, but I still think of you. I would've offered to get together, but I've turned things around. I'm very happy now. Hope you will be too.*

John was so matter of fact. There was something very different about a guy's advice than if I had talked to my sister or my friends. Men distilled things down into very simple black-and-white viewpoints. He was right. I had to move on. I just had to figure out the first step.

As I looked at my puffy face in the mirror, it hit me: I was tired of being a fake blonde. It was time to be a real brunette. I got dressed and into my car. I knew my salon would never be able to take me the same day, so I drove to the mall and went to the one that took walk-in customers.

"I want to go darker," I told the girl at the counter, who happened to have blonde hair with streaks of blue and green. She raised her eyebrow at me, as if to ask *why would you ever want to do that?*, but then shrugged and led me to one of the chairs.

"How dark are we talking?" she asked, smacking her gum.

"My hair is naturally light brown. I want to let it grow out and I don't want roots. Can you do that?"

"Let me get a hair color chart." She put it in my lap and I pointed to the one I thought looked most like my natural color, at least from what I could remember.

"Well, that's going to be different," she said.

"I certainly hope so," I said. Everything was going to be different from here on out.

# 42

My doorbell rang, and I ran to get the door, expecting that my mailman had a package to deliver. I was trying to remember whether I had ordered anything recently as I opened the door and saw Jason standing there, a bouquet of flowers in his hand, looking nervous. I was speechless.

"Wow! Look at your hair! You look beautiful."

"Thank you," I said, and I'm pretty sure I was blushing. Of all the people who would see me with brown hair for the first time, I was most worried what Jason would think if and when he ever saw me again.

"Can I come in?" he asked. I still didn't say anything, but opened the door wider and gestured for him to enter. He handed me the flowers and sat on my sofa. I filled a tall glass with water to put the flowers in, set it on the counter and joined him on my couch.

"Thank you for the flowers," I said.

"I love you, Kristen. I made a terrible mistake and I'm sorry. I came here to ask whether you'd give me a second chance."

"I don't even know what to say. You were so angry."

"You could say yes?" he replied, more asking than commanding.

"Yes," I said, leaning forward to hug him.

"Whew," he said, fake-wiping his forehead. "This is even scarier the second time, but I have to do it." He got down on his knee in front of my lap and pulled out my engagement ring, holding it up in front of me.

"Kristen, would you do me the honor of becoming my wife?" he asked. I nodded and he slid the ring back onto my finger. I burst into tears.

"Why are you crying?" he asked.

"I'm just so relieved. Everything felt wrong when we were apart. I didn't even realize how much you and the girls have become my family."

"You're right. Everything did feel wrong. I missed you. Ellie missed you. Even Miriam seemed out of sorts. And by the way, thank you for the driving lessons. I don't know if she's really shown her appreciation to you, but she told me you're a way better teacher than I am."

"Wow, I'm surprised. You know, I figured at least Julia would have been relieved that I was out of the picture."

"Not at all. Julia knows the girls need stability. I was wrong to treat you the way I did. I asked you to be a mom to the girls, and you were doing so well. I got defensive because I didn't deal with something I should have, and my ego got in the way. You handled the situation with Miriam very well."

"I did mess up, though. Husbands and wives don't keep secrets from each other, especially about their kids, and I think my desire for Miriam to trust me overshadowed my good sense to realize that you need to know what's going on with her."

"Let's make a promise to be honest in everything from here on out. And with you becoming my wife, I know I need to focus on your needs more. I haven't acknowledged enough how much you needed to adapt to my family. All the hard work and change has been on your part. I'm sorry I haven't recognized that."

"Thank you."

I stood up and pulled him up for a long hug, resting my cheek against his chest. I felt relieved, happy, and a little bit resentful that we had wasted all this time apart.

"You wanna go shopping?" I asked when we let go of each other.

"For what?"

"I read this article that said assembling furniture helps people communicate better."

"That sounds fine with me," he said.

An hour later, we were choosing a wardrobe big enough for his clothes and mine. It's not like I had a ton of clothes, but his closet was already full and so was his dresser. Jason may have had more clothes than I did.

We somehow managed to wedge the box in the back of his car and drove back to his house to begin our joint project.

"I think we need to have lunch before I'm ready to tackle this," I said. "Would you like a sandwich?"

"Sure. I'll get started on this."

"No, you won't. We have to do each step of it together. That's the idea. It's a communication exercise. I think that's the one thing we've been lacking sometimes."

"All right. Well, then I'll help you make sandwiches too. Does that work?"

"That works great. Just like we will, I hope," I said, kissing him on the cheek.

# 43

A few days later, I pulled the girls' pajamas out of the dryer at Jason's house. I remembered that when I was little, my mom would warm up our pajamas on cold nights so we could climb into warm, soft clothes after our baths. I brought them upstairs and knocked on their doors.

"I have something for you," I called out. Ellie's door popped open immediately. I handed her a warm bundle, her pjs folded neatly.

"Oh, they're so soft! And they smell so good. Thank you, Kristen!" She gave me a little hug around the waist and I put my arm around her shoulders and kissed the top of her head.

"You're welcome, sweetie." Just then, Miriam poked her head out from her door, her hair wrapped in a towel from her shower.

"I warmed up your pjs for you," I said, holding them out to her.

"Wow, thanks. What is this, a luxury hotel?"

"No, just a little something my mom used to do for me when I was a kid. I thought you two would enjoy it."

Both girls retreated to their rooms to put on their warm pjs, and I went downstairs to join Jason.

"You're a sweetheart, you know that?" he asked, pulling me close to him on the sofa. I didn't answer, but snuggled my head against his shoulder. He was watching another one of his treasure-hunting shows and I zoned out, leaning against him with my legs curled under me. He absentmindedly stroked the top of my shoulder with his fingertips. I couldn't imagine feeling happier than I did at that very moment; sitting with my husband-to-be, his – our – girls at home relaxing, everyone in a good mood.

The next day when I stopped at Jason's house after work, there was a card for me on the kitchen counter. I didn't recognize the handwriting on the envelope, but I knew it wasn't Jason's. I opened it to find a picture of a skeleton with hearts all around the border. Inside, the card said "I love your guts" and was signed by Miriam and Ellie.

I almost started crying, but mentally kicked myself. *What is wrong with you, Kristen, turning into a ball of mush?* Becoming part of such an emotional family was cracking through my hard shell. I wasn't used to being around people who were always cuddling and saying "I love you," but it felt like something I wanted to get used to. This was the first time the girls had said anything like that to me. I liked the funny, light-hearted approach and saw Miriam's wry sense of humor.

They were at Julia's for the night, but I couldn't wait to show Jason the card. I started pulling things out of the refrigerator, trying to figure out what would be good for our dinner. Cooking sometimes overwhelmed me, but I was getting used to the idea of making sure we had balanced meals with plenty of veggies. I was eating more vegetables than I ever had in my life – including scary-sounding ones like Brussels sprouts.

An hour later, as we sat down to a broccoli and chicken casserole with side salads, I showed Jason the card. He had the same look I did when I opened it, like he was going to tear up but stopped himself.

"That's really nice," he said a moment later, handing it back to me.

"It's definitely going in my keepsake box."

"You know, I think it's about time we started getting the wedding planning in motion. And you moving in."

"I know. Well, I was afraid to bring it up because I didn't want to jinx anything. Sometimes I can't even believe how smoothly everything has been going, even with Miriam. It's like she doesn't hate the idea of us getting married!"

"I'm sure there will be bumps in the road, but we got this," Jason said, pulling up my hand to kiss it softly.

"I'd like our wedding to be small, simple," I said, finally allowing myself to daydream about what it would actually be like to marry Jason.

"That's one of the things I love most about you," he said. "My first wedding was a spectacle. Almost three hundred people. I barely knew half of them. Julia went into hyper-planning perfectionist mode for more than a year ahead of time. It was awful. It felt like the marriage itself was nothing compared to the wedding reception. I was hoping you didn't want that kind of a wedding, but I didn't want to say anything, because I am old-fashioned enough to believe it should be the bride's day."

"That is the opposite of the kind of wedding I want. I'd really like it just to be my immediate family, if that's okay with you," I said.

Jason had told me early in our relationship that his parents had both died and he was an only child, so other than his daughters, he didn't have much family. My family was small too, and I appreciated that we wouldn't have to feel obligated to invite anyone else if we really said family only.

"That is more than okay with me. That sounds perfect. Can we get married at my church? Will you join?"

"Yes and yes. How about you take care of the church and I take care of the reception? Does that sound good?"

"Or should it be like assembling the wardrobe – we have to do it all together because it improves communication?" he asked.

"Good point. *We'll* arrange for the ceremony and *we'll* arrange for the reception."

"You're so smart. I knew there was a reason I wanted to marry you," he said, winking. I playfully punched his arm.

"There are lots of reasons to marry me. How about because I'm an all-around goddess?"

"That too. So, my goddess, when are you moving in with me?"

"I'd say, officially, after we're married. I think it would be better to give the girls some time to adjust if we took this step by step, and I want to do things right."

"I can't wait to make you my wife," Jason said, pulling me into a hug.

"I can't wait to be your wife," I answered, but in the back of my head, I worried a little. What if he changed his mind again? What if the girls were awful about things once we set a date? What if Julia turned into a super-bitch about it? These were all things that could keep me up at night if I let them. I tried to push the fears aside and enjoy the moment.

# 44

Jason insisted that Julia was okay with us getting married, but she certainly was inserting herself into our lives more often lately. She called and texted several times a day, and Jason always responded immediately. "It's just easier this way," he said. I was pretty sure she was regretting her decision to leave him now that he had found a new partner, someone who seemed to find him very desirable.

Sometimes it felt like Julia and I were vying for the role of wife. I wasn't sure how much of that was Jason's fault for the way he handled things. I was still getting used to the idea that he had to be in regular contact with his ex because of their kids.

Miriam and Ellie were disruptive to our relationship too, but it was a more welcome disruption. Jason had told me from the get-go that he was a father. I knew what I was signing on for, even if I didn't fully understand it at the time.

I never looked at Jason's phone or asked him what Julia was saying, but I wanted to. It would be too hypocritical after our blowout over Adrienne's message to me. I wondered if she vented to Jason about me.

"Does Julia say bad things about me?" I asked him, sounding as casual as I could.

"No, of course not. Well, not really. I mean, you know, she's having some trouble with the idea of me getting married again, but you shouldn't be worried about it."

"She left you! How does she have a right to feel upset? Did she think you were just going to pine away for her forever?"

"Probably," he said, chuckling. "She does have that kind of an ego."

"How do you expect me not to worry? What if she sabotages things? What if she's poisoning the girls' minds against me?"

"Kristen, stop." Jason pulled me into a hug. "The girls are old enough to think for themselves and it's clear that they love you, or at least are starting to love you. They are used to you. You should have seen what a mess we were when you and I were apart. It was like the house stopped functioning. I don't know how we ever made it before you came into our lives."

That made me feel better. I hugged him, feeling comforted. I said a silent prayer for Julia to leave us in peace. It was hard enough to become a stepmom without an adversary.

Over the next week, my prayer seemed to have been answered, but not in the way I wanted. I felt like a cartoon character who had found a genie's lamp and rubbed it, only to find that every wish made things worse instead of better.

Jason was trying to hide it, but I could tell his vision was getting fuzzy because he'd reach for a glass and his hand would miss it. I saw him walking down the hall from the back and he looked like a drunken sailor the way he was swaying to one side.

"We need to get you back to the specialist," I said a few times, though he kept shaking his head no.

"I'm fine; don't worry," he said.

Doctors make the worst patients. I tried to think what a wife would do because I was going to be one soon, and with hands shaking, I called the neurologist and made an appointment for him. I had never seen Jason go through a relapse. Even when he first started coming to the spa for massages, he was entering a period of remission, and we were lucky enough that it had lasted all these months.

When I told him I'd made an appointment, he first seemed irritated, then relieved. I noticed he was more emotional lately. He was given to tearing up anyway, but now he seemed less in control of his feelings.

"I'm scared," he confessed one night, as we were snuggled under the covers in his bed, facing each other.

"I know," I said, rubbing his arm softly. "I am too."

"No, it's not the MS I'm scared of right now, although that's always in the back of my mind. I'm afraid you're going to change your mind about me like Julia did. Have you noticed that as soon as this happened, she disappeared again? Not one text or phone call in a week. It's like she sensed that I'm weak and she ran away again."

I didn't know what to say. I was filled with love and compassion and fear, all roiling together in a gelatinous blob of emotion. Of course I was scared. What if this was it? What if he went on one long decline from here? Julia was a doctor. She knew much more about this than I did and she wanted no part of it, even though they had children together. Did I really want to possibly take on the role of not only stepmom, but possibly also a caretaker to an invalid? Tamara's words "I think you're making a huge mistake" rang through my head daily. My own family was less opinionated, but I could tell they had their reservations, for multiple reasons – good reasons. What would I tell a friend in this situation, if I were being honest?

"I won't change my mind," I said, kissing him on the forehead. "I love you and that's enough."

# 45

I drove us to Jason's neurology appointment. Jason had muscle weakness and conceded that it wouldn't be a good idea for him to drive. He cut back his hours at his office, working mornings and coming home to nap all afternoon. He stopped taking new patients and advised his neediest ones that they might want to look for a doctor who could be more available.

He'd get up for dinner, watch TV for a bit, and go back to bed. He slept more restlessly at night than he used to. I was losing sleep too, not only from worry, but also from trying to sleep next to someone who was sighing a lot, pulling the covers up, then kicking them off, his legs twitching. I felt guilty, but I started spending more nights at my own apartment, even though they were nights the girls were with their mom and I'd normally be with Jason. The nights I did stay at his house, I'd often end up taking a pillow to sleep on the sofa just to get a few hours of uninterrupted sleep, although it was also a restless sleep because I worried what was going on with Jason in the bed upstairs.

I pulled into a suburban shopping plaza with parking strips right in front of the stores and offices. The neurology office had large windows shaded by vertical blinds and a glass door with the doctors' names stenciled in white at eye level. We were going to see Dr. Mortinson, Jason's longtime friend and a former residency colleague.

The first thing I noticed when we walked in was how immaculate the place was. The second was how quiet it was. Unlike Jason's office, which was cheerful but messy with toys in the corner that no one allowed their kids to play with, and piles of women's magazines that looked a bit raggedy, and bright stripes of colors on the walls, this office was hushed and peaceful. No one else sat in the soft waiting room chairs, no TV blared from a stand near the ceiling. Jason checked in with the receptionist, who recognized him right away. I sat down, prepared to wait like you usually did at a doctor's office, but Jason ushered me to follow him to the back and led us to Dr. Mortinson's exam room. Here again, I noticed the contrast: No medical posters on the walls, no prescription drug company doodads that seemed to litter doctors' offices, not even an exam table. Instead the room had a side counter with a sink and cabinets and a few chairs. Nothing would mark this as being different than a small office's conference room.

Dr. Mortinson knocked and stepped into the room, wearing a button-down oxford shirt and khaki pants rather than the typical white lab coat. I instantly felt more at ease when I saw his wide smile as he greeted me and patted Jason on the back (softly, I noticed, not like the typical male slap on the back).

It seemed like most medical offices were set up to remind me that I was a patient at the mercy of someone with more expertise and more money than I had. I waited varying lengths of time to be seen, the receptionists sat behind glassed-in desks, everyone wore intimidating looking scrubs or uniforms, and exam rooms were decorated with horrifying images of blackened lungs, strange disease conditions, or skin lesions in various stages of cancer.

In contrast, this office was set up to make the patient feel like a customer or an equal human being. I took note because an idea was forming in my mind that Jason and I could open our own integrated health clinic where he offered general medical services, on a schedule he could set himself, and we would offer nutritional counseling and yoga too. I wanted a business that would serve the whole person, not just a disease, and one that empowered individuals to feel that they could take part in their own health care.

"Nice to meet you, Dr. Mortinson," I said softly.

"Oh, just call me Morty," he replied. "Everyone else does. Thank you for calling. I don't know whether you've ever noticed that Jason can be a little... how shall we put it... stubborn?"

"No, of course not," I laughed. Jason watched our conversation without trying to argue on his own behalf. Honestly, he looked pretty tired, not himself at all, and I sensed that Morty could see the difference too, because he quickly settled into a more clinical mode.

"So what's going on with you, Jason?" he asked, as we all sat down. "When did you notice the flare-up beginning?"

Jason paused and then looked over at me, wordlessly asking whether I could answer these questions for him. His posture was one of defeat, leaning forward a bit, head down.

"It was about three weeks ago," I answered. "First it was his vision getting blurry. Then his balance. And from there he seemed more and more tired and weak. I've never seen him like this since I've known him."

"You are definitely in the midst of a recurrence," Morty said. "I'd like to check your vitamin D levels. Have you been outside much lately?"

"No. It was a pretty unpleasant winter," Jason answered. "I guess between working and not wanting to be outside, that could be a problem, right?"

It was so hard to watch Jason, who usually spoke with confidence and vigor, almost trembling. He looked like any other patient with a medical crisis. It didn't matter that he was a doctor and understood his physiology better than most people. Maybe that was a worse position to be in. I only knew what I saw right now. He knew all of the possibilities that lay ahead.

After a brief physical exam that I watched closely, Morty offered some more advice, this time talking more toward me.

"We will review his medications after we get the results of his bloodwork. In the meantime, there are complementary therapies you might want to pursue. There's a lot of work out there about using nutrition in MS management. It's not scientifically proven because it's not a drug, but stuff like avoiding artificial sweeteners and sugar, dairy, processed foods. Do you have time to help Jason monitor what he eats, maybe cook more of your foods at home?"

"Definitely. I'm not a great cook, but I've been learning. I want to do everything I can to help."

"You found yourself a good woman," Morty said. I blushed a little. I wondered what he thought of Julia. Apparently she hadn't been willing or didn't have the time to explore alternative treatments. "Jason, you go ahead out. I want to talk to Kristen for a moment. I'll call you with your results in the next day or two."

"Thanks, Morty," Jason said, shaking his hand. I watched him close the door behind him and my heartrate immediately skyrocketed. Is this where he was going to tell me Jason was dying? He could see my fear because he immediately used a more soothing tone with me.

"Kristen, you did the right thing making an appointment. Jason thinks the world of you. Every time he's been in here, he's over the moon. I am hoping your commitment level is high, because you're going to have some struggles ahead. He was absolutely devastated when Julia left. I would hate to see him go through that again. She kicked a good man when he was down."

"You have nothing to worry about," I said. I felt bad that people on all sides of us were making this difficult, questioning whether we were doing the right thing. Getting married was hard enough without the guilt trips, the doubtfulness of friends and family, and the resistance of Julia. "I'm going to take care of him."

Morty looked satisfied with my answer. He rubbed my shoulder as we stood up, then walked me out to the waiting room. I gave Jason a hug.

"Ready to go home?" I asked. He nodded and reached for my hand.

# 46

"We have something to ask you," Ellie said, looking angelic as Miriam stood behind her.

"Sure, go ahead," I said, feeling surprised to see them looking so uncertain. Ellie and Miriam were used to getting what they wanted, and they usually asked for things with a high level of confidence.

"Could we be part of your wedding? Like bridesmaids, maybe?"

"Oh, Ellie, of course you can!" I was so relieved in that moment. I had struggled with the idea of asking them to participate, had sought Jason's opinion on the matter, but we were both unsure of whether it would be too uncomfortable for them or make them feel disloyal to their mother. It shouldn't have, considering she left him, but kids don't think that way. That's the rational adult way of looking at the situation, not the emotional child straddled between two households.

"Could you *not* make us wear ugly dresses, though?" Miriam asked.

"Of course not. You girls can pick your dresses. How about if we shop together to find something you both like? We can have a girls' day out."

"Can we go to lunch too?" Ellie asked.

"Definitely," I replied. No surprise that Ellie was more interested in the food and Miriam wanted to look fashionable. "Just one question: Have you talked to your mom about this yet? I wouldn't want her to be upset."

"Well, we didn't tell her yet because we wanted to make sure it was okay with you first," Miriam said. "There was no point telling her if it wasn't going to happen anyway."

"That makes sense," I said, although I worried a bit that she had the foresight to see that her mother was probably not going to be happy about it. I said a quick prayer that Julia would not make this a problem.

"So would you want to go shopping today?" Miriam asked.

"I'd love to, but I'm just worried about your mom."

"Don't worry. We'll talk to her tonight."

"How about your dad? Shouldn't we tell him?"

"Let's surprise him," Miriam said. "We'll see how the shopping goes today and then we can tell him about it at dinner tonight. Just tell him you have plans with one of your friends or something. I think he could use some good news."

"What do you mean?" Ellie asked, but Miriam brushed over it.

"Where do you want to go for lunch, Ellie Bellie?" she asked, rubbing her little sister on the head.

"I don't know what I'm in the mood for yet. I need some time to think about it," Ellie said.

"All right, well, if you two really want to go today, let me call the shop where my gown is and I'll see if they can take us this morning."

Two hours later, after Miriam had tried on at least fifteen gowns, we had a winner. I did my best to be patient and look interested in each dress that Miriam modeled for me, coming out of the changing room to twirl in front of the three-way mirror before finding some fault with what she was wearing. Ellie had given up trying on dresses after the first three and sat on the carpeted floor, completely bored. I thought Miriam looked absolutely smashing in every one of them. She was a beautiful young woman with perfect hair and skin. She had amazing posture from years of ballet, and although I thought she still looked a bit too thin, she certainly had the figure for clothing. I wondered if she was really that self-critical or she just wanted to try on everything in the store.

Finally she came out in a pale peach gown with spaghetti straps and a bodice cut straight across the top that flowed into a simple A-line tea length. It looked a lot like her ballet dresses, although less flowy, so it made sense that she finally found something she was comfortable wearing. I could see the dress would be a bit less flattering on Ellie, but she was a nine-year-old girl who didn't care a bit about clothes, so she just shrugged her approval when Miriam asked what she thought.

The tired-looking saleswoman took measurements for both of the girls and wrote up an order slip. I signed and made the deposit.

"Would you two like a special sneak peak of my wedding gown?" I asked. "No one else has seen it yet except Adrienne and my mom." Ellie tried to look politely interested, although I could tell she couldn't wait to get out of the shop, but Miriam clapped her hands together and squealed, "Oh, yes, could we?"

The salesgirl only sighed a little bit as I asked her to pull mine out. I reassured her that I wasn't here to try it on, just let the girls see what it looked like. She brought the gown back a few minutes later, unzipping the bag and hanging it on one of the dressing room doors.

"Oh, Kristen, I want one just like this when I get married," Miriam said, her eyes shining as she gazed at my unembellished ivory satin gown. I could tell she was envisioning her own wedding, not mine, as she reached out to softly touch the fabric, but that's okay because I think all girls do that. It was funny how Miriam and I had much more in common, being the girly-girls we were, yet Ellie and I had a much more easygoing relationship.

The salesgirl zipped the gown back into the bag and Ellie looked relieved.

"I've decided about lunch," she announced. "Let's get pizza."

Miriam and I both groaned at the same time. I'm sure we were both thinking the same thing: the carbs, the cheese! But I had promised Ellie it was her choice, and she was awfully patient for two hours of dress shopping.

I drove them to Antonio's, the best pizza place around. If you were going to eat pizza, you had to have the real stuff. Antonio was a third generation pizza maker who had somehow made it to Mountain Ridge from New Jersey after a dispute with his brother. Unlike the franchise chains, he imported all his cheese from Italy and made a new batch of homemade sauce each morning. How did a non-foodie like myself know all this? You couldn't walk into his shop without hearing more details than you ever needed to know. The only thing he was secretive about was the recipe for his sauce. He claimed his brother stole his sauce and that's why he had to get away from the family shop. Anything else – from his father-in-law's salary to his sister's divorce – was public domain.

We ordered a pie and side salads and water (because I insisted no sugary stuff to Ellie) and sat silently. I still hadn't mastered the art of small talk. Jason was so good at getting them to open up and get the ball rolling, but there were still awkward silences when I was alone with them as I struggled to think of things to say or to ask them about. Miriam looked uncomfortable and

Ellie looked listlessly around us as though she were a visitor to a museum exhibit she wasn't especially interested in.

"Dad's not doing too well, is he?" Miriam finally asked.

"What do you mean?" Ellie said. Being nine, she was probably less attuned to the changes Jason had been going through, and he tried extra hard for her not to see him off balance or taking his naps.

I looked at Miriam and she nodded. She agreed that we need to tell Ellie at least some of what was happening with their dad.

"Well, you know your dad has multiple sclerosis, right?" I asked. Ellie nodded. "Okay. Here's the thing: When someone has MS, it can be unpredictable. Your dad is lucky to have a type that comes and goes. They call it relapsing and remitting. That means he has times – weeks or even months at a time – where he is feeling good. But the past few weeks he has been having a flare-up. That means he has some changes in his body that are making him very tired, and he's having a little trouble seeing and with his balance."

"Is he ever going to get better?" Ellie asked.

"He is always going to have MS. He is going to have times he's better. The good news is, he should live as long as a person without MS. But I think you're old enough to know that we don't know when his good times and when his tough times are going to be, or how long they'll last or how bad he'll be feeling."

"Oh," Ellie said, looking down. Miriam was holding back tears; she understood more about the prognosis. I wanted to cry too, but I knew I had to keep it together for the girls. They needed to see that the adults in their lives were handling this setback calmly. The problem was, I had no one to cry to. Jason needed me to be strong, and I couldn't bear to hear "Are you sure you want to *marry* him?" from my mother, my sister, or my friends.

"Listen, ladies, let's enjoy this pizza and go home and tell your dad the good news. He is going to be so excited that you want to be part of our wedding. Ellie, you can tell him that part, and Miriam, you tell him about the gowns you picked out. Sound like a plan?"

"I just hope he doesn't cry again," Miriam said. She was rolling her eyes, but she was also smiling.

"If he does, it'll be happy tears," I said. "This means the world to me, and I know it will to your father too."

# 47

The doorbell rang and I heard insistent knocking. I didn't want to answer Jason's door, but he was lying down upstairs, taking one of his marathon naps. I crept up to the door and peeped through the glass panel at the top. There was Julia, a tight expression on her face, raising her hand to knock again. I didn't want her to wake Jason, so I yanked open the door just as her knuckles were about to make contact. This threw her off balance so that she had to take a step forward.

"Oh, Kristen, it's you. Listen, I need to talk to Jason and he hasn't been answering his phone. Is he here?"

"Hello, Julia, how are you?" I asked, hoping my good manners would call attention to her lack of etiquette. It didn't.

"Is he home?" she demanded.

"He is, but he's asleep right now. I'm sure that's why he didn't respond." And it was at least partly true. He and I had discussed the way he seemed to be at her beck and call, and he agreed that he needed to wean her off the notion that she could reach him instantly day or night if it wasn't an emergency. We had all learned our lesson about being available from Ellie's broken wrist, but most of the time Julia called or texted, it was about non-urgent matters, or she wanted to vent about something.

Before Jason lay down for his nap, he had received a few texts from Julia along the lines of *I need to talk to you asap*. He assumed it was because the girls let her know they wanted to take part in our wedding. "I can't deal with this right now," he told me. "I'm just too tired today."

So now I had to deal alone with an enraged Julia, who was standing on the door step, trying to look past me. The girls were up in their rooms, so they weren't going to serve as a buffer either.

"I don't believe you. Why would he be asleep at" – she looked at her watch – "four in the afternoon?"

"Julia, are you completely in denial? Can't you see that he's had a relapse? He's exhausted all of the time."

"He's avoiding me."

"Honestly, he's not trying to avoid you. We've barely seen him either. He goes to work in the morning, comes home and sleeps all afternoon. His body needs it right now."

"I *need* to talk to him. Right now."

"How about you come in and talk to me, and I promise I will relay to him whatever you want him to know." I felt like a celebrity's publicist fending off an intrusive reporter. She was apparently so desperate to unload whatever was bothering her (I'd bet anything it was the wedding) that she brushed past me. I followed her to the living room and she sat on the sofa while I sat catty corner on a club chair.

"So what's on your mind?" I asked.

"The girls. Your wedding. No one even asked me until after the fact. My daughters came home and told me you took them dress shopping and already ordered bridesmaid dresses. It was completely unfair for you to railroad them into participating and then not even have the decency to ask me how I felt about the whole thing."

Uh-oh. This was tricky territory. I knew I should have cleared the air with Julia before we went shopping. And since I wasn't there, I had no idea how the girls had approached the topic with their mother. Had they told her it was my idea instead of theirs, hoping to soften the blow? I tried to avoid the part about whose idea it was to go dress shopping and instead aimed for a conciliatory approach.

"I'm sorry, Julia. That was insensitive. You're right."

Julia looked at me for a moment, her eyes narrowing as she studied my face. I was sorry. I agreed that the situation wasn't handled well. But I also felt the girls were old enough to make that decision on their own. She stood up suddenly, pacing toward the stairs before I caught on to what she was doing.

"I'm talking to their father. I don't care if he's asleep; I'm waking him up," she said over her shoulder as she bounded up the steps. God, the woman was fast. I raced after her, but didn't reach her until she was already in Jason's – our – bedroom, poking him on the shoulder. I stood in the doorway, taking in the strangeness of this scene: Jason's ex-wife in what used to be their bedroom, sitting on the edge of their – his – our bed. The intimacy of her sitting on the bed felt so threatening to me. I wanted to shove her aside and say "You dumped him. He's *mine* now." But I was paralyzed, watching to see what would happen next. Jason stirred, opening his eyes and looking disoriented when he saw Julia sitting next to him. He half sat up, asking, "What's going on?"

"Jason, I can't stand this. Your girlfriend talked our daughters into participating into this absurd pageant of a wedding you're planning to put on and I want it stopped."

"She had nothing to do with it!" he said. I felt movement behind me and turned around to see both Miriam and Ellie also listening in.

"Stop it, Mom," Miriam said, walking over to sit on the other side of the bed, laying an arm protectively over Jason, who was now in the middle. "It was our idea, not Dad's, not Kristen's.

I'm sorry you can't handle it, but we want to be in the wedding. Right, Ellie?" She looked over at us, and Ellie cautiously nodded her approval, looking at the floor. I could tell she didn't want to disappoint her mother.

Julia looked back and forth at the two of them. No one said anything. She shook her head slowly, her cheeks a little flushed from anger, and abruptly got up.

"So that's the way it's going to be," she huffed. "Your new, perfect family. I'm glad it was easy to replace me."

She stormed out. Ellie burst into tears, and Jason beckoned her over. I stood at the doorway, watching him console Ellie on one side, while Miriam sat on the other. He looked up at me and tilted his chin up, motioning for me to join them on the bed. I gingerly sat next to Miriam and she put her free hand on my leg.

"It'll be all right," she said. We weren't a perfect family, but Julia was right about one thing: We were a family.

# 48

"Daddy, wouldn't it make more sense for me to get a new car than a used one? It would be safer and you wouldn't need to worry that I'd break down somewhere."

I hated when Miriam said "Daddy." I don't know if he noticed, but it was always Dad unless she wanted something; then, all of a sudden her voice was high and babyish, and it was "Daddy, could I please..."

"Honey, these cars are only a year or two old. They are in excellent condition. I can't see spending a couple of thousand extra."

"But I really, really like this one," she said, running her hand over a sweet little Mitsubishi. "Don't you love it too, Ellie?"

Ellie just shrugged. She was about as interested in car shopping as she was bridesmaid gown shopping. This didn't pertain to her and she had asked whether I would stay home with her, but I insisted we all go together. For one, it was a "family activity," and second, I was hoping to be the voice of reason in Jason's other ear because I knew Miriam was going to talk him into spending more than he had planned.

"Jason, can I talk to you a minute?" I said, tugging his sleeve. I led him away from the girls and spoke in a hushed voice. "What if we gave Miriam my car and I got one of these used cars? I'd be happy to have one. I don't need a brand new car, but any of these would be better than what I have now."

Jason looked dubious.

"I don't know. I did promise to buy her a car."

"Yeah, but you didn't promise her a new car. And shouldn't the wife be driving something better than the sixteen-year-old new driver? I thought all kids started on a beater car. Adrienne and I had to share a hunk of junk until she moved out. Then I drove it until I finished massage school and got a job and could buy my own car. And I've had the same one since. It's still running, but I think it's time for a step up."

"I don't think Miriam would like that."

"Jason, are you concerned at all with what I'd like? Because I don't think it's fair that a kid is going to be driving a nicer car than I have." What I couldn't say is that all the savings I could put aside were going into my new business fund that I was waiting to discuss with Jason when I felt a little more prepared.

"How come you were okay with driving what you have until the prospect of my daughter getting a car?"

"I don't know. Maybe because I feel like the girls *always* come first and get the best of everything, and I'm wondering when I'm going to come first."

"That's not fair," Jason said, stepping back.

"Really? It's not? I thought when we were dating, okay, of course you're going to prioritize them over me. But now we're about to get married, and nothing's changed. Am I going to be your wife and still come in third place?"

"You're being ridiculous, Kristen. There's no third place. You're all the same to me."

"You can say that all you want, but your actions speak differently."

"Fine! We'll buy two cars today. I'll buy Miriam a used car and you a brand-new one. Will that make you happy? Then you'll have one that's better than hers. Jesus, Kristen, you sound so petty when you get like this. You have no right – and no reason – to be jealous of my daughters. Sometimes I feel like you try to drive a wedge between us, especially Miriam and me."

"Do you even realize how hurtful you sound right now? Why don't you try putting yourself in my place for once? This has been so hard for me, and I've stuck to it no matter what. I wasn't a mom, but I handled difficult things and I've built a relationship with Miriam and Ellie. I feel like you don't give me credit. So what if Miriam's mad that she doesn't get a new car? It will be a good lesson that you don't always get what you want. They are a little bit spoiled; even you would have to admit that."

I could see out of the corner of my eye the girls looking intensely uncomfortable watching us argue. The salesman had also backed away and was standing at a distance, leaning against the plate glass window under the eve of the office. I could only imagine that he had witnessed many fights in this parking lot. Large purchases could bring out the worst in people.

"Jason, look, there's going to be a million things like this in our future. Let's compromise. Buy Miriam a used car and I will keep driving mine for now. But when mine finally dies, I need you to help me buy another one. Deal?"

"Deal," he said, and we shook hands on it like we were the ones making the transaction. "I'm really sorry. You were right about all of it."

He hugged me and we walked hand in hand over to the girls. Miriam took the news that she wasn't getting that beautiful little new Lancer with only minimal pouting because at least she was getting a silver Ford Focus with less than ten thousand miles on it and the all-important new car scent inside. As for me, my Toyota Corolla was getting put to the test for claims that they'd roll into the hundreds of thousands of miles.

# 49

One reason I didn't have the money to buy myself a new car was because I had been saving up for a dream that was becoming more and more clear with each passing day. As excited as I was for our wedding, this idea crowded even more of my brain with so many thoughts and ideas that I was constantly writing them down on little scraps of paper. I wasn't the most organized person, but I at least tossed all of the notes into a shoe box and wrote with Sharpie on the lid: Whole Body Health.

On a Saturday morning when Jason looked fairly energetic, I pulled out my box and sat next to him at the kitchen counter while he was reading the newspaper.

"I have a proposal for you," I said, my heart beating a million miles an hour.

"I thought that was my job," he replied, kissing me.

"No joking around. This is something different, something I've been thinking about for a while and I am really hoping you will like the idea."

I showed him the box.

"What is this?" He looked inside at the grocery receipts, the junk mail envelopes, and a few napkins with notes scrawled all over them in pencil and various colors of ink.

"I know right now it just looks like a heap of nothing, but these are all my ideas for a business I would like to start with you. You could be the doctor, I could be the massage therapist, and we could hire a nutritionist and a yoga teacher and run our own integrated health clinic. Maybe we could even get big and have a health food store or a juice bar there or something. There's so much we could do. I know you haven't been feeling the best, but I could do most of the starting things up. You could set your own hours, keep it as limited as you need." I finally had to pause after saying all of that in one breath.

"Whoa," he said, taking my hands in his. "Where are we going to get the money for this? Or find a place to rent? Neither of us has ever run a business."

"You're the one who taught me that having faith in something can make it happen. I was the one who always believed the worst. I never thought I could make my dreams come true, and you showed me that I can."

"I guess that's true, but we have to be practical. I don't like to bring this up, but you know as well as I do that my prognosis is unknown. What if I can't work? What are we going to do for income?"

"That's exactly why we need to do this now. I bet the girls would help us out. Even Ellie. Miriam says she wants to be a dietician. Wouldn't it be great if we had a business for her to come to when she finishes school?"

"Wow, you've really given this thought, haven't you?"

"Every single day for weeks now, Jason. I may finally have found my purpose. Before I met you, I remember constantly thinking, "Is this all there is?" Then you and the girls took up so much of my time and my heart, but I realized there was still more I needed to do and I think this is it. Seeing you go through what you do makes me want to help other people. I want to bring dignity and compassion and self-agency to health care."

"Listen to you with the big words." Jason kissed the top of my hand. "Okay. How about we start putting the idea out there, asking if anyone wants to help us out, knows a good space we can rent. Does that sound like a plan?"

"Definitely! I know we can do this together."

We told Miriam and Ellie what we were planning and I was thrilled by how they excited they seemed. Both of the girls volunteered to help in whatever capacity they could, and Miriam looked flattered when I told her I was hoping she'd be our nutritionist once she got her degree.

At church, Pastor Dawn announced our plan, asking the congregation to pray for our endeavor. By that afternoon, we were looking at warehouse space in the nearby industrial park that a fellow parishioner who worked with the chamber of congress knew was available.

It was a brand-new building, occupied on the other side by a packaging company that hired disabled adults to count and place products from other nearby industries into cartons for shipping. The industrial park was as beautiful as such a place could be, with open grassy expanses on two sides. The back of the building faced a forested area that marked the edge of the park. I envisioned picnic tables out back. The only downside was the lack of windows in the building. In my head, our office would be so light and airy that we wouldn't even need the lights on in the summer. But we had to start somewhere.

The church's crafting committee offered to help decorate, a man who owned a local office supply center gave us a discount on furniture, and the youth group volunteered to plant flowers outside the building and make a hand-painted sign. I had never felt so cared for by a whole community before.

Adrienne and my parents seemed really pleased, in their own quiet way. This was the first time I ever truly felt like my mom and dad were proud of the decisions I had made. I gave them so much to be ashamed of, the way I screwed up in school and then the boyfriend that I couldn't even bring home for Christmas. I'm sure they worried a little about what would happen to Jason and how I'd handle it, but when they saw me forging ahead confidently, they dropped the subject of maybe not getting married.

Sometimes I worried that the stress and the change in routine would make Jason even more tired, but he seemed to be thriving, despite his exhaustion. I didn't want to jinx it, but it seemed he was slowly getting better. As I worked on his muscles a few times a week, I could feel them loosening up again. Every night when I prayed for him, I pictured him dancing with me at our wedding.

# 50

The laundry was piling up, there were constantly dishes in the sink, the trash can was overflowing, and the lawn badly needed to be cut. Instead of healthy, homemade meals, we were eating a lot of takeout. Jason was exhausted constantly, but so was I, from lack of sleep, working full-time at the spa, and trying to manage the house and the girls on my own. Not to mention the final details of pulling the wedding together and our new business venture.

"Girls, we need a family conference," I told them one morning after not even being able to find a clean bowl for some cereal. I had reached the end of my rope. The girls sat on the stools on one side of the kitchen counter while I stood with a notebook and pen on the other. Bossy mom was not a role I was accustomed to, but things had to change or we'd all go crazy. They looked at me warily, not expecting anything good.

"You know your dad is having a flare-up and can't do all the things he'd normally do for you and the house. I am trying to make up for what he can't do, but it's too much for me to handle on my own. I need your help."

"But this is our summer vacation," Ellie grumbled. "We're supposed to get some time to relax."

"Ellie, you'll still have plenty of time to do what you want, but I need help. If your dad is going to get better, we have to do everything we can to make sure he doesn't feel stressed out.

When he sees the house falling apart and knows he can't do anything about it, he feels worse."

I hated playing the guilt card, but I did know how loyal the girls were to their dad. I figured that while they may not be motivated to help me, if they thought their dad wanted them to do more, they'd make an effort. Julia and Jason had spent years spoiling their girls and now I was the one paying the price for it.

"Okay," Ellie said.

"What do you want us to do?" Miriam asked.

"How about we make a list of things that need to be done on this paper and then we'll start volunteering for the jobs we most want to do?"

"I don't know how to do laundry or dishes," Ellie said.

"I will teach you. Remember when you didn't know how to clean your bathroom? You do a decent job at that, at least most of the time. And Miriam, you're going to need to know how to do your own laundry soon enough. When you go to college, that's going to be your responsibility."

"All right. I'll do the laundry. And the dishes if you need me to. But I am *not* doing outdoor work. I hate being outside," Miriam said.

"Ellie, how about we do the outdoor work together? You can do some weeding while I cut the grass. I will show you which ones are weeds."

I washed enough dishes to make a decent breakfast. While the girls ate, I brought Jason a tray with some toast and strawberry jam plus a scrambled egg and some orange juice.

"I heard you girls talking downstairs," he said. "I hate this. A man provides for his family."

"Jason, you provide everything we need. The best way for you to get better is to rest when you are tired. Later on, I will help you with some stretches, and if you feel up to it, we'll take a short walk. But you know the heat and humidity are killer. Stay in the air conditioning."

"Thank you. I feel so guilty," he said, tearing up a little. The prednisone made him emotional.

I held his face in my hands and looked deeply into his eyes.

"I know you would do anything for me," I said. "I'm just showing you my love. And besides, it's about time these girls get off their asses and do something. It's not going to kill them to do a little housework."

He laughed then and I kissed him on the forehead.

"Rest up and we're going to have a good dinner tonight. No more junk. We need to get you healed up in time for the wedding and our honeymoon." I winked at him. It was hard to be so brave and light-hearted in front of him when I really wanted to cry and ask how we were ever going to get through this, but knowing he needed me to be strong made it a little bit easier.

By five p.m., the house was looking decent again. I had recruited Adrienne to come over and help with dusting and vacuuming, promising I'd come help her with her house sometime when she needed me. Miriam had washed, dried, folded and put away four loads of laundry. She ran the dishwasher through and took out the trash, making a big show of holding her nose when she opened the big trash bin in the garage. I managed to start the lawn mower after trying for about ten minutes and wrenching my back in the process. Ellie pulled a bagful of weeds and only a few of them weren't actually weeds. We all took showers and then I asked Ellie to come with me the grocery store to stock up. By now, she had become good at figuring out what was healthy and what wasn't.

The three of us steamed a head of broccoli and prepared a rice pilaf and broiled a piece of salmon. I wasn't much of a fish lover, but I would eat just about anything if I knew it might help Jason. Ellie went upstairs to tell him dinner was ready, and he came down looking refreshed and surprised to see how orderly everything was again.

"Wow, you girls had a busy day," he said, patting Ellie on the head.

"We want to help you get better, Daddy," she said, looking up at him.

"I am getting better; I can feel it. Thank you," he said. I prayed that he was. As proud as I had felt about our combined efforts to take over the household, we still really needed him too.

# 51

Ugh, why did *she* have to be there? I was taking yoga classes twice a week, still at the beginner level, but with each class, my confidence grew, as well as my flexibility and strength. I often reached a state of flow where I wasn't thinking about anything but holding each pose. I wasn't evaluating my body or comparing myself to anyone else in the class or wishing I was more advanced, but today Julia was killing it for me.

We hadn't spoken since the day she stormed out of Jason's house, angry about the girls participating in our wedding. Of course, she looked as beautiful and perfect as ever. I thought about my looks less and less these days, and as a result, I felt happier. I avoided women's magazines and their editorial messages of "you're beautiful the way you are" wedged between pages and pages of ads insisting that I wasn't good enough without buying this product or that one to slow the process of aging. However, something about Julia brought out the competitive side of my nature.

I saw her looking at me out of the corner of her eye, even though I had positioned my mat on the other side of the room from hers. I did my best to ignore her, but my budding discipline of focus was shattered for this class. I hoped she wasn't going to be a regular here because I had few places in our small town to avoid seeing her. She was always turning up at Jason's house or grocery shopping when I just ran in to get a loaf of bread or pumping gas when I pulled in to fill my car.

I guessed that this was her first class because she looked uncoordinated and confused, much the same as I did when I started. All the running and lifting weights I did weren't a major help to the practice of yoga. She had to watch Mindy closely, whereas I had reached the point of being able to move fluidly into each pose just by listening to her soothing voice. Julia looked frustrated. I was glad there was at least something that Ms. Orthopedic Surgeon wasn't naturally good at, but then I felt guilty and renewed my concentration. Yoga wasn't a competition, and trying to one-up Julia wasn't going to make me happy either.

No matter what, she was the mother of Jason's children and she would always hold a place in his heart for that. I had to make the best of it. Even though she made it clear she was upset, at least she didn't directly tell the girls she didn't want them to be in the wedding. They felt bad, but they were still excited to be bridesmaids.

As class ended, I quickly rolled up my mat and slid my feet back into my flip-flops so I could escape without bumping into Julia, but as I was walking out of the room, I heard her call, "Kristen, can you wait just a second? I was hoping to talk to you." She was sitting on the floor lacing up her sneakers. My first instinct was to pretend I didn't hear her and keep going, but I stopped and went back to stand over her, waiting to see what she'd say.

"I wanted to apologize," she said, standing up now and clumsily holding her loosely rolled mat.

"Okay," I said. What else was I supposed to say?

"I felt blindsided by the whole thing, but that's not an excuse. Of course the girls would want to be part of the wedding. It's healthier for them anyway. If Jason has to get married again, I can't imagine anyone better than you."

"Thank you," I said. Now I was in shock. Was she heavily medicated or what? First she apologizes, and then she compliments me. She looked at me expectantly. I guess it was my turn to say something. "It means a lot to me to have your blessing. I know you're their real mom, but I feel honored to have a place in their lives too."

"You're handling things better than I could have. I mean with Jason's health being unknown and all. Miriam told me how you taught her how to do the laundry. I guess that's something she should have known before now, but at least they are being helpful."

"They are wonderful girls. You and Jason have done a great job with them."

"I'm afraid that if you become more important in their lives, it means I will be less important to them."

"That could never be true, Julia. Can't you think of me as a bonus mom? I'm not trying to replace you. I wouldn't want to. I know they're your girls. I just want to hold them in my heart."

"I know they need you too. I can't promise I'm not going to get bitchy now and then because this is really hard for me. But even when I do, keep it in the back of your mind that I'd rather you be there than anyone else."

"Thank you." I turned to go, but she kept talking.

"I have regrets. I wish I had handled things better, but there's too much water under the bridge now. Jason is so happy with you. I'm not going to interfere with that."

I felt relieved, but there was fear underneath the surface. She had just about admitted she wished she didn't leave him and that she could have him back. What if she openly asked Jason for another chance? He valued marriage so much. Would he put that ahead of what we had, even though she had left him? I wondered if he'd give her another chance, if the opportunity arose. I wanted to get away from her as quickly as I could.

"Well, it was nice to talk to you, Julia. I've got to run or I'll be late for work."

"You know, I don't even like yoga. I just came here to talk to you."

I laughed with her, but I felt enormously grateful that I probably wouldn't see her here again. I needed at least one Julia-free sanctuary. I would tell Jason that she apologized, but I was never going to mention the rest. I hoped it would just disappear and we'd be married and live happily ever after without any ghosts from the past to disrupt our life together.

# 52

Tamara's words burned: "I think you're making a huge mistake," she'd told me. I was angry because I felt like once you make a decision, your friends should support you. She and Heather both seemed lukewarm when I told them that the wedding was back on with Jason. I was hurt, but I understood they were looking out for me. It made sense at first because they had a point – maybe he would flake out again over some issue with his daughters.

But now, months later, with things going better than ever, I think they should have admitted that it was worth giving things a second chance. I wanted them to be happy for me. I wondered in the back of my mind if this was one reason I didn't want a big wedding. Who would stand up for me as a bridesmaid, other than my sister?

I had asked them to come over and help me pack up all of the stuff from my apartment that I wouldn't need before the wedding. As we sorted through my clothes, I offered several items to them before some went in the giveaway pile. Most of my outfits that I had worn to the club were in that pile.

"I miss fun Kristen," Heather lamented. "Even your clothes are boring now. You turned into one of *them*."

*Them* meaning a mom, I take it.

"Heather, I'm still fun, just in a different way. Why won't you try yoga with me, or come over for dinner some night? Or we can still go out sometimes. I just don't want to go to clubs and bars anymore. It's not me."

"It always *was* you, until you met Jason. That's what I don't like. You've let a man turn you into a different person," Heather said. Tamara remained quiet, but she clearly was in agreement, nodding her head with pursed lips while she folded shirts.

"He didn't change me, Heather. *I* changed. I wanted to change. Even before I met him, I wasn't happy with my life. Please don't be offended by that. I love you guys and I always will. But that night in the club, when that girl called me 'mom,' do you remember that? I realized I do want to settle down. I want to have a home and healthy meals and a career. I don't want to keep pretending I'm still a crazy kid."

"You even changed your hair," Heather said. I felt like I was on trial. "Did Jason tell you to do that too?"

"No! I didn't even tell him ahead of time that I was going to. He didn't seem to care either way what color my hair is. One of the things I love about him is that he sees me for what's inside. All the other guys were just looking at me on the surface."

"The way you talk makes us sound so shallow," Heather said.

"Heather, no! I am so happy for you, that you still have the energy to be out late and manage to get up on time for work. I admire how amazing you always look. Just because I changed some things around in my life doesn't mean I think any less of you. I'm not judging you, so please don't judge me."

We continued sorting and packing in silence. The two of them seemed so sullen that I wished I hadn't asked for their help.

"We're almost finished here. How about I take you out for dinner to celebrate when we get everything into the car?"

"Sure," Tamara said unenthusiastically.

"Yeah, if you have time," Heather said. "Maybe you need to be home for dinner with your new family."

"Knock it off, Heather! I wouldn't have asked you if I didn't have time. I appreciate you coming over to help me and I appreciate everything you've done in the past couple of years to get me through all my love-life failures. If it were you getting married, I'd be happy for you."

That's when Tamara said it: "I think you're making a huge mistake."

I looked up from the coffee mug I was wrapping in newspaper.

"Why, Tamara? Because we broke up once? Because he already has kids? Because he has MS? I told you, we've been working on all of that. I knew it wasn't going to be easy helping him to raise two teenage girls, but they are used to me now. They even gave me this card," I said, reaching across the kitchen table to hand it to them.

"That's gross," Tamara said, looking at the front. "It's like they're making fun of you."

"They are not! Do you think it's easy for a teenaged girl to tell her stepmom she loves her? I think this was the perfect way to break the ice."

"You know they're going to make your life miserable," Tamara persisted.

"Honestly, sometimes they do. But Jason is worth it and so are they. Marriage is working through all the hard stuff. I was always in it for the easy stuff. Now I'm ready for all of it, good and bad. I love him. Don't you get that? I thought I loved John, but it was so different."

"Are you going to have babies with him?" Heather asked.

"I don't know."

"I mean, see, even that. You agreed with us that you never wanted to have kids. Now all of a sudden you have two and you might even have more."

"So what if I change my mind? We probably won't. Jason's right that we only have a few more years of the girls in the house and then things will settle down for a bit, at least until there are grandchildren. But if we decide differently, what's wrong with that? People change."

"Grandchildren! Oh, my God, Kristen."

I taped up the last box and picked it up.

"Enough. Let's go out and celebrate. I'm as freaked out as you are about how quickly things are changing, but we don't have to let it affect our friendship. Dinner and drinks on me!"

We grabbed as many boxes as we could carry, piled them into the trunk and headed out for some Mexican food and margaritas. Once we had a drink and some appetizers, the mood lightened considerably. Tamara and Heather had made good points and I didn't want to ignore what they were saying because a lot of it made sense. But I guess that's why they call it "taking the plunge." There's no way to wade into marriage.

# 53

"Adrienne, would you take Drew back if he said he made a huge mistake and wanted to start over?" We stirred our coffees and put the spoons down at the same time. I sat at Adrienne's counter while she washed dishes at her sink. I never understood where all the dishes came from until I started hanging around Jason and his daughters. When I was on my own, I was washing maybe three cups and plates a week.

"What kind of question is that? He couldn't wait to get out. He would never ask for another chance."

"But if he did..."

"I never really thought about it. I guess not. Because if things had gotten that bad, I don't think we'd be able to fix it anyway. What brings this up?"

"Just some stuff Julia said yesterday about having regrets. I'm afraid she's going to tell Jason she wants to come back and he'll dump me."

"Oh, Kristen. I don't think he'd do that. I really don't."

"But he's all about his family. Maybe he'd think it would be better for the girls."

"It would be confusing for them. They seem happy with you. I'm sure it's a more peaceful household now than it was with her there. Besides, she left him because he was sick. You're right there with him. How could he forget that?"

"I hope you're right. I'm afraid I'll lose him. It was awful when we were apart. Everything felt wrong, like I had lost my purpose."

"No person should take away your sense of purpose. But I do understand what you mean. After Drew left, I was adrift for a long time. It was like if I wasn't a wife, what was I? I knew I was still a mom, and that's what kept me going. You need to hold on to an essence of you that doesn't rely on him. The beautiful pain of love is knowing you could lose the object of your affection at any time."

"When did you get so smart?"

"It's called getting old," she laughed.

"So how are the boys doing? How's Jonathan?"

"Great to all three. Knock on wood, but everything has been going so smoothly lately."

"Do you want to marry him?" I asked.

"No, at least not right now. I'm happy seeing him on weekends and it's easier with the boys. They have to go deal with the chaos of Drew and Amy's every weekend; at least they know when they're home with me that everything is still the same. But it's not just them. I don't know if I can get used to the idea of living with a man again. I like my independence. Some of my friends tell me they have to ask their husband if they want to buy a new pair of shoes and I'm like *what*? I'm the one who decides what I can afford. And I get the whole closet and the whole bed to myself. That would be hard to give up."

"You're making me feel a little nervous. I already have a case of the jitters."

"You're going to be fine," she said, lightly punching my arm. "You and Jason are good together. I don't think he has one controlling bone in his body, does he?"

"Well, no, but we're not married yet."

"A tiger doesn't change his stripes. You've worked through the issues with Miriam and Ellie, you're coping with his MS. If you can handle that, you can handle whatever else comes your way." She gave me a hug and practically pushed me out the door. "Unless you're here to help me clean, you best be on your way."

I took the hint.

"There's plenty of that to do where I just came from," I said.

I drove back to Jason's, wondering whether it was normal to feel nervous about getting married. It was like a secret club I couldn't join. Everyone who was married just laughed about it and my friends who weren't had no clue. I couldn't exactly talk to Jason because he was skittish about the way Julia had abandoned him. I didn't want it to get into his head that I might do the same.

And I wouldn't, would I? I wasn't the type to quit. When Jason had his little fit over Miriam, which is how I chose to think of it now, I didn't quit. I took my ring off, but I didn't really want to break up. I was hoping he'd put it right back on my finger. So why would I quit now?

I had to stop worrying that he'd leave me or I'd leave him and simply trust that we'd be okay. I made myself think about our business instead of our wedding, and that cheered me up. We had so much to look forward to, the joint venture of not only being husband and wife, but also helping other people take better care of themselves and be more proactive about their health. That would be my mission.

# 54

I woke up in a state of bliss. The sun was peeking above the horizon and I could see blue sky through my window. It was finally our wedding day. I stretched my arms above my head and pointed my toes until they reached the tucked-in sheets at the bottom of my bed. I sat up and looked around my empty room. There was nothing in here now but the bed and a laundry basket with the few things in I'd need for getting ready. My wedding gown hung in the closet and I touched it gently before pulling out my yoga mat.

By now I was practiced enough at yoga to follow the routine at home on the days I didn't have class. It was a quiet meditation to start my days, and I thought about how much I enjoyed waking up early and feeling clearheaded, compared to the past, when I was constantly getting up right before work and grabbing a soda on the way in to clear my caffeine headache. Now my days were structured and routine, but instead of feeling older and set in my ways, I felt younger and healthier than I had in years.

When I finished my morning vinyasa, I rolled up my mat and texted Miriam: *Did he leave yet?* Jason had promised to get out of the house for the morning so that the girls and I could have breakfast and get ready together. He spent last night with them, taking them for his last single-dad dinner, although we had promised them together that they would still get plenty of alone-time with their dad. I knew they'd need breaks from me and I'd need breaks from them, and I was determined to keep our relationship as strong as possible by avoiding the resentment that kids of divorce feel about the new person who steps into their lives.

Julia had backed off since her apology. The girls were going to spend a few days with her while Jason and I had a brief honeymoon, and then the schedule would go back to normal. If she was guilt-tripping the girls or making it difficult for them, they didn't tell me. I'd asked a few times, "How's your mom doing?" and they'd always answer "fine." I didn't need to pry into the details of their relationship with their mother.

A minute later, my phone pinged back with a message from Miriam. *Happy Wedding Day, K! Yup, he just left. Come over.* I loved that the girls had taken to calling me K. Having a nickname made me feel like family. I had started calling them Miss M and E. I didn't really like the Ellie Bellie nickname, even though both her parents called her that.

A few seconds later, I got a text from Jason. *How's my lovely bride on this beautiful morning? I can't wait to see you light up the church. I'll be waiting for you at the altar.* I texted him back, *Can't wait to see you too, my handsome groom. I'm looking forward to that kiss.*

I put my laundry basket and yoga mat in the car, then came back to carefully lay my gown over the backseat. The girls were waiting for me, and they helped me carry my stuff inside.

"We made breakfast for you!" Ellie exclaimed. I was thrilled to see them both looking so happy and excited.

"Thank you," I said, kissing her on the top of the head and giving Miriam a brief hug. It was taking a while for all of us to get used to the physical affection, but it got easier with practice. "Did your dad get some breakfast?"

"Yes, we fed him too; don't worry," Miriam said. "He went to his office to get some paperwork done." Sometimes I loved the way Jason could single-mindedly focus on something and block everything else out. Other times I hated it.

"So what's for breakfast? It smells great in here."

"We made a flaxseed oatmeal blueberry coffee cake," Ellie said proudly.

"Wow, yummy *and* healthy. What a treat." I grabbed myself a cup of coffee as Ellie cut me a large slice and sat at the kitchen counter while the girls looked at me expectantly.

"What? Am I forgetting something?"

"No," Miriam said. "We're just not sure what we should be doing now."

"Just chill for a minute. Pretty soon we're all going to need showers, or did you take one already?"

"Nope, but you can go first, then me. Then Ellie."

"Why am I always last?" she complained.

"Because you need the least time to get ready," Miriam said.

Nearly two hours later, we had all taken showers, dried our hair, and gotten into our gowns. I zipped the girls' dresses for them and Miriam fastened the line of buttons running up the back of mine while I held my hair up.

"Are you going to wear it up or down?" she asked.

"I think down. What do you think?"

"That sounds nice. You have beautiful hair. I like it better brown too."

"Thanks. This is my real color."

"You weren't as nice when you had blonde hair." "Really?"

"Yeah. Sorry to say that, but it's true. I thought you were so fake when I first met you. I was wondering what my dad was thinking, because that's not usually his type."

"How does your dad have a type? I thought it was just your mom and then me."

"Well, yeah, but she's so accomplished and professional. Don't take that wrong, please. I have so much more respect for you now. You helped me, you helped my sister, you help my dad. But I didn't know it was going to be like that. I figured you'd just take him away from us."

"It's okay. You know my sister is divorced. It's hard for the kids when their parents are trying to move on with their lives."

"That's what I like about you. You get it. Even though your parents are together, somehow you know what it feels like to be me."

Just then, Ellie walked in carrying my flowers.

"Are you going to toss your bouquet?"

"No, Ellie," I laughed. "Aren't you a little young to be getting married?"

"I am now, but someday I'm going to. I'm going to have three boys and a girl."

"Wow, you'll be busy," Miriam said.

"How about you, Miriam? Do you want to get married someday?"

"No. Well, maybe. I really don't know."

"That's okay. I didn't think I'd be getting married either, but when you know, you know." And all of a sudden, in that moment, I *knew*.

I finished putting on a light coat of mascara, looking at my glowing reflection, and turned around to see Adrienne come through the doorway, looking as pretty as she did on her own wedding day.

"You look awesome!" we said at the same time, rushing into each other's arms.  And then, "Jinx!"

We pulled back and checked each other out, trying not to get tears in our eyes and ruin our makeup. Miriam took a few sister pictures of us and then I took some of her with Ellie.

"Are you ready, girls? It's time to get to the church. You're driving, right, Miriam?" I tossed her the keys.

"Awesome, yes, I am definitely driving," she said.

"Let's go see your dad."

We blasted "Going to the Chapel" in the car, signing along loudly. I didn't have a limo to take me to my wedding, but I couldn't have imagined a better way to get there than with the girls who loved me.

# 55

As we pulled up in front of the church, I paused for a moment before getting out of the car. Even though we'd been planning for months, it still didn't seem real that the day was finally here. Miriam and Adrienne went in ahead to make sure everyone was ready while Ellie stayed back with me. I think she heard my breath quickening because she took my hand and squeezed it. Her hand was warm and soft.

"You got this," she whispered. I smiled then, because how many times had I said those very same words to her at the gym? I squeezed her hand back and we swung our arms back and forth a few times while I held a small bouquet of magenta cornflowers in my other hand.

Miriam came back to the door and nodded, and I walked up the steps with Ellie, taking a deep breath. Rather than my father, I had asked the girls to walk me down the aisle and then stand with us for the vows. I hoped my dad understood. I had explained to him that I felt like I was too old and too modern to be "given away," and that Jason and I wanted to include the girls in our ceremony to make it official that we were becoming a family. He grunted and shrugged, which translated to "fine with me," or at least I think so. I remembered how intensely uncomfortable he looked walking with Adrienne at her wedding. He kept dabbing his sweaty forehead with the pocket square in his suit jacket.

Our pastor happened to be a classical guitarist, and she played the traditional "Canon in D" as the girls and I walked up the center aisle toward Jason. Miriam kept giving me little tugs to hold me back because I was walking too fast. Even though the only audience was my sister, her sons, her boyfriend, and my parents, it seemed indecorous to rush up the aisle. As we got halfway up the aisle, I could see the tears in the corners of his eyes.

"Keep it together," I had told him the last time we talked. "If you lose it, so will I, and we don't want to be one of those weepy couples wiping their noses with the backs of their hands as they say their vows, do we?"

"You have a way of being so gross sometimes," he said.

"Thanks," I laughed, kissing him on the nose.

But as I got closer, I could see he was doing a good job of keeping it together, just like I had asked. The girls and I finally made it to the front of the church, and even though it was my instinct to kiss him right away, I held back. Instead, I handed my flowers to Ellie and let him take both of my hands in his.

"Good morning," Pastor Dawn boomed, and then, realizing she didn't need to talk so loudly for such a small group, she turned her voice down. "It is one of the greatest pleasures of my calling to perform a marriage ceremony, and I do so in great joy today, knowing that I am playing a small part in bringing together two of the kindest and most loving people I have the privilege to know."

I could hear my mother sniffling, and saw Adrienne nudging her and pulling out a packet of tissues to hand to her. I looked back at Jason, who was smiling at me, his eyes shining.

"Dearly beloved, we have come together in the presence of God to witness and bless the joining together of this man and this woman in holy matrimony," Pastor Dawn continued. "The bond and covenant of marriage was established by God in creation, and our Lord Jesus Christ adorned this manner of life by His presence and first miracle at the wedding in Cana of Galilee. It signifies to us the mystery of the union between Christ and His Church, and Holy Scripture commends it to be honored among all people.

"The union of husband and wife is intended by God for their mutual joy; for the help and comfort given each other in prosperity and adversity; and, when it is God's will, for the procreation of children and their nurture in the knowledge and love of the Lord. Therefore marriage is not to be entered into unadvisedly or lightly, but reverently, deliberately, and in accordance with the purposes for which it was instituted by God.

"Into this union, Kristen and Jason now come to be joined. If any of you can show just cause why they may not be lawfully wed, speak now or forever hold your peace." She paused for a moment to look up, but the church was silent. I thought about how, in the movies, someone always came rushing through the doors to object right at this moment, and I hoped that it wouldn't be Julia today.

"I charge you both, here in the presence of God and the witness of this company, that if either of you know any reason why you may not be married lawfully and in accordance with God's Word, do now confess it." Jason and I smiled at each other and squeezed hands.

"Kristen, will you have this man to be your husband; to live together with him in the covenant of marriage? Will you love him, comfort him, honor and keep him, in sickness and in health; and, forsaking all others, be faithful unto him as long as you both shall live?" Pastor Dawn asked.

"I will."

"Jason, will you have this woman to be your wife; to live together with her in the covenant of marriage? Will you love her, comfort her, honor and keep her, in sickness and in health; and forsaking all others, be faithful to her as long as you both shall live?"

"I will," Jason said confidently, looking deeply into my eyes.

"Will all of you witnessing these promises do all in your power to uphold these two persons in their marriage?"

"We will," my family said quietly.

"Please repeat after me," Pastor Dawn said, and Jason said the words back to me.

"In the name of God, I take you, Kristen, to be my wife, to have and to hold from this day forward, for better, for worse, for richer, for poorer, in sickness and in health, to love and to cherish, until we are parted by death. This is my solemn vow."

When it was my turn, I repeated the vows, thinking of how many brides had said these words and how I meant every word of them truly in my heart. I hoped the better days, the richer ones, the healthy ones would outnumber all the others, but I was ready for whatever may come.

Pastor Dawn held up our rings.

"Bless, O Lord, these rings as a symbol of the vows by which this man and this woman have bound themselves to each other; through Jesus Christ our Lord."

"Amen," Jason and I said. She handed him my ring, which he placed on my finger.

"I give you this ring as a symbol of my love, and with all that I am, and all that I have, I honor you, in the Name of the Father, and of the Son, and of the Holy Spirit," he said.

I took Jason's ring from Pastor Dawn and pushed it gently back on his finger.

"I give you this ring as a symbol of my love, and with all that I am, and all that I have, I honor you, in the Name of the Father, and of the Son, and of the Holy Spirit," I said, smiling at him and looking down to see the gold band on his finger for the first time. So many times I had looked at his hand, picturing a wedding band on his finger. Sometimes I was surprised I never crashed my car for all the times I looked at the engagement ring on my finger while I was driving. Now I'd have two rings to distract me.

"Now that Kristen and Jason have given themselves to each other by solemn vow, with the joining of hands and the giving and receiving of rings, I pronounce that they are husband and wife, in the name of the Father, and the Son, and the Holy Spirit. Those whom God has joined together, let no one put asunder."

Miriam and Ellie each gave a reading, from 1 Corinthians and then from Colossians, their voices clear and strong. When they finished reading, Pastor Dawn continued with something special we had requested after first making sure that Miriam and Ellie liked the idea. However, it was a surprise for the rest of my family.

"These sacred vows are not just between Kristen and Jason because, not only will they be a new couple, but a new family," Pastor Dawn said. "Miriam and Eleanor, will you please join us now for the special family rites of this wedding." They stepped forward between us, and I began speaking.

"Miriam and Ellie, thank you for sharing your father with me, loving me, and allowing me to love you as my own daughters. We promise to love and support you as a family. These necklaces are a symbol of our love and devotion to the two of you." Jason placed a gold chain with four hearts on it, two gold, and two silver, on each his daughters. They matched the necklace he had given me for Christmas. Miriam touched the hearts on hers as he fastened Ellie's.

"I love your guts," I whispered to the girls, and they giggled.

"Kristen and Jason, having witnessed your vows of love to one another, it is my joy to present you to all gathered here as husband and wife," Pastor Dawn said. "You may kiss the bride," she told Jason, although it wasn't necessary because he was already pulling me into a big hug and a tender kiss. Normally we were reserved in sharing our affection publicly, but it felt just right at that moment.

The girls walked arm in arm down the aisle before us, and we followed. Jason's balance was a little off, but I don't think anyone else noticed the way he leaned on my arm for support.

# 56

Jason drove us to the restaurant where we would hold a mini-reception before taking off for two nights to a resort in the Catskill Mountains of New York. Miriam was heading for the front seat as we walked to his car, but she saw me hesitate a few steps back, and opened the door for me instead. She climbed into the backseat with Ellie. I turned around to wink at the girls, who both looked tired and happy.

"Are you doing anything special with your mom this weekend?" I asked.

"She's taking us to a Broadway show, but she won't tell us which one," Miriam said.

"I hope it's *The Lion King*," Ellie piped in.

"That'll be such a treat. I can't wait to hear all about it," I said. Jason was humming to himself.

We sat at one big table with my family, enjoying salad and sandwiches. After lunch, we cut a small coconut cake, sharing a piece together while Adrienne passed slices to everyone else.

"Before we end our little party, I'd like to ask Kristen for a dance," Jason said, standing a bit unsteadily. My eyes filled with tears. Even though he seemed to be improving a little bit each day and heading toward another period of remission, it was more than I hoped for that he'd be able to dance with me at our wedding.

He nodded to our waitress, and a moment later "If I Needed You" began playing over the sound system. He held out his hand to me. I stood up to and put my hand in his, and let him lead me to a space between the tables. There were other people having lunch at the restaurant, and they all turned to watch us, but for a few minutes, all I could see was Jason. Everything around us was a blur as though we spinning on the Scrambler at an amusement park. I could feel the warmth through his suit with my hand on his back and my other hand wrapped in his.

"I love you," he whispered, closing his eyes.

"I love you too," I whispered back to him, but I kept mine open because I didn't want to miss a second of what I hoped would be the first of many dances with my husband. The word *husband* kept running through my mind. I never knew until this moment how much it would mean to me to call him that. I looked at his closed eyes, his nose, his lips, his chin, and down to our hands. I pivoted his slightly so I could see the gold band on his finger. This was the most perfect moment of my life so far. I hoped there would be others, even better than today, but it was hard to imagine. I thought about my family, about Miriam and Ellie, and even about Julia, wishing them all the greatest happiness and joy that life could bring. The song ended and the spell broke as everyone at the tables cheered for us, but I still had that woozy feeling of waking from an amazingly pleasant dream.

We hugged everyone in my family goodbye and gestured for the girls to come with us. We had two stops left to make before we were on our way: one to drop off the girls at their mom's, and then to change clothes and pick up our packed bags at our house.

Julia came out to the car when we pulled up to her house.

"Congratulations," she said, trying to sound cheerful while looking inconspicuously at our ring fingers.

"Thank you, Julia," Jason said. "Enjoy Broadway."

"We will," she said, wrapping her arms around the girls and pulling them in tight. I could see tears in her eyes, but she was smiling. "You two look gorgeous," she said to them. We watched the three of them walk inside before Jason headed toward our house. Now I could call it "our house" and not feel self-conscious. We already met with an attorney to sign a prenuptial agreement that would add my name to the deed of the house and then leave it in our wills to our children.

I needed Jason to unbutton my gown, which took him a while with the weakness in his hands, but we were patient. He kissed the back of my neck as I held my hair out of the way.

"I know I've said it before, but do you know how beautiful you are? Not just on the outside, but on the inside too? I could not have imagined a better partner and wife than the one standing in front of me now."

I turned my head to kiss him.

"Thank you," was all I could manage to say. He finished unbuttoning and I carefully slid my gown over my head and put it back on its padded hanger.

"Want to consummate our marriage?" he said, winking at me.

"What, right now? Here?"

"What better place? We're home. I'm sure we'll be consummating all weekend, but isn't this the best place to start?"

"I believe you're right, husband," I said, laughing, trying out the new title for the first time.

"Come here, wife," he growled, and then laughed at himself trying to sound sexy.

# 57

The alarm went off and I rolled over and stretched. Jason groaned as I nudged his leg with my toe. Who knew I'd be the morning person in this house? Some things you had to live together to figure out. Even waking up on Mondays was easier than it ever had been because I knew I'd be busy doing work I loved all day. There would be people who needed me and counted on me, and together, Jason and I could share our gifts. We purposely kept our business small so that every person who walked through our doors would feel cared for, but word of mouth helped keep every time block full most days. Miriam had made a website for us, Ellie tended to the flowers outside, and we had slowly recruited a small staff that included a yoga instructor, a nutritionist, and a nurse. I continued to give massages and learned to do the bookkeeping.

"Wake up, sleepyhead," I said, kissing his cheek and tickling him a little bit. He grabbed my hands and held me still.

"Not yet," he mumbled. "Just a few more minutes."

"Lots to do today!" I chirped. Who was this cheerful, chipper morning person? I barely recognized myself these days, but I loved it. I used to drag myself out of bed, always in a bad mood, never talking to anyone until I had at least one cup of coffee or a large soda coursing through my system.

I had basically enjoyed my work at the spa, but a lot of days I felt bored and unmotivated. I felt like I only saw a sliver of my clients, even though I saw them practically naked, because I was only treating a symptom, muscle soreness and tightness. I wanted to teach them how to eat better and exercise and lower their stress levels, but what kind of a hypocrite would I be when I was living on fast food, alcohol, and caffeine? It had only been thanks to good genes and forced workouts that I didn't look on the outside like I felt on the inside back then.

Now, every day brought new challenges. Starting a business felt like what I imagined it must be like to give birth, to see something go from the seed of an idea in my heart to a child toddling off, growing and changing every day. Sometimes things felt scary and out of control, but I also felt more fulfilled and contented than I thought a person could. I wondered so often how could I actually be making money for this?

"Who are we seeing today?" Jason asked, finally opening his eyes a crack.

"One of your super-duper favorites, Lucinda, is first thing this morning," I said. I knew that would wake him up. Lucinda was a six-year-old girl who had overcome a tremendous number of obstacles and still had a long way to go. She was born with fetal alcohol syndrome, but fortunately adopted by a very patient and proactive family who believed it was their mission to take in children from the foster care system. We worked with her and her family monthly on a special diet, as well as teaching her calming yoga postures for when she found herself angry and wanting to tear things up. Jason had called her teachers at school and explained that if they let her go to the back corner of the room and do a few stretches when she got agitated, they'd have far fewer confrontations to deal with. So far, the new plan was working well.

When she was focused and happy, she was the funniest kid around. I imagined that if her family had been inclined, she'd be a YouTube sensation. I was glad, though, that her family didn't indulge her in that way, but held her to the same expectations as their other five kids.

Besides her yoga and nutrition, I worked on her muscle tension at least once a month. Massage is essential for keeping balanced, but it's only one part of the whole picture.

At home, it's not really all that *Brady Bunch* with Miriam and Ellie the way I had expected it would be. Of course not. Miriam is a moody teenager, and poor Jason when she and I both have PMS at the same time. There's a lot of door slamming going on in our house. And some stomping around, eye rolling, and good old-fashioned yelling. Ellie's still a little young for that, but she's getting in the game. Jason knows when to go hide in his study and watch manly documentaries.

Even with a stepmother in the house (and I prefer to be called a bonus mom, thank you very much), there's a lot of love too. I think about our vows to the girls every day and besides working hard at marriage, I work hard at being a mom because I know it's worth it. I love Jason, and therefore I love his children, whether they're technically mine or not.

After our busy Monday, we sat down to dinner together, as we did most nights. Ellie made a salad, but the rest was picked up from the prepared foods counter of the grocery store. Thank goodness for whoever decided that home-cooked meals from the supermarket was a good idea, because it's been a godsend. We still get some vegetables and I don't have to cook them. As we passed the plates, I couldn't help but think about a night almost two years ago when I was peering into another family's window, feeling insanely jealous and left out and very sure that I'd never have a family like this of my own.

# About the author

Grete DeAngelo wrote nonfiction for half her life, all the while dreaming of writing the same kinds of books she likes to read under the covers on Saturday mornings. She teaches high school history and research writing. Past experiences include selling vacation packages, answering letters to the editor, and filing blueprints in a vault. She lives with her family in Pennsylvania.

# Acknowledgements

Thank you to my first readers, Aaron Floryshak, Fred Holland, Kathleen Haentjens, and Susan Miller, for their valuable insights and attention to detail. I also want to thank several people who let me interview them for their expertise on many matters covered in this book: Sara Hodon Karnish, Dr. Lisa Ferry, Karen Steber, and Dr. Jerry Kline. The kindness and generosity of people never fails to amaze me. I also want to thank the Lehigh Valley Writers Group, especially Amy Deardon and Laurel Wenson, for their encouragement and advice.

# Also by Grete DeAngelo

Please visit the author online:
www.gretedeangelo.com

Find all of her books here:

Please go to the next page for a preview of *Giving Myself Away*,
the story of Kristen's sister, Adrienne.

## *Giving Myself Away*

## **Chapter 1**

*Please God, don't let me be pregnant*, I whispered to myself, though I no longer believed in answered prayers.

"Excuse me, ma'am?" said the pimply CVS clerk as I dropped an armload of items onto the counter, a few of them skittering toward him.

"I didn't say anything, did I?" I asked, hoping I hadn't been talking out loud again.

"No, uh..." He pointed behind me to my six-year-old son, who was unwrapping a pack of gum.

"Tyler, stop that this instant!" I snapped, grabbing the gum from him and slapping it on the counter. "Sorry about that," I said to the clerk. "We'll take that, too, obviously."

I paid for my items, most of which I didn't really need, except to distract the kids from the fact I was buying a pregnancy test. My period was six days late, and at age forty-two, it seemed unlikely that I'd suddenly hit menopause. Still, this was crazy. Women in their forties don't get pregnant, at least not by accident.

At thirty-two, when I had Nicky, I already felt like I was old, and by the time I had Tyler at age thirty-six, I was considered a "high-risk pregnancy." How many times have I read tabloid headlines in the grocery store checkout line about this forty-something celebrity or that one seeking fertility treatments or adopting a baby? So here I am in my forties, so done with having babies, on the pill, and not sexually active – well, not *really* sexually active – and my period's late. This has to be stress, I kept telling myself. The anxiety, the fatigue, the feeling that I have two giant melons for boobs, that all goes with the usual PMS territory.

We stepped out of the quiet, cool protection of CVS into the blazing sunshine. July in Pennsylvania is the best month of the year, if you ask me. The days are long, the nights are warm, and it feels okay to be lazy because it's summer. I loved grilling hot dogs with the kids and watching them play in the sprinkler in our backyard while I sat in the shade with a good book. I was hoping we could do that later.

The boys and I got into my new and completely impractical black sports car. Everyone else my age is driving a minivan, but I'd rather die. Ever since I traded in my hatchback wagon for this two-door pretty baby, I'd become pretty strict. No more eating in the car. My last car always had Cheerios and Goldfish crackers crushed into the seats, but Happy Meal toys and school papers never littered the floor these days. This was my single-person car, the one I should have owned before I had kids, not after. I could finally understand the midlife crisis convertible that everyone joked about when they'd see a balding doctor revving up his Mustang at the traffic light. I never exactly fit into the perfect hair, perfect makeup, perfect outfit suburban mom mold, but I do even less so now that I'm divorced.

I love the way my car stands out when I line up between all the minivans at Saturday soccer games, but I feel as out of place at the playground as my car looks there. I see the way some women glare at me if I even so much as smile at their husbands, not that I want their husbands anyway. They look as domesticated as their wives, wearing knit polo shirts in various pastel shades (gad, even pink!), cargo shorts, and boat shoes or sneakers without socks. They sport the casual tan of men who work eight to five and go outside only on weekends to cut the grass, grill, and golf.

When we got home from CVS, I managed to distract the boys with the candy I'd bought them while I extracted the pregnancy test and tiptoed into the bathroom. I got a two-pack so I wouldn't have to make another perilous trip to the drug store if one was faulty. The package said if there are two pink lines, it was a positive result, as in pregnant. I was a veteran at this. I'd used these before, but every time I had, I'd wanted there to be two pink lines. I reassured myself about the times I'd sworn I was pregnant, had all the symptoms, even the "implantation cramps" everyone online talked about, but no, they'd be just regular old cramps and Aunt Flo would arrive a few days later. I peed on the white side of the stick and folded up a piece of toilet paper to lay it on the sink. I couldn't stand even looking, so I put the test face-down and left the bathroom, closing the door behind me. I figured I'd give it a good five minutes so there wouldn't be any doubt.

I went to the kitchen to make a much-needed cup of chamomile tea. I was kind of sentimental and I still had the pregnancy tests from my two boys tucked away with other old mementos in a box under my bed. I don't know if that's weird or not, keeping things you'd peed on, but I couldn't bear to get rid of them any more than I could throw out the tiny hospital bracelets they'd worn when they were born. I would pull out the plastic strips on Tyler's and Nicky's birthdays and ask them whether they could believe they ever fit on their arms, and when they'd say no, I'd show them their baby pictures to prove it. Even though I was relieved at all the milestones the boys had reached, especially the ones that involved brushing their own teeth, wiping themselves, and getting dressed on their own, I still cherished the little mementos of their babyhood and the closeness we'd once shared. They still tolerated my barrage of hugs and kisses, and even sought out my affections sometimes, but I knew it wouldn't last much longer.

The boys were racing around the house playing pirates. Nicky had a wooden spoon for a sword. Tyler's was smaller and white. Wait...

"Mom, why is Tyler holding a pregnancy test?" Nicky asked.

I don't know if I was more horrified that my six-year-old boy was brandishing a urine-soaked stick, that my ten-year-old knew what it was, or that there were two distinctly clear, dark pink lines on the results window.

# Chapter 2

I've been separated for twenty-four months now, divorced for seven. If you're wondering what happened, my husband cheated on me. And here's the pathetic part: I wanted to stay with him anyway. So did he leave me for a younger woman unblemished by motherhood? No, he left me for one of those soccer moms who has three kids. I thought there was a rule that a husband couldn't leave you for someone who has more kids than you do.

There were signs, but I did what any loving wife would... I ignored them all until it became so obvious that I had no choice but to acknowledge that the love of my life no longer loved me. I guess some wives would know right away that something was wrong, but Drew and I had married relatively late. We were both thirty, and by that time, we had developed a lot of long-term habits that didn't bode well for comingling our money. We valued our privacy and kept our finances separate. So I wasn't the kind of wife who would be reading his credit card statements, looking for jewelry he'd bought but never gave me, or smelling his shirt collars to see if there was a lingering scent of women's perfume on them.

Plus, he had to travel a lot for his job, even out of the country. He sells surgical instruments. The best ones are manufactured in Switzerland and Israel, so he frequently needs to go on buying trips. I never worried much because there aren't that many women working as orthopedic surgeons or selling bone saws. So where'd he meet Amy? Online, of course. I wasn't even snooping, but he left an instant message chat log on our computer that he apparently forgot to delete.

*R U married?*

*Let's just say my wife is out of the picture.*

What the hell does that mean, I'm "out of the picture"? And why was that good enough for Amy?

Confronting Drew wasn't pretty. I'm not good at meeting adversity head on. I do everything I can to avoid arguments. This is undoubtedly the trait that most annoyed Drew.

"I thought women were supposed to be the talkers," he would say. But in our relationship, he was the one who wanted to discuss everything and tell me all his feelings, and I was the one who clammed up. Every time we argued, I'd go hide under the blankets in our bed, remembering my dad's well-worn phrase: *You can't beat a dead horse.* So I knew about Amy for almost two weeks before I brought it up with Drew. I used that time to plan what I'd say and also to observe his behavior. He did seem quieter at home and sort of distracted. He spent a lot of time checking his phone, and he never left it out of his sight. When he was sleeping, he had it locked, and he changed the code from the last four digits of his phone number. I know this, because for the first time in our marriage, I started snooping. I smelled his clothes every time I did the laundry, but they smelled the same. The biggest change was that he actually became more helpful around the house, especially when it came to running errands.

"I'm going to run to the store and get some milk, Adrienne. We're running low," he'd said one night after dinner.

*We have two gallons*, I thought. He was gone for twenty minutes ("long line," he said, even though it was a Monday and I happen to know the store is practically dead then). I couldn't take the suspense anymore and I needed to hear it from him. I was still hoping for some kind of reassuring, believable explanation for why I was "out of the picture" and what Amy (I only knew her as SunFlower92 then) meant to him.

"Drew, I need to talk about something," I said, as he bent into the refrigerator to put the new milk in the back.

"You need to talk? Well, that's something new," he said, winking at me. He seemed awfully relaxed for someone committing adultery.

"Who is SunFlower92?" I asked, scrutinizing his face for signs of lying. I had gone online to read up on what a liar's face looks like and learned that people often blink more, close their eyes, or stare at you unblinking while lying... how's that for definitive?

"Oh, she's just a nurse from one of the surgical groups I sell to," he said casually. "I barely know her, but she asked me for my IM address one time and got in touch."

"Okay... well, why were you telling her I'm out of the picture?"

"What? What are you talking about?"

"You left a chat log on the computer and I read it. Are you cheating on me?"

"No! Of course I'm not, hon. I was just having a bad day; that's all. I've never even seen her except through work."

"What's her real name?"

"Amy. I don't even know her last name."

I wanted so much to believe Drew. I needed to believe him because he was my other half. I mean that almost literally because we'd been together since we were fourteen. Yep, eighth grade. Drew had his friend Kevin pass me a note in English class asking me if I wanted to go out with him, and I wrote *yes* and made my friend Isabelle pass the note to Kevin so he could give it to Drew. I furtively watched Drew unfold the note and read my one-word reply. He smiled and looked over at me.

Going out with Drew in eighth grade meant wearing a silver chain his mom had bought for him and sitting with him and his friends at lunch. Lunches consisted of fart jokes and watching the boys throw food at each other. We didn't talk much at school, and although we talked on the phone sometimes at night about all the sex we'd have, neither of us exactly understood how it worked.

By the time junior year rolled around, we were known as the kids who were going out forever already. We both had our own casual friends, but everyone pretty much left us alone and I'd sit on Drew's lap or right in front of him whenever I could. He somehow learned about sex, or at least a little bit about it. I liked the way it made me feel mature and different from all the other girls who weren't doing it yet, but truth be told, it kind of hurt and I was always terrified of getting pregnant. We used condoms, and when we needed more, I'd wait outside a drug store while Drew went in and bought them. Looking back, we probably weren't ready, considering it was a huge embarrassment to even discuss birth control. I couldn't ask my mom about going on the pill because I knew she'd kill me, or at least disown me, if she knew I needed it.

Drew went to the local university because his dad was a professor there and he got free tuition. He probably wouldn't have gotten in if it weren't for his dad because his grades were only so-so. My grade point average was a lot higher and my school guidance counselor advised me to go somewhere else, but I just wanted to be with Drew. I couldn't even imagine what it would be like to go off on my own when I'd already had him by my side for four years. So I went and majored in business administration like Drew and we took most of our classes together. I was in charge of organizing our school work and he took care of our social life. We studied in the library together and I wrote a few of his papers for him when he said he couldn't handle them. He made sure we always had somewhere to go on Friday and Saturday nights. Usually it was some off-campus house where we'd drink cheap beer out of plastic cups and shoot darts. I'd sit on a lumpy sofa staring at Def Leppard and Metallica posters and all the dart holes in the wall around the dartboard wondering how my social life could be so lame. There were poetry readings and lectures from ambassadors and scientists and chorale performances all the time on campus, but if I went to them it was alone because Drew said he got enough culture from classes and he just wanted some downtime on the weekends. I couldn't totally blame him because his parents had dragged him out constantly from an early age to see modern art exhibits and hear speakers talk about the effect of pesticide use on tree frogs, and I guess I'd be burned out too by the time I was old enough to pick what I wanted to do.

My parents were different. They were both college educated, but they seemed to think television shows provided everything you'd need as an adult for edification and relaxation. They were retired and rarely went anywhere but out to breakfast, grocery shopping, and the occasional movie. I couldn't understand how sitting around at home could make them so content. Anytime

I was home for more than a day without leaving the house, I'd start feeling a little edgy.

Drew and I never lived together before we got married. He rented a half-double with two of his college buddies in what could only be described as a slum, and I lived in my own tiny apartment that was marginally nicer. When my mom came over one night to drop off some cookies she'd baked she asked me if I had a vacuum. Of course, I told her. "Well, do you ever use it?" she asked.

Finally when we were thirty, Drew proposed. There were a lot of jokes at the reception about how it was "about time." I didn't mind because I always knew we'd get married, and once Drew was ready, everything would work out for us. If I had known when he proposed that we'd get divorced later, I probably still would have married Drew. He had a way of convincing me that everything was all right, so when he told me Amy was a work associate, I believed him, right up until July fourth two years ago, when it became so blatantly obvious that I would have to get a divorce if I wanted to maintain any shred of self-respect. The irony was not lost on me that we got separated on Independence Day.

Please visit the author online:
www.gretedeangelo.com

Find all of her books here: